THE GARLAND KEEPERS

Manohar Malgonkar (1913-2010) was an eminent post-Independence writer whose contribution to Indian writing in English is immense. A remarkable storyteller and a keen observer of social and political realities, Malgonkar is notable for his military thrillers, historical novels and adventure fiction. His major works include *The Men Who Killed Gandhi, A Bend in the Ganges, Spy in Amber, Combat of Shadows, The Garland Keepers, The Sea Hawk, Shalimar, The Princes, Cactus Country, Distant Drum, Bandicoot Run* and *The Devil's Wind.*

ALSO BY THE SAME AUTHOR

Combat of Shadows

Spy in Amber

THE GARLAND KEEPERS

MANOHAR MALGONKAR

RUPA

Published by
Rupa Publications India Pvt. Ltd 2013
7/16, Ansari Road, Daryaganj
New Delhi 110002

Sales centres:
Allahabad Bengaluru Chennai
Hyderabad Jaipur Kathmandu
Kolkata Mumbai

First published by Vision Books Pvt. Ltd in 1986.

ISBN: 978-81-291-2473-9

10 9 8 7 6 5 4 3 2 1

Typeset by Ninestars Information Technologies Ltd, Chennai

To Durga Bhagwat, Ramnath Goenka,
A.D. Gorwala, C.R. Irani, H.R. Khanna and
V.M. Tarkude, who stood guard when the lights went out

AUTHOR'S NOTE

The Emergency, which forms the background for this story, is not the 1975-1977 Emergency, but a fictional one, supposedly imposed some years later. Similarly, the National Democratic Front is not either the Janata Party or any one of the Congress factions, and the Great Leader is only a creature of the author's imagination. At that, since all fits of national epilepsy must show some common outward symptoms, some of the events described in the book may have a passing resemblance to those that took place during the days of that earlier seizure. This would be no more than a coincidence.

Burbusa
12 July 1978

Manohar Malgonkar

The principal deity in the temple may be garlanded only by the head priest or his deputy, a monarch only by those in the first circle of nobility. When garlands are removed, they are passed on to the most favoured among the courtiers, whose privilege it is to keep them.

—the etiquette of flowers

'The strongest chains binding the prisoners were their universal submission and total surrender to their situation as slaves.'

—Alexander Solzhenitsyn

PROLOGUE

Between Chinari and Uri on 8 April 1948

THE five man patrol had been out since dawn. They had crossed the Jhelum a little before noon and stopped for a rest. On the bank of the river they had made tea and eaten their rations. Then the commander had told them they could lie down for half an hour.

Naik Fida Ali had thought of taking a bath. That had been his undoing.

He stripped and plunged in and scrambled out squealing, all in a matter of seconds. The water was cold as ice and the current nearly swept him away. He stretched out on the hot shingle to dry himself and shut his eyes. He thought he heard Mir Khan say something in Pushtu to the Captain.

Mir Khan and the Captain were known to be clan-brothers. Even though still in their twenties, both had seen more war service than many veterans, and each in some way was believed to have saved the other's life. They had been together in Libya in the campaign against the Afrika Korps, and as fellow prisoners in Bengazi. They were Miwand Pathans, over six feet tall and strong as oxen. They were clan-brothers first, and after that comrades-in-arms, before they were officer and other rank. Out on patrol, they were like a team, the leader and his deputy.

Fida Ali opened his eyes and saw them both looking at him in a way that made him feel hot with shame. Then Captain Jamal Din got up, like a camel after its sleep, Fida Ali thought, and came loping over the flint stones and lay down beside him. He held out a packet of cigarettes and after both had lit up, said, 'When we get to the hut this evening, I'll send the others on sentry-go. We share the hut, eh?'

Fida Ali's stomach muscles contracted and his body cringed as the meaning of the proposal became clear. He sat up with a start, flung the cigarette away, and began pulling on his clothes. The other leered, blowing smoke through his nostrils.

Fida Ali had little in common with the other men of the patrol. They were Pathans, he, a Kashmiri who, only a few months earlier, had belonged to the Maharaja's Gilgit garrison. At times he thought he hated the Pakistanis, who had now become his comrades, even more than he hated the Indians who had overrun Kashmir.

A crazy thought flashed through his brain. He would pick up his Sten and blow up the evil, hawklike face of his patrol commander—or better still, that satanic blood brother of his, Mir Khan. Even without looking, he was conscious that all his four companions were watching him closely. Were they all in this?—he wondered—looking upon him as some kind of an outlet for their perverted sex urge? The Pathans' preference for boys over girls was well known; some of them flaunted it even, as an attribute of virility, of manliness.

But he was not a boy, he told himself. He was a young man twenty years old, well brought up and educated. They were illiterate tribesmen from the hills. Except of course the Captain. But they were different from him in other ways too: bigger made, stronger, older, immeasurably more experienced, and dirty—god, how they stank. A bath to them was an eccentricity. They had performed brave deeds and won medals and killed men in battle and raped their womenfolk. He was merely a man who wore uniform, a soldier who still had to kill an enemy.

He did not know that, within the course of the next day, he was fated to kill two men. Of the two, at least one could never be regarded as an enemy.

Now, as though some message had passed between them, the other four were squinting at him and twirling their moustaches. The Captain leaned forward and ran his hand over his shoulder. 'You have the most beautiful body I have ever seen,' he said very gently.

High overhead, a Himalayan kite gave a mournful whistle. The hills rose majestically on all sides, craggy and forbidding. They were said to be alive with Indian snipers. Why did not one of them put a bullet through the black eyes staring unblinkingly as though trying to hypnotize him. 'I shall never do it,' he said with vehemence.

The matter-of-factness of the answer shook him. 'If you do not cooperate, the others will hold you down. They've done it before...'

How often had he not heard of that particular boast in the langar, of the number of Hindu and Sikh women they had raped. His lips felt dry. 'I will...I'll run away,' he croaked.

The Captain reared like a snake. 'Scum!' he spat out a gob of saliva. 'How dare you even talk of deserting? Have you not taken an oath of loyalty to Pakistan and Islam?' The voice shook with patriotic fervour. 'And you know what the kaffirs do to our soldiers they take captive? Cut off their genitals and leave them to rot on a dungheap for the ants and bugs.'

By now Fida Ali had put on his clothes and was lacing his boots. The Captain had still not finished his tirade. 'And even that will be merciful to what I shall do to you—with my own hands. We shall post you as a deserter. A firing squad will be waiting for you when you choose to come back—no matter when—looking for your father or mother or whatever foul things that have bred you. Don't you know that the most despicable crime for a warrior of Islam is desertion?'

Like some vulture squawking, Fida Ali thought; primitive man ranting about the only things his puny brain could grasp. He felt a contempt for his superior officer, this man whose name was spoken of with awe in the regiment, as its most promising, most daring officer.

And even as he was watching him, a change had come over him. Like an actor slipping into a character role at the rise of the curtain, the Mullah or street corner pedagogue that he had just been, turned into a career army officer, alert, cool, wholly professional. Captain Jamal Din unfolded his map case, studied a map briefly and snapped the case shut. He got up and scanned the route with his binoculars, and then shut his eyes for a few seconds as though he was saying a prayer. Then he gave the order to march. 'Let's go, bhaijan. Chalo!'

~

He had prayed, pleaded, sobbed like a child, howled like an animal. It did him no good. They were not to be denied. His splendid, unblemished body of which he had been so vain, was subjected to its most degrading violation.

All night, he lay awake, thinking, dreaming of vengeance, of blowing his own head off, and every now and then, bursting into uncontrollable sobs. He knew there was nothing he could do to them; and he was too much of a coward to end his own life. He also knew that he could never go back to face his family, friends, comrades; everyone would know, somehow even strangers would know.

The awesome night-time stillness of the mountains was desecrated by the sounds of snoring, the pine-scented air was thick with the foul smell of their exhalations. He prayed for an Indian shell to land on the hut and finish them off.

It was still pitch dark when the Captain stirred as though in response to an internal alarm. He glanced at his watch and nudged one of the others awake. Someone made tea while Mir Khan came and sat beside Fida Ali and untied his hands and rubbed his wrists gently to restore the circulation of blood. The touch of his calloused fingers had made Fida Ali's skin prickle with revulsion and caused a shuddering sigh to escape his lips.

No one said a word to him, but they spoke and joked among themselves as though this was just another day. They drank their tea and munched their biscuits and sucked their boiled sweets. Then they lit cigarettes while Captain Jamal Din studied his map. Then he flashed his torch all round the hut and made them pick up the cigarette butts and bits of paper and bury them outside. He glanced at his watch, closed his eyes for a few seconds, and said, 'Let's go, bhaijan. Chalo!'

Mercifully, it was still quite dark. Otherwise it was almost certain that the hawk-eyed Captain would have noticed that Fida Ali had not buttoned down his shoulder flaps.

They were rounding an abutment in the hill path, and they

were marching well spaced out because of the danger of mines. Fida Ali had managed to lag behind the others. Even as he was walking, he had unslung his Sten. Now he was holding it fast against his side and aiming it at the man walking in front of him, Havaldar Mir Khan.

The others had rounded the bend. The man immediately ahead was a black shadow sliding past an enormous grey rock.

He pushed forward the safety catch and pressed hard on the trigger. He saw the shadow jerk backward first and then plunge forward as in a dive. He flung away his Sten in the same movement as he shrugged off his webbing harness. By the time they had realized what was happening, he had bolted down the khud.

There was a yelling behind him, and curses, and someone let loose a burp of Stengun fire into the hillside. Then he heard Jamal Din's voice rise above the abrupt silence, like the howl of some animal in torment, 'Come back, Fida Ali! I can see you. I'll blow your head off if you don't come on the double. Double, I say!'

Squatting behind a rock, he knew he could not be seen, and that the Captain was bluffing; bluffiing even as he was scanning the ground to locate him and listening for telltale sounds. Fida Ali sprang up and made another dart down the valley, and heard the curses, anguished and terrifying, 'Napak shaitan! Deserter! Murderer! Yah Allah…I swear I shall dig out your roots and kill you like a rat, wherever you might be hiding! Coward. Scum! Bred by pigs…'

At the foot of the hill, he was out of range of the Stens. As he lay down on his back to regain his breath, the thought crossed his mind: having a man deserting from his patrol must be the very first black mark on the Captain's glittering record; a disgrace far worse than having one of the men of his patrol killed.

In the distance, over a mountain edge that stood like a paper cut-out against a steel-grey sky, he saw a faint brightness. So that was the east. He only had to march in that general direction. Within twenty miles, he would have crossed into the enemy-held territory and placed himself out of the clutches of his brothers-in-arms.

~

The sun was now in the West, low and big and slightly misshapen.

The young Dogra who stood on a ridge turned a full circle. He realized that he was hopelessly lost.

He grinned and shook his head, wondering how he had managed to lose his way, for the journey from Margan onwards to within a few miles of Gulmarg was almost along the main tourists' route. It was his anxiety to keep away from the main routes that had made him miss a turning.

'A stranger is apt to be shot down without warning,' he had been cautioned. All soldiers were believed to be trigger-happy. 'And if you see a military encampment, don't go near it. Take a detour.'

Just outside Margan, a military jeep full of black men in green uniforms had stopped him to ask him who he was and where he was going. They did not speak either Kashmiri or Hindi. So he had tried his high school English and discovered that they were from Kerala, which was somewhere at the other end of India.

Actually, even though he was a citizen of the State of Jammu and Kashmir, the Srinagar valley had always been like a foreign land to him, the world beyond the Nanga Parbat. He belonged to Gilgit, a good two weeks' march across the main Himalayan range and along a track that was icebound for half the year.

Gilgit. A land more rugged, bleak, inhospitable, yet breathtakingly beautiful, and above all, holy; the chosen land of the gods. Half the male members of his family were monks.

He alone of three brothers had been singled out for being sent to the world beyond; to be educated, to become a lawyer or a doctor in the Maharaja's court. There had been great rejoicing in his family when he had passed his matric from the Partap Singh High School in Srinagar. But within days of that, he had been sent right back to Srinagar to secure admission in the Government college. He must not take the risk of the route becoming snowbound.

He was still in Srinagar, waiting for his college to be opened, when he had heard that the troops in Gilgit, who were commanded by especially chosen and highly paid British officers, had rebelled. Overnight, Gilgit, a province of the Maharaja's domain, had become a part of the new country called Pakistan.

It was as though the world had collapsed, all its landmarks suddenly vanished. The Nanga Parbat which had shone above their village like an eternal lamp, overshadowing everything else, had gone up in smoke. Whatever the rest of life had to offer him, a higher education and the glittering rewards it was guaranteed to bring, held no appeal for him. He wanted to go back to the family's traditional calling and become a monk.

It had taken him nearly three months to secure admission in the Math of the Thirteen Order at Deoban which had had a mauling during the recent war. Four of the monks had been killed and some of the institution's buildings had been burnt down by a raiding party, and that was the only reason why they were admitting four novitiates to the order at the rate of one a year.

He was dressed in stout canvas boots, woollen trousers and jacket and a turban, and he carried with him a goat-hair blanket and a whitewood staff. He had been particularly told not to bring any books with him, or clothes. He would be given the Math's robes. In a cloth bag he carried some fruit and a block of jaggery.

Even though he knew he had lost his way, he was not really worried. For him the day of horror had come and gone: nothing would ever be quite as shocking as the realization that he could never go back to that segment of paradise that had been his homeland. What did it matter whether he reached the monastery in which he proposed to spend the greater part of his life, a day or two late? He had been told that in the Math, there were neither clocks nor calendars.

He sat down, watching the setting sun. He closed his eyes and recited a silent sandhya to the departing day.

When he opened his eyes, he saw a shadow against the melon-red orb, like a worm in an apple, he thought. The man must have been there all the time, but sitting so still as to resemble a rock. He was now getting up and coming towards him, folding his hands in greeting.

He wore some sort of an uniform. He squatted down in the dust a few feet away and said, 'I have not eaten for a whole day. Have you got anything to eat, brother?'

It was good to hear Kashmiri spoken, even though the accent was unfamiliar. 'Yes, certainly. I have some fruit and jaggery.'

The man in the khaki uniform gratefully accepted the food. He ate in silence for a few minutes and wiped his lips with the back of his hand. 'I had food in my haversack,' he said by way of explanation. 'But

I lost it.'

'You are a soldier, then?' the Dogra asked.

'Yes,' the man answered, keeping his eyes averted.

'Which battalion?'

'I am not allowed to tell that to a stranger.'

'I was asking because the only troops I saw this morning were from South India. They could not be your battalion.'

'No, they could not,' the soldier said, gazing at the distant peaks. But he did not volunteer further information about himself. He ate a pear, skin and all, and licked the juice off his fingers. 'And you, brother, what is your name?'

'I am called Pulakashi.'

'And what are you doing alone in these inhospitable parts?'

Pulakashi grinned. 'I'm going to become a monk,' he said proudly. 'You know, the Order of the Thirteen.'

'I don't. Why thirteen?'

'Because there can be no more than thirteen at the monastery at any given time.'

'Is it near Uri?'

'No. In the same range as Gulmarg. I should have been there now, if I had not lost my way.'

'You cannot get there tonight, then.'

'There is no hurry. Tomorrow will do—or the day after. Not like college, or your parades.'

'Do they know you, brother?'

'No. But I have a letter, telling me to come.'

The soldier broke off a bit of the hard jaggery and put it into his mouth. For a minute or so he sucked contentedly, then he stretched out his legs.

'Is that blood on your trousers?' Pulakashi asked. 'Have you been in battle?'

The soldier's face flushed and he sat up as though he had been stung. He placed his floppy jungle hat to cover the splotches of blood. 'That is a heavy stick you have,' he commented, as though to change the subject. 'Shines like silver.'

'Whitewood. It will keep away snakes.'

'At this place you are going to. Will they teach you in any

language you know, or only Sanskrit?'

'Hindi, I believe. And English too. But at first, I don't think anyone will speak to me at all, in any language. And as for me, I am not supposed to say anything to them for a whole year.'

'Really?'

'It is the rule. Novice monks have to take a vow of silence. A whole year.'

'I would not like to go to that sort of place,' the soldier muttered almost to himself, and then asked, 'Have you a cigarette?'

It turned out that the other did not smoke. Presently it became dark, and the two men stretched out in the lee of the hill. It was very cold where they were, about eight thousand feet above sea level, and realizing that the soldier was shivering because he only had a thin sweater over his cotton blouse, the other gave him his blanket to cover.

It must have been a couple of hours later. The moonlight was very bright. The aspiring lama heard a sound and opened his eyes. Silhouetted against the burnished sky, he saw a shadow. A man standing sky high, and raising a stick which seemed to glow with a light of its own. He screwed his eyes tight as though to shut out the nightmare when the blow fell which broke his skull.

CHAPTER I

It was well past midnight, and the air conditioning in the airport building had either been switched off or stopped functioning. A voice over the loudspeaker crackled indistinctly. 'Air India flight AI 1372 to Mauritius and Nairobi is now ready for boarding. Will all passengers...'

The girl in the belted raincoat shook her head with impatience and glanced at her watch. She might have been an off-duty air hostess which was the impression she sought to create, because she was in the PASSENGERS-ONLY part of the building, and was anxious to finish her business before anyone discovered that she was not a passenger.

A porter came in with two brown imitation-leather suitcases and hoisted them onto the weighing machine. Smart luggage, the girl thought; must be travelling first class too, to take that much baggage.

A woman came in, waited upon by an official in white uniform and wearing two gold stripes on his shoulders. She was perhaps in her forties; handsome, well-preserved, and self-assured.

While the man behind the ticket counter was checking her ticket and filling out her boarding pass, the girl in the raincoat who had been standing beside the untenanted British Airways counter, took out from her pocket a rectangular metal box no bigger than a cigarette lighter. She bent her head over the counter and aimed the Minox at the woman with the smart luggage. She made three exposures and slipped the camera back into her pocket.

'Have a good trip, ma'am,' the Air India man said to the woman as he handed her her ticket and boarding pass. She nodded her thanks, said good night to the man who had escorted her, and sailed through the door marked Immigration. The man who had accompanied her, waited until the porter had finished tying labels to her suitcases and placed them on the conveyor belt. Then he opened an unmarked door behind the counter and went in.

~

The customs inspection room was cavernous, airless, and dimly lit. The conveyor belt that came in from the ticket enclosure rolled right through the room and onto the tarmac outside where the train of luggage vans waited. Two officials in white uniforms, who were standing well apart, kept pointing to odd pieces of luggage for inspection. These were immediately pounced upon by one or the other of the team of porters and carried over to the inspection counters.

The two brown suitcases came riding over the belt, and with them walked the two-striper who had accompanied the woman to whom the suitcases belonged. A porter made as if to pick up one of them but checked himself when the officer made a gesture with his hands, no more than a flick of his fingers.

By that time everyone in the room had got the message. The suitcases were privileged. They were not to be subjected to checks.

~

Outside, near the check in counter, the girl in the raincoat, her purpose now achieved, waited for a chance to make her getaway. Through the glass front she followed the lights of cars as they drove up, unloading passengers. Her face lit up as a large black car with a flag came and stopped at the entrance. She beamed and waved out as to a friend and walked briskly through the door as though to greet the important personage who had arrived.

Once outside the building, she darted for the domestic entrance side and jumped into the first taxi in the rank.

~

A few minutes before noon on the next day, a motorcycle roared along Rajghat Road. The rider crouched low over the handlebars, enjoying the sensation of speed. A traffic policeman threw a salute as the machine flashed past, its speedometer needle hovering between seventy and eighty.

The man on the motorcycle was a police officer. His name was Om Prakash Agarwal, and he had been recently promoted to the rank of Deputy Superintendent as a special recognition for his efficient handling of the Dorabji bank fraud case.

The motorcycle slowed down as it turned into one of the new housing colonies and came to a stop near a gate which bore a signpost:

SURANA LIMITED
CHAIRMAN'S OFFICE

It was a double-storied house with a garden.

The rider parked his machine and walked in. The uniformed durban at the gate saluted as he strode past. He went through the waiting room in which three men with bulging briefcases sat smoking, and pushed open a door which was marked PRIVATE.

It was a small room. The girl who was at the airport sat at a table, speaking into one of three telephones. A nameplate on her table said

MISS NETRA AGARWAL
SECRETARY TO CHAIRMAN

'...in a conference at the moment,' she was saying. 'And he has three more appointments before lunch, Mr Satham. He rests for an hour after that. What? Oh, in that case, I could fit you in for—will ten minutes be all right?'

She looked up, flashed a smile at her visitor and pushed the cigarette box towards him even as she was saying into the telephone, 'Ask for Miss Netra Agarwal. That's me. I'll whisk you in. Fifteen forty it is. Yes, Mr Satham, I'm making a note.'

She made a face at the telephone and wrote down the appointment on a pad. 'Some big bug in the party—treasurer or something,' she explained, and then in an accusing voice said, 'Fine brother you are, sending me into the passenger's lounge. God, was I scared!'

'How did it go?'

'Swimmingly.' She opened a drawer and took out the Minox. 'Three exposures.'

'Thank God! I was beginning to get desperate.' The way he made a grab for the camera made the girl ask, 'Don't tell me you're in some sort of trouble.'

'Up to here,' he told her, touching his adam's apple. 'But may be this will help sort out things.' He kissed the Minox and put it into his pocket.

'I do wish you had not got involved in that bank fraud case,' she said anxiously.

'Oh, I'll be all right,' he reassured her. He got up and patted her shoulder. 'You have been a real help. Just do one more thing for me, will you? I've been trying to get Superintendent Lal all morning. Ring him and tell him I want to see him...that it's urgent. Oh, any time at all, day or night. Okay?' He dashed out of the room.

Even as she was waving at his back, one of her telephones had begun to ring.

~

Manekji Hormusji Dorabji, ex-army Captain and now a convicted swindler, sat on a hard wooden bench in his cell in Tihar jail and frowned at the *Statesman* crossword. He cocked his head as he heard footsteps and voices. The door leading to his corridor squeaked as it was opened.

He was undergoing a five year prison term for having conned a bank into parting with the rupee equivalent of a million dollars in currency notes. He had got away with the money but, for some inexplicable reason, had lingered in the capital, wandering aimlessly, or so it seemed.

He was caught the same night with the money still in his possession. He had confessed his guilt and was convicted.

In prison he had had time to brood. He had complained that he had confessed under coercion and promises of reward made to him by persons in authority whom he was prepared to name. He had managed to interest a lawyer in his case and demanded a fresh trial. The High Court had granted his plea and offered to release him on bail pending a retrial.

Then Dorabji had done a strange thing. He had declined bail. The impression he gave was that he felt he was safer in jail than as a free man outside. He was permitted no visitors except of course his lawyer and the police officer who had been in charge of investigating his case.

The door into the corridor squeaked again as it was shut. Dorabji cocked his ears to listen to the sound of the padlock being put on. It was customary in this part of the jail for the corridor doors to be kept locked.

Steps approached his cell. A warden appeared and unlocked and threw open the door with something of a flourish. 'Deputy Sahib,' he announced.

'I'll be a little time,' Deputy Superintendent Om Prakash told the warden. 'Don't wait here. I'll call you when I am done.' He waited till the warden had locked the cell door and gone out of earshot. 'Don't like the look of that man,' he said without turning. 'Far too oily.'

Then he lowered himself on the bench, and taking an envelope from his pocket handed it to Dorabji.

~

After he had come out of the corridor, the warden stood motionless for a few seconds. Then he strolled to the adjoining corridor which was set aside for violent cases. He went through the routine precaution of locking up the corridor door behind him, and then walked on tiptoe till he came to the cell that was directly behind Dorabji's.

It was exactly the same shape and size as Dorabji's except that this one had a solid steel door which had a window that was more like a peephole, three inches by six. He went in, locked the door with his passkey and fastened a piece of black cardboard which he carried in his pocket against the peephole.

Then he sat comfortably on the wooden bench and pulled out from under it a plastic box in which nestled a set of headphones. He put on the headphones and began to listen.

~

Dorabji's fingers had trembled as he opened the envelope. Inside were three photographs, each one the size of a playing card. They showed a woman standing at the Air India counter at the International airport building.

'The same?' Om Prakash asked.

Dorabji gave the thumbs up sign. 'Oh, absolutely. That's Mukti Bahini. But how did you discover her?'

'You put me on to her. You told me that you were to deliver the money to a woman; a woman who would be waiting for you in a car at the gate of Jantar Mantar. That you had been given code signals to identify each other.'

'I know. But I had no idea what her real name was or anything—what kind of a car she would come in, where she lived. Oh, I had seen her before, when I had given her a suitcase full of money. That time she was waiting in front of the stadium car park, in a taxi. That's all I told you.'

'You told me something else,' Om Prakash reminded him. He handed the prisoner a cigarette and lit it for him. 'You said that when you put the suitcase in her taxi, there was other luggage in the taxi which had made you think that she was going abroad.'

'That's right. Another suitcase, an airlines bag, a raincoat—the cab stank of perfume.'

'A raincoat in Delhi in the middle of March. Obviously someone taking an international flight. I pursued the hunch. The same woman was going to meet you this time…'

'At the Jantar Mantar gate. The bitch wasn't there, and I was stuck with all that dough.'

'You were late—two hours behind time,' Om Prakash pointed out.

Dorabji reacted with venom. 'That's because that swine bank manager didn't show up till one-thirty!'

'I know, I know,' Om soothed him. 'So I made inquiries to find out what last-minute cancellations there were on the day you…on the day of the bank fraud. There were seventeen.'

'Cancellations? So many!'

'Thirteen were a group booking. Party of students from Japan. That left four. Of them, only two were women.' Om held up two fingers and smiled. 'After that it was easy. I checked up with immigration control whether one of these women had travelled abroad on that day when you met that first time—in March. Only one. This woman.' He tapped the envelope with his fingers.

'Smart,' Dorabji said with approval. 'Where had she gone?'

'Mauritius.'

'And her cancelled ticket this last time? Also for Mauritius?'

'Right. So I kept a watch. Waited till the name appeared on the passenger list to Mauritius again. Then had her photographed—in the airport building.' He reached out and collected the photographs.

'But she was a stooge, Mr Agarwal,' Dorabji pointed out. 'Like myself. You still don't know who the people behind her are—the men who give her the orders.'

'Don't I?' Om Prakash said. 'I can tell you I believe I have broken this case. It is all in my case diary...'

'Really, Mr Agarwal?'

Om Prakash nodded. 'That's where these photographs...' he stopped in mid-sentence. 'What's that?' he asked, springing to his feet.

There was a commotion in another part of the jail. Yells of rage and screams and ominous thuds and the sound of things falling. A bell began to clang and someone was shouting at the top of his voice,

'Stop that! At once! Khamosh! Khamosh!'

'Gang warfare,' Dorabji explained with a shudder. 'For supremacy. Even here. We have a big fight at least once every week. They'll stop soon enough when the guards make a lathi charge and break a few heads.' He threw away the butt of his cigarette and crushed it underfoot. Then he asked, 'Who's she, Mr Agarwal?'

~

In the adjoining cell, the warden suddenly sat up. For a second or two he remained motionless. Then he whisked off the earphones and sprang to his feet. He put away the earphones in their container and slid it under the bunk. Then he opened the door of the cell and ran to the scene of trouble where the other footsteps were converging.

~

'Her name is Ekanti Ma. Does it ring a bell?'

Dorabji shook his head. 'And yet—I've heard the name.'

'Swami Rajguru's chief disciple...'

'Oh, my God! *The* swami. You don't think he's in this.'

Om Prakash grinned.

'And she is his chief disciple?'

'In other words his procuress,' Deputy Superintendent Om Prakash said irreverently. Then he got up and yelled for the warder.

'But...but Mr Agarwal,' Dorabji stammered. 'If the Swami is at the back of this, does it mean that the people who have made him their guru also...?

'Shhh!' Om Prakash warned, and gestured in the direction of the approaching footsteps. 'See you in a couple of days,' he said in his normal voice. 'Meanwhile, keep your chin up.'

~

It was now late in the evening. In her office, Netra Agarwal was making yet another attempt to make an appointment with Superintendent Lal.

'Can you take a message for him, please. It's urgent. I am speaking on behalf of my brother, Deputy Superintendent Om Prakash Agarwal. Yes, yes, Mr Lal knows him well. He wants to see Mr Lal this evening...what? He's not expected back till midnight? Oh, help! No, no. I shall try again, myself.'

CHAPTER 2

THE battered old Fairchild Packet made a tight turn over the target area. A thousand feet below, the lake glimmered like a sheet of gun metal. Visram Lal could only just make out the outlines of the three bungalows facing the lake. He would look a perfect fool if they dropped him in the lake, he thought. Later they would pretend that it was all a prank.

Only a selected few police officers were given training in the Inter-Services Commando School, on the theory that, in case of war, they would prove more useful as agents operating behind enemy lines than the officers of the defence services. Barely half an hour earlier, the Range Commander had given him his briefing.

The RC, Avinash Batra, was the head of what the army called its Dirty Dogs. He held the rank of Colonel. According to Batra, it was no more than a routine exercise, what they called 'Enter shooting'. They were going to drop him by parachute almost on top of the target, which was a lakeside bungalow where two enemy agents were supposed to meet once every week. All he had to do was to kick open the door and blast away before they could draw their guns.

The RC was not in uniform. He must have come straight from some dinner party, for he was wearing a well-cut sherwani and a glossy black cap at a jaunty angle. Decked up like a Lucknow pimp, Visram thought.

'You'll hit ground at three minutes after ten,' the RC had told him very professionally. 'Remember there's no moonlight to speak of. One minute to get your bearings and another to finish the job.

The jeep will be in the drive at five minutes past. It's engine will be running. It will not wait for more than—shall we say, ninety seconds?'

'That should be enough time,' Visram Lal had answered, and then added, 'I am taking a Beretta, Colonel.'

The other had shrugged disapprovingly. 'I'd never let one of our own chaps out with one of those things. But…some people will never learn.'

It was the same every time. The instructors were sold on the revolver; preferably the Webley Scott .38. An automatic to them was something invented by Hollywood to film cops and robbers; a stage prop that was bound to develop a stoppage just when you were in a tight spot.

He, Visram Lal, swore by the Beretta; and he was allowed the latitude to choose his own weapon merely because he was an outsider.

'Even after you enter, the light will be dim,' Batra told him. 'Only a kerosene lantern, I believe.'

'What's so special about the exercise?' Visram Lal asked. 'To me it looks like a piece of cake. In, bang bang, out.'

The man in the knee-length black coat and the fancy cap smiled. Even the smile was condescending, Visram reflected.

'All our exercises are pieces of cake,' the Colonel had answered. 'If—if our operators are prepared to take the unexpected in their stride. Here. Sign.'

Visram had scribbled his signature across the next-of-kin form and walked out of the RC's office.

Now the plane had circled the lake and was turning again, losing height gradually. There was a shrill beep and a red light in the roof had begun to blink. They were on the final approach. Visram patted his holster and touched his belt buckle in a nervous gesture. He hitched up his parachute harness and wiggled his toes inside his American-Marines' ankle boots with their soft rubber soles.

Two men in Air Force overalls who had been sitting slumped in bucket seats in the rear of the plane rose and stood on both sides of him. It was their business to shove him out of the plane if he failed to jump on cue. He had been told that they had had to use force every once in a while.

The tail swung gently from side to side. The door rolled away with a metallic whirr and the sudden inrush of air caused the plane to lurch. By the time the plane had steadied again, the red light had stopped winking and a mechanical voice had taken over. 'Ten seconds to go.'

Visram Lal stood up. He braced his feet against the metal edge of the gaping hole and held on tightly to the struts on both sides. He wondered which of the two men behind him was going to come out with the stock joke.

It was the one on his right, coal black and with the face of a rhesus monkey who said it. 'If it doesn't open, bring it right back, sir. We'll give you a brand new one.'

Visram held up the thumb of his right hand in answer.

'Five seconds. Four. Three. Two. One second. On!'

Almost by reflex action, he had pushed himself into the blue-black rectangle. He glimpsed the metallic underside of the plane flying side by side and then suddenly found himself hurtling away as the force of the air bowled him over and over. The lake was coming up at an alarming rate. God, had the stupid bastard dropped him over the lake after all! He cursed as he tugged at the ripcord. He saw the chute fly up like a ribbon of smoke and braced himself for the jerk that knocked the air out of his chest. After that he was floating down, and he could see that the wind was carrying him towards the edge of the lake.

That damned navigator certainly knew his job. When his feet touched ground and he rolled over, he was barely two hundred yards from the end bungalow. He unclipped the belt and wriggled out of his harness and saw the chute go billowing towards the babool trees.

~

The breeze was now behind him. He lay on his stomach in the moist grass, trying to get back his breath and taking a look at the target. There was not a light anywhere, and nothing seemed to move. No sound either, not even the customary dog barking. Then he heard the thin wail of music coming from the middle bungalow which was his objective, and set off at a crouching run, pressing his hand against the gun almost for reassurance. It was amazing how much one could see, just by the light of the stars.

He remembered the briefing. Five steps to the veranda. Then three doors. He had to go for the door on the right. As he reached the veranda steps, he dropped down and peered cautiously across its width. No light came from any of the doors. He padded silently up the steps and across the width of the veranda.

He kicked open the door and darted in, sideways, holding the Beretta close to his hip, cocked, determined to take the man on the left first and then turning and finishing off the second. Even in the dimness of the soot-grimed lantern, he could see the two men, exposed, waiting to be struck down. It took him a second or two to realize why he had not shot them at sight, why his finger had remained frozen on the trigger.

Both men had been dancing to the music of a small transistor, and each held a woman in his arms.

The music went on. Pubescent voices moaned and wailed in ecstasy. The four figures which were cardboard cutouts set up to represent the men and women for the purpose of the exercise mocked the man who had come in with a gun to mow them down. And then the room reverberated to the roar of gunfire as six bullets hit the wall only inches above Visram Lal's head and brought down a shower of chipped plaster.

And then the room was flooded with light so that a camera could record the exercise on film, and Colonel Batra's voice from an inner room said, 'Okay, Mr Lal. That will be all.'

~

In the jeep, going back to Delhi, Visram Lal stared resentfully at the man who was driving. Over his immaculate evening dress, Colonel Batra now wore a plastic cape with camouflage paint. He also wore old-fashioned motoring goggles.

Visram Lal was fuming at the fiendish trick that had been played on him. The bastard had sent him on an exercise whose purpose was said to be to kill two enemy agents, and then had presented him two women to kill along with the men.

They were passing the Qutab Minar when Batra said, 'You were dead, you know, several times over.'

Visram Lal did not answer. He would never do it, and to hell with them. He could never bring himself to shoot women in cold blood—even if they were consorting with enemy agents. If it had been four men instead…

'If it had been four men, I would not have hesitated,' he told Batra. 'Chanced that the third or certainly the fourth would have shot back. But women… No.'

'Others have done it.'

'Only because they knew that they were firing at cardboard dummies.'

Batra shook his head. 'The whole point of the exercise is that you must act as though you're dealing with actual men and women. In any case, it was a real situation we duplicated. A British agent was para-dropped to kill two Germans. When he went in, he found that each was accompanied by a woman. He shot down all four.'

Visram Lal made a face. 'The British have their own code.'

'It was during the war,' Batra explained.

'I could never bring myself to do it—not even if there was a war on.'

'Chivalry has no place in my calling,' the Colonel said pompously.

'Thank God it is not my calling,' Visram retorted.

The Colonel had turned as though he had been stung. For a few seconds he must have wrestled with his self-control and then come out with it. 'At least my calling has not become a dirty word.'

Visram looked away into the distance; at the black dome of some Mogul tomb cutting into the blue-black sky.

'You take your orders from palace flunkeys, not from your superiors—and no written orders at that. Two men whom both of us have seen as clerks now crack the whip and you jump, send your minions to plant bootleg whisky or foreign money in someone's house and carry out raids. You bug telephones and put cameras into people's bedrooms to record their sex life. You send perfectly normal people to the loony bin just because they have dared to talk back to that budding Idi Amin who has become your lord and master. You wake up citizens in the middle of the night and march them off to some Gulag horror where you torture them to extract confessions. You hush up a bank fraud of millions because you are terrified of the gang at the top, and then sign blank warrants by the dozen to send innocent people to jail!' He stopped, as much because his voice had cracked as because he realized that he had said too much. His chest was heaving.

'Go on,' Visram prompted. 'Surely there is more.'

For a long time, Batra did not say anything. Then he said. 'I am sorry. I expect I have already said enough to be sent to Tihar jail for the rest of my life.'

'Well, a couple of years certainly.'

'I'm sorry,' Batra said again. After a while, he asked, 'You're not carrying some sort of a recording device, are you?'

'No. I left mine at home.'

'But then you're not RAW, are you?'

'I've got one of the new fangled RAW recorders, as it happens.' Visram told him.

'And at that I don't suppose you need one, really. I mean, you could just run me in, could you not?'

'Oh, easy. It was pretty strong stuff, you know; particularly about budding Idi Amin. Is that what the services call him these days?'

'When they're minding their language.'

Visram laughed. 'I'm sorry I made that crack about—your calling.'

'Well, we do get pretty callous, I suppose,' Batra admitted. 'After all dirty tricks is our business...'

'But you haven't become a dirty word, yet.'

'Not yet.'

After that they did not say anything till they were nearing the President's estate. Batra said, 'Going back to that exercise today. You want to be put on again?'

'No. It'll be the same again. I won't kill women.'

For the rest of the journey, Visram brooded about what the other had said. God, what a pass things had come to. At the crossing near Safdar Jung's tomb, he had himself dropped. He would walk the rest of the way.

~

No. 49, Arjun Singh Park, is one of the smaller flats in a three-storey brick building constructed during the last days of the Raj, and which is exactly similar to five other buildings clustered round a rectangular lawn. The building has no lift, and all its eleven flats are occupied by Government officials. By the time Visram turned into the gate, none of the windows showed a light.

No. 49 was on the second floor, a bachelor flat, which consisted of two spacious, high-ceilinged rooms and a bath and a balcony overlooking Lodhi gardens.

Near the entrance, Visram saw a parked motorcycle, a powerful machine with an extra-large exhaust and wide handlebars supporting a jumble of special fittings. A speed-nut's dream, a brute of a machine that came into its own only while roaring on the highway at ninety-plus, Visram thought. It was painted either black or some dark shade of green or blue—he could not be certain in the dim light coming from the street lamp about fifty yards away.

A man was waiting for him on the second floor landing. The light from the stair lamp was dim, and the man had clicked his heels and saluted before Visram recognized him: Om Prakash Agarwal who had been an Inspector under him in Bilaspur when they had both started service.

Agarwal was now with the Delhi police, and that very month he had been promoted to Deputy Superintendent over the heads of scores of others who were senior to him, because he had managed to nab within a matter of hours, M.H. Dorabji, the culprit in the most sensational case of the year: the seven million bank fraud.

It was true that, in his fledgeling years, Om Prakash had looked upon Visram Lal as his guide and mentor. But that had been eight years ago. Their paths had drifted and now they belonged to different departments which were often at rivalry with each other, Visram to the Special Branch and Om Prakash to the Delhi Police. What was more, there had been a good deal of clucking of tongues in and out of the service, about Om's handling of the bank fraud case. Full recovery of the stolen money and a confession by the thief all within a matter of hours, and the resulting conviction had been achieved within fifteen minutes.

It was said to be the quickest trial in the history of jurisprudence.

Whether it was or not, Om's part in the whole affair smacked of extensive manipulation.

Visram's first reaction was one of annoyance. He stood frowning in front of his own door, the key ring in his hand, his mind divided between the demands of service cameraderie and a reluctance to soil his hands with something that was patently unethical. 'Did you want to see me?' he said, and glanced pointedly at his watch.

'Yes, sir.'

'What's it about?'

Om Prakash gave a nervous allround look but did not say anything, which made Visram ask, 'Have you been waiting long?'

'About an hour.'

'It's nearly midnight,' Visram muttered as he opened the door. 'Come in and take a seat. God, you look washed out! I just want to get out of my overalls.'

He went into the bedroom and, opening a drawer of his dressing table, put away the Baretta. He changed into a bush shirt and trousers and even as he was bending over the drawer, picked up a gleaming plastic object, the size of a double pack of playing cards, and slipped it into his pocket. It was the latest in sensitive tape recorders, an instrument made by Halicrafters especially for the CIA. A dozen had been brought into the country under special licence by the Research and Analysis Wing, or RAW. This one was officially on loan from RAW to the special branch.

'Would you like a drink, Om?' Visram called out from the bedroom. 'Or are you still a TT?'

'Still TT, Mr Lal. How well you remember. No, never touch the stuff.'

How few of us can say that of ourselves, Visram reflected as he joined Om in the front room.

~

'I came for advice, Mr Lal,' Om Prakash began. 'Didn't know who else to turn to. It's about the Dorabji case.'

Visram Lal winced. He did not want to have anything to do with the Dorabji case. It was not his concern. Not even his department's concern. It was common talk among policemen that the Dorabji case was the kiss of death.

'But it was one of those open-and-shut cases,' Visram pointed out.

'That's just it, sir. I opened it; I also helped to shut it.'

'Then why reopen it?'

'Because I have come to realize that the man was no more than a stooge in a colossal racket.'

'But why come to me?' Visram asked impatiently.

'You're the only man in this service whom I can trust, Mr Lal.'

Visram stopped Om with a gesture. 'Before you tell me anything, I want you to understand that there can be nothing confidential between us. I mean, in case the question arises, I will have to reveal why you came to see me and what you had to say.' He knew he was speaking as much to the gadget in his pocket as to his visitor.

There was an awkward silence. Om's face had blanched as though the blood had drained from it. He gave a nervous flick of his tongue and took a deep breath. 'I really did not think you would say that, Mr Lal,' he said.

'But, Om, you ought to know the rules: If any of us have a problem—a professional problem—we must take it to our superior, whoever it is we take our orders from.'

Om Prakash gave a hoarse laugh. 'Who do we take our orders from?' he asked in an undertone. 'A voice that comes over the telephone and says it is transmitting palace orders. We dare not question. We jump to attention and do whatever we're told.'

Visram flinched. Here it was, for the second time within an hour. He wished Om had not been so indiscreet, or that he did not have the recorder switched on. What was being taped would help to save his own skin all right. But it was like setting up an ambush for poor Om, the man who had come to him so full of trust.

Shame was an emotion to be shunned in his profession. He was assailed by it all the same. Visram glanced at his watch again. Twelve minutes to midnight. 'Just a sec,' he excused himself and went into the bedroom. He switched off the recorder in his pocket, and came out holding two glasses of water. 'All right. Tell me.'

Om Prakash was near the door, picking up a paper which he hastily shoved into his pocket. He looked sullen and resentful

'What's that you've got there?' Visram asked.

'It's nothing really. Just a note I had slipped under your door in case I missed you.'

'Hand it over, then.'

But whatever had driven Om Prakash to come of him for advice must have been too tenuous to have withstood that initial rebuff. He shook his head and said, 'I don't think I'd better. It was a foolish impulse.'

'I don't know. All of us find ourselves in need of advice, every now and then.' Visram said soothingly. 'Here, drink this.'

Om Prakash obediently gulped down the water and put away the glass on the table. 'Look, Mr Lal, I am sorry I came. I had no business to.'

'Will you answer one or two questions?'

'You are my superior in rank. I cannot not answer.'

'And for no other reason?'

Om Prakash did not answer.

'And will you give me that bit of paper which you had already slipped under my door?'

'Again, only if you order me to.'

'All right. I order you,' Visram said very curtly. 'Come on, hand it over.'

For a second or two he stared defiantly at Visram, and then suddently took out the paper and held it out. Visram put it into his pocket and asked, 'All right. So Dorabji retracted his confession.'

'That came out in the papers, Superintendent.'

Visram thought for a few seconds before going on. 'Tell me, why did you keep on with the investigation even after the case had been buttoned up? The man had made a confession and had been convicted. And you had been promoted as a reward.'

Om Prakash gulped. His adam's apple went up and down. 'Somehow the two things are connected, Mr Lal. Because I was rewarded, promoted out of turn, I wanted to deserve the reward—by finding out the truth.'

'And what were you able to find out?'

'The truth, I believe.' He put on his helmet and saluted. 'Can I go now, sir?'

Visram was conscious of disappointment, of a mistake made, of a confidence turned away. But then there was no other way he could have handled it, he told himself. He had had a long day and was utterly exhausted. He would call him tomorrow and give him an opportunity to unburden himself. 'All right, Om. Good night, and the best of luck.'

Om Prakash hesitated. He said, somewhat stiffly, 'Since we are strictly on an official footing, sir, can I have that paper back?'

God, the man was really behaving most strangely, Visram thought. 'All the more reason why I cannot give it back,' he said. 'You had meant it for me, had you not?'

Om Prakash gave him a resentful look. Then he turned about and almost ran out of the room. Visram bolted the door as the other went down the staircase.

The first thing Visram wanted to do was to erase whatever he had recorded of their talk. He brought the recorder and placed it on the table beside Om's empty glass. But something held him back. Then he remembered that he had not heard the motorcycle start.

There was a gentle knock on the door. Visram went and opened it, but held it on the chain. Om Prakash stood outside, looking, in the overhead light, oddly sinister. Then Visram realized that he was staring at the tape recorder as at a time bomb.

'So you put down everything on tape?'

'Not everything. Anyway, I was about to rub off whatever there was. Why don't you come in?'

Om stood where he was, rocking on the balls of his feet, staring disbelievingly at the little gun-metal package made by Helicrafters.

'I came for that bit of paper,' Om said.

'I haven't read it yet. If you will wait a minute…'

'That's just it, cant you understand, for God's sake? Once you have read it, there's no point in my retrieving it.'

'Oh, stop being silly, Om,' Visram snapped. 'Come in and let's talk things over.' He took off the chain.

But Om did not come in. He pointed a finger at the tape recorder and made a spluttering sound. Then he turned on his heels and went pounding down the steps looking as though he was chasing a gigantic spider that was his own shadow.

Visram shut and bolted the door. Even as he unfolded the note, he heard the motor-cycle engine growl and roar into full life. Om Prakash had scrawled with a felt tip pen in neat blue letters:

Destroy after reading. If it becomes necessary to find the case diary, it is with my sister, Netra Agarwal, who lives at 12A, Golcha Marg. She is Vinay Surana's Secretary. It is dynamite.

Even after he had finished reading it, Visram could hear the drone of the powerful engine as the motorcycle sped away into the night.

Visram did not know what to make of the message. The case diary, of course, must contain whatever Om had been able to find out about the Dorabji case. But it was an official document. It was wrong of Om to entrust it to his sister's care.

He would contact Om in the morning and sort out things. For the moment, all he wanted was a night's sleep. He took a shower and changed into a loongi. He carried the recorder into the bedroom, thinking that he would erase the tape. But his eyelids were heavy with sleep, so he decided to leave it till the morning. Then he remembered that he had not burned Om's note either.

He was asleep the moment his head touched his pillow. But even in his sleep, he thought he could hear the roar of Om's bike.

~

The road to Palam was a broad black ribbon rushing at him, and it was totally deserted. This was the sort of challenge that Om had always revelled in. He would give the petrol tank of his BSA M 20 a fond pat as though it were a horse, and then give it its head, deliberately preventing himself from peeking at the speedometer but knowing, by the force of the breeze against his cheeks as much as by the howling of the engine, that he was doing close to ninety miles an hour.

Not today. He was doing a sedate forty, and he was cool and relaxed as he had not been for a long time, and sitting well back in his saddle and thinking that he had not eaten for a long time.

That outburst in Lal's flat had somehow cleared a mental block. Now he was at peace with himself because the realization had dawned on him that he was on the brink of making a fool of himself.

He had no business trying to dig up the truth when he knew that a lot of very powerful people were interested in supressing the truth. That was no way to get on in life. If a man like Visram Lal whom he had looked upon as some kind of a model to copy, was prepared to accept the palpable inconsistencies of the bank fraud case, what business had he, a relative underling, to take up cudgels on behalf of a scapegoat who was being sacrificed.

And yet. Would Superintendent Lal still have quoted departmental propriety at him if he had read the case diary?

He laughed aloud. The question was academic. Visram Lal had not read the case diary. He was not likely to read it, ever.

Because he, Om Prakash Agarwal had made up his mind to destroy it.

He saw the lights coming from the opposite direction when they must have been at least a mile away. He dipped his own light and was answered by a matching courtesy. Now they could both pass each other at the speeds they were travelling at. The road was broad enough.

They could not have been more than a hundred yards apart and Om was thinking to himself that the lights of the oncoming vehicle were set higher than in most commercial lorries, when they were turned on full, blinding him with their glare. And then he saw them veer to his side of the road.

He cursed and braked and swerved, and threw out his legs for balance. He yelled as the realization came to him that there was no way of avoiding a head on collision. In his last millisecond of conscious thought, Deputy Superintendent Om Prakash Agarwal of the Delhi police wondered if the great ten tonne conglomerate of hurtling metal was being deliberately aimed at him.

CHAPTER 3

To Visram Lal, it seemed that he had been asleep only a couple of minutes when the ringing of the telephone awoke him. The watch by his bedside said it was a little after 3 a.m. He lifted the receiver and growled, 'Yes?'

'Superintendent Lal?' someone was saying in that lifeless, catspaw voice of the telephone attendant that is an office peculiar to Indian officialdom. 'Hold the line please. Mr Pashupat wants to speak to you.'

God, did the man never sleep? Visram wondered as he shook himself awake and put on the light. Then he switched on the recorder that he had kept on the bedside table and shifted it closer to the receiver, knowing to himself that what he was doing was enough to earn an instant dismissal from the service or even a term of imprisonment under the newly enacted Maintenance of Internal Security Act, or MISA, which empowered the Government to send any person to prison without giving reasons or without even making a formal charge.

Mr R.A. Pashupat was one half of the uncle and nephew team that had rocketed into prominence over the past year, since the Emergency had been declared. They were the watchdogs of the palace. No one could enter unless they gave the nod, and all orders emanating from the Great Leader were passed through them over the telephone. Nothing was ever written down. Anyone who did not obey was transferred to punishment postings, dismissed or sent to jail.

Pashupat was the nephew; the uncle was B.G. Kaul. Both had been thrown up from the nethermost cellars of the gigantic Kafka castle that housed the nation's administrative intestine. Here, vast armies of faceless clerks laboured among ceiling-high piles of files, and became increasingly attached to them as they mouldered and grew old together. Until finally, the clerks retired and died but the files went on, undyingly, spawning more and more of their kind to serve as the love objects of a new generation of clerks.

From this subterranean world, the two had shot up as by a process of fermentation. Their rise to a position of power that was rated as being higher than that of Cabinet ministers was one of the freak phenomena of the times.

They were now accepted as the surrogate voice of a supreme authority, unchallengeable because no one could reach beyond them to find out what the Great Leader at the top of the pyramid really wanted done. All orders were passed through them, all messages were received through them. They were the only inlet and outlet, the guardians at the gates of an iron fortress. It was they who summoned Cabinet ministers and kept them cooling their heels, they who chastized the senior-most civil servants as though they were erring schoolboys, made transfers, ordered dismissals and arrests, held back or cancelled trains or air services.

Kaul and Pashupat, caricatured in clandestine circulars as the Owl and the Pussycat, the palace flunkeys who also wielded the palace whips, apart from the Great Leader and the Great Leader's son, the most dreaded individuals in the land.

'Speak to Mr Pashupat, please.'

Visram Lal could imagine the man at the other end of the line, in the side room of the modest bungalow that was the centre of the nation's capital. A tubby little man with a moon face and half-moon moustaches under a blunt, broad nose. A natty dresser who fancied himself as a ladies' man, with a voice that was never ruffled; it was the same when he was tearing strips off an industrial magnate or ordering a midnight arrest.

Pashupat was a man of the world, even a bit of a gay dog, unlike his uncle, Kaul the Owl, who professed to be a philosopher and spouted quotations from the Gita. The Owl, with the hooded eyes behind thick lenses, a huge man who padded about in soft rubber chappals and wore flowing white kurtas and pyjamas, resembling some ungainly fowl whose lips were always wet with paan juice.

Through the receiver, Visram could detect other voices in the room at the other end, and as he was wondering to himself who the others might be who were awake at this time of the night and what crisis had caused them to gather together, one of the two voices that customarily gave out what were said to be Palace Orders came over the line.

'You had a visitor, Mr Lal,' Pashupat said.

So they had put a tail on Agarwal. 'Yes,' he admitted.

'What did he want?'

'I never discovered. As soon as I found that he wanted to talk to me off the record, I told him it wasn't on.'

'Ask him where Agarwal is' he heard another voice saying to Pashupat. It was neither the voice of the Great Leader nor of the Heir Apparent, and yet Visram reacted with a tremor of fear; a resonant, stern voice, male, and of someone who could obviously give orders to Pashupat. Visram had the impression that they had hooked on the receiver at the other end to a loudspeaker gadget so that everyone round the table could hear what was being said.

'Yes, go on,' Pashupat was saying.

'I'm afraid there's nothing more, Mr Pashupat. He left soon after that.'

'Cagey, isn't he?' the other voice said. *'They're all the same.'*

'Surely, Mr Lal,' Pashupat said. 'As a senior police officer, was it not your duty to listen carefully to whatever Agarwal had to say and then make a report to the appropriate authority?—instead of warning him not to say anything indiscreet.'

That was the new ethics of the times; reporting the indiscreet utterances of your friends and neighbours was a duty—in fact it was one of the points of the Thirty-Point programme. Visram suppressed a curse. He said, quite mildly, 'I didn't know he had done anything wrong, Mr Pashupat. Has he?'

'Not very forthcoming, is he?' he heard the other voice say. *'I think you'd better tell him what's happened.'*

There was an ominous pause, and then Pashupat said. 'I'm

afraid there has been an accident. Agarwal ran his motor-cycle straight into a lorry.'

'Oh, my God!'

'Stinking of booze, when they found him. You'll have to come and tell us how much he drank in your place. Must have been already roaring tight when he turned up—all that.'

All what, for God's sake? Visram asked himself. He could see what they were asking him to do. Help them establish that the man was drunk, when he knew that Om had never touched alcohol in his life.

'We'll sort all that out in the morning, shall we?' Pashupat said.

Visram slid the tape recorder within inches of the earpiece and said, very distinctly. 'But I know Deputy Superintendent Agarwal never touched alcohol, Mr Pashupat. In my flat he only drank water.' At least he had got that bit down on tape. His hands were already sweating.

'*I told you he'd be difficult*,' he heard the third voice say.

'Agarwal never touched a drink in his life. I would swear to that,' Visram said again.

'We'll go into all that tomorrow, shall we, Mr Lal. I know you're trying to...to cover up for a brother officer. Most praiseworthy, of course but...well, there's something more important I have to ask. He didn't leave any papers with you, did he?'

'Papers?'

'A file. It is missing. He had stolen it. It has official secrets.'

'He left nothing with me, Mr Pashupat.'

'Did he say anything about a file—or any other document?'

He was prepared for that question and was able to answer, very evenly. 'No, Mr Pashupat.'

'Well, well. Sorry to have woken you up. Come and have a chat tomorrow—oh, today, really. Around eleven, shall we say? Oh, Mr Lal. He has a sister somewhere in town, hasn't he? Someone will have to tell her. You don't know where she lives, do you?'

'No, Mr Pashupat. I didn't even know he had a sister.'

'A step-sister, I believe. She works as the Secretary of one of these big business magnates, doesn't she? Mr Birla or Mr Jain.'

'I really don't know, Mr Pashupat.'

'There is so much that you don't know, Mr Lal, for a senior police officer. I am really surprised.'

On that rebuke, the line went dead. Visram could not help remembering that only three years earlier, Pashupat used to address him as 'sir'.

~

No matter what the crisis was, self-protection took priority over everything else, Visram Lal thought ruefully; instinct reinforced by training dictated that. A few minutes spent on tidying up saved endless complications later on.

He extracted the tape from the recorder and inserted a spool with recorded music. The tape on which he had recorded a bit of Om's talk and then the conversation with Pashupat, he tucked away in the folds of a shirt in his cupboard.

On his table there was that mysterious message from Om Prakash. He snapped on his cigarette lighter, burned the note, and flushed the ashes down the toilet.

Then he began to dress. Trousers and turtleneck shirt and tennis shoes, then a wind-cheater jacket. As he was putting on his clothes, he kept thinking that it would not take them long to find out Om's sister's address. They knew she worked as the secretary for a big-name industrialist. All that they had to do was to make a dozen or so telephone calls...or ask the telephone people for it.

He grabbed the directory. It was possible that she had a telelphone at her residence. There were literally hundreds of Agarwals, so perhaps he had a slight edge over those who did not know her name and address. There it was: Miss N. Agarwal, 12A, Golcha Marg-17. He dialled the number.

Impatiently he listened to the burr at the other end, wondering how long it would take her to wake up and also exactly how he was going to tell her that her brother had died in an accident and warn her about the case diary. He heard the receiver being lifted and a woman's voice saying hullo.

'Miss Netra Agarwal?'

'Yes. Who is it?'

'My name is Lal. Visram Lal. Your brother may have spoken...'

'But...who did you say? Mr Lal from the police?'

'That's right. Your brother and I were together in Bilaspur.'

'I know that, Mr Lal...'

'Look, Miss Agarwal. I'd better come and see you because...'

'See me? At this...'

Then he heard a gasp and the sound of a scuffle. 'Miss Agarwal? Are you there, Miss Agarwal?' he said and cursed as he heard another sound, something between a moan and a sigh. Then the line had gone dead.

He thought of ringing again and decided against it. He put down the receiver and ran out of the room. As he was locking the front door, his telephone began to ring. He turned back and watched the instrument for a few seconds and then picked up the receiver.

'Railway inquiries?' a male voice was asking.

He said something stuitably rude and banged the receiver down. It may have been a genuine wrong number. On the other hand, it may have been someone trying to check up if he was still at home.

He would have liked to strap on his Beretta, but decided against it. He was too senior in the service to get involved in a shootout with housebreakers, and in any case he was in the wrong department to go looking for burglars in the middle of the night.

He opened his steel cupboard and took out his Vienna police helmet. It was like a skin-diver's mask and equipped with a special neck-piece reinforced with thin metal strips; the whole thing looked like a French Foreign Legionaire's headdress. He had found it useful in the past.

~

The house that Netra Agarwal lived in was one of several similar houses in the locality that belonged to one or the other of the Surana companies; a neat, two-storied bungalow with two garages. The ground floor was occupied by the company's drafting office, and the first floor, which could be reached by an independent staircase, had two flats. One of these was vacant, and the other was occupied by the Chairman's secretary.

The telephone, also paid for by the firm, was in the entrance lobby, and it was not at all unusual for it to ring at odd hours. The

Surana companies had business connections all over the world, and after office hours, all business calls to the head of the firm were routed to his secretary. People in America or Europe often put through calls without realizing what time it was in India.

It had taken Netra no more than a minute to answer the ring. It was not a foreign call however; it was the man she had been trying to contact most of the previous evening. And he was just saying something about coming to see her when someone had crept from behind and placed a hand over her mouth and tried to wrench the telephone away from her.

Then the light went out, which gave her the impression that there were two men. She had lashed out with her foot and caught the man's wrist and heard his moan of pain. Then the other man had joined in overpowering her and wrenched the receiver from her hand. She had heard the click of the receiver being put back on the cradle, and someone was saying to her in a hoarse whisper: 'Don't resist. Nothing will happen to you!'

They had put on the lights then, and all that she had time to notice before they bandaged her eyes was that both men wore black masks, like tight black stockings pulled over their heads and in which holes had been cut out for the eyes and nostrils. After that they had tied her hands and feet and gagged her mouth with a scarf. Then they had lifted her bodily and deposited her in her bed.

Then one of them dialled a number and asked for railway inquiries, and after that they had proceeded to search the flat.

~

At this time of the night, a speeding car could be heard from a good mile away, and Visram had no desire to advertise his arrival in Golcha Marg. He drove as far as the Jor Bagh police station, identified himself to the Duty Havaldar, and borrowed one of the station's bicycles. After he had reached No. 28, he left the bicycle near one of the signposts advertising the Thirty-Point programme that had mushroomed all over the capital, and walked the rest of the way.

No. 12 stood in its own garden. 12 A must be the first floor, and he could see the door of the staircase. He clambered over the wall and walked across the lawn surrounded by dark bushes. The door had a brass nameplate. For a second his fingers hovered over the bell-push and drew back. If the house had been broken into he did not want to advertise his arrival.

Gingerly he tried the door handle. The door swung open without a sound, almost as though it had been left unbolted for someone to go rushing in. He took a deep breath and kicked open the door, but instead of going in, turned on his heels and fell into a crouching stance.

A shadow had sprung up from the bushes. An upraised hand came down in a chopping motion. He tensed for the blow but did not duck. He reeled at its impact at the same time as he heard the sharp squeal of pain emitted by his assailant. The edge of his hand must have landed smack against the reinforced neckpiece.

By then he had swung into the attack. Little tricks practised over and over again in the combat school came into play almost automatically. His left elbow crashed into his assailant's ribs and then he closed in and his right knee knifed up and lifted the man clean off the ground. He saw the man fold up and totter even as he heard someone behind the door flying up the stairs. He went in and kicked the door shut with his foot and followed the man up the stairs. A strong smell of mogra hung in the air where the man had been waiting. He paused at the landing and groped for the switch. He put it on and off, just to get his bearings. If the other man had a gun, it was better to take him on in the dark. He heard a moan and moved at a crouch towards a dark rectangle that was a door. He went in and paused, trying to listen hard for the sounds of breathing when the blow fell. He threw up his hands to gain balance and caught a whiff of mogra before a blackness descended.

~

He was lying on the floor, staring at the ceiling fan. Gingerly he touched the side of his head and winced. The special helmet may have saved his skull from cracking, but there was heavy swelling which pressed into the side of the helmet. Carefully he peeled off the helmet and felt an instant sense of relief. For a few seconds, he lay back, trying to get his bearings. There were bird calls in the trees outside. It was morning.

He stretched out his hands and feet and wriggled his fingers. At least he was not trussed. He sat up and looked round.

Through the open door of the bedroom he saw the girl lying in bed in flimsy nightclothes, inert. Was she dead?—he wondered. With the instinctive policeman's anxiety not to touch anything near a dead body, the first thing he did was to go to the window and pull the curtains. An early morning light filled the room.

The girl must have heard him move. She was making sounds and heaving in bed to attract his attention. He went in and untied the bandages round her eyes and mouth and then the cords around her wrists and ankles. He threw a counterpane across at her and as she busied herself, rubbing her wrists and ankles to get back their circulation, went into the bathroom. He soaked a hand towel with water and brought it out. She wiped her face with it and sat up in bed, blinking.

'For a minute I thought you were dead,' he said.

She made no answer. He made a quick tour of the flat. Everything was in disarray. The carpets shifted, the sofa and chairs overturned, the drawers emptied, the books from the shelves lying on the floor.

'So they didn't find it,' he said to her.

She frowned. 'Found what?'

'What they were looking for. Om's diary.'

'Of course they didn't,' she snapped. 'I wasn't going to leave it in my flat.'

'Where is it?'

She shot a disbelieving glance at him. 'You don't think I'd tell you that? You of all people!' She flounced out of bed and began to tidy up the room.

'Why me of all people?'

'You're Mr Lal, aren't you?'

'Yes. I believe Om told you that I was to be given the diary in case...'

'Oh, had he? Well, Mr Lal. It is true that he had. But he telephoned late last night, after midnight, just to say that you were not to be trusted. Said you had let him down, that you got him to say things and taped the talk.'

'The bloody fool!' Visram muttered. For a second or two he started at the girl in annoyance and then asked, 'How many were they?'

'Who? Oh, two, I think.'

'I don't suppose you saw either of them?'

She shook her head. 'No, I didn't. They were wearing masks. But you didn't either, did you—see them?'

He ignored her question, and glanced at his watch. It was ten to six. 'When does someone arrive? Your maid or cook or whoever.'

'After seven. My maid. The servants' quarters are at the back of the park.'

'I'd better clear out before she comes, hadn't I?' Then he braced himself and said: 'Look, something terrible has, happened. I don't know how to...'

She clutched her throat. 'Oh, no!' she gasped. 'You mean they've killed him?'

'I'm afraid they have,' he said, not knowing who she could be meaning. She slumped into a chair and hid her face. There was nothing he could do. The maid would arrive in an hour. Meanwhile he had his own work to do. As he went out of the flat and towards the stairs, he heard her exclaim, 'So he wasn't talking nonsense!'

Then she had begun to sob.

CHAPTER 4

The bicycle leaned against the Thirty-Point hoarding.

Visram rode to the Jor Bagh station house and trundled it into the veranda. 'I've brought your bicycle back,' he called out to the Duty Havaldar who was dozing in his chair, and slipped out before the man could come out and see the bruise on the side of his head.

He had been thinking about Om's diary. Dynamite, he had called it. It had cost him his life. Someone who had been following Om had rung up to say that he was on his way home to Palam. They must have been studying his movements for days.

And anyone who was hiding that diary was just asking for trouble—big trouble.

That silly girl.

It was a pretty fair guess that she had put it away in one of the company's safes, or a bank locker. But that did not mean that they would not get hold of it. All they had to do was to fake an income tax or foreign exchange charge and carry out a raid of the Surana properties. They could then legitimately open bank lockers.

But they would not go to all that trouble unless they had made sure that he, Visram Lal, did not have the diary. Somehow he had to make them believe that Om had handed the diary to him, and that, after reading it, he had destroyed it. It was up to him to create such evidence.

A police officer of Visram's seniority has special resources. Over the next couple of hours, he had called at half a dozen addresses, from Maharani Bagh to Chandni Chowk, and managed to collect six bottles of Remy Martin brandy with diplomatic, duty-free labels, and three hundred and three U.S. dollars and eighty Swiss francs. From a well-known smuggler's agent, he bought a flashy gold Pulsar watch. He would even have been able to get hold of any number of gold biscuits if he had had the money to pay for them.

He was back in his flat soon after nine. He scrambled three eggs and made toast and coffee. After eating his breakfast, he shaved and took a hot shower. Then he stashed away his illegal possessions in various odd places in the flat before stretching out in his bed and lighting a cigarette.

Now the one thing he lacked was Om's diary—or something that might have looked like it.

The diaries issued to the investigating officers of the Delhi police were five inches by nine inches and bound in brown calico. Each contained a hundred numbered sheets, and resembled one of those cloth-bound books published by the Writers' Workshop in Calcutta, except that the binding favoured by the workshop was maroon handloom material.

And suddenly he was sitting up.

He took out a book of plays from his book case. It was the correct size and shape. He ripped out the pages, tore them into shreds and burned the bits in a kitchen pan. Then, with a pair of scissors, he cut the cloth cover into several pieces and set fire to them, taking care to see that they were not completely burnt. After that he emptied the ash and the charred bits into a waste-paper basket.

Here was evidence that he had destroyed a case diary by burning.

He rang up his office to say that he would not be coming in the morning because he had to report to the Great Leader's house. Then he slept for an hour. Before he left his house, he took out the tape he had made the previous night and slipped it into his pocket. If they skin-searched him, it was just bad luck. But he did not want to leave it lying around in the house.

At eleven o'clock he presented himself in the small office in the modest, whitewashed bungalow on Asafjah Road from which, the Owl and the Pussycat, as the front men for the Great Leader, ran the affairs of the country.

It was Kaul the Owl who saw him. It seemed that Pashupat

had still not come to the office. Resting after his all-night vigil, Visram Lal reflected. Anyway Mr Kaul seemed to know all about the purpose of the interview.

'Oh, yes,' Visram told him, knowing that whatever he was saying was going on tape. 'I got the impression that Deputy Superintendent Agarwal had had quite a lot to drink before he came to see me.'

The Owl clucked his tongue and swallowed paan juice. 'I'm told he never stirred without a hip flask.'

'Quite possible.'

'And then the drinks in your room. How many?'

'I really cannot say. I left the bottle with him while I went to wash and change. I had been out most of the evening, on an exercise with the Combat...'

'Well, such a pity, really. An excellent officer. But then...drink makes animals of men,' he quoted a Sanskrit proverb, and shook his wattles in disparagement. 'Perhaps it would be just as well not to say he was drunk, don't you agree?'

'I suppose I won't be asked to give evidence, at the inquest.'

'There will be no inquest, Mr Lal. Surbinder, the DIG, is handling it personally. A most...er, helpful officer. He has assured me that everything will be handled with the utmost discretion.'

Visram had met the new Deputy Inspector General who had been brought from outside the state, and heard how he had become a tool in the hands of the Owl and the Pussycat.

'You'd better wait in the compound,' the Owl said, dismissing him. 'I'll check up if we have any more need to consult you.'

Did that mean that the new DIG was already busy searching his flat for the diary—Visram wondered as he strolled out of the presence. He went and told the guard commander at the gate that he would be sitting on a bench under one of the trees, in case he was needed.

There were at least half a dozen cars on the main road, and three of them had ministerial flags on them. Four cars were parked inside the compound wall, and since a small white odd-looking car was among them, Visram surmised that these must belong to the inmates of the palace. In the veranda sat several men with large bellies and khaddar caps. Outisde on the street, there were perhaps a hundred men and women who had come to catch a glimpse of the Great Leader.

In their usual place under a kikar tree, sat the half a dozen Gauleiters of the Dropout Brigade, which was composed of tough young men drawn from the slums and paid—so the rumour went—from political funds. It was their job to act as cheerleaders and to storm the meetings of the Opposition. In a situation where a high school dropout had become a national hero, the Dropout Brigade had become a law unto itself. A creation of Kaul the Owl, it was his boast that he could mobilize a thousand men in any place in Delhi at half an hour's notice, all of them carrying the proper placards and shouting the proper slogans, ready to create a road block, or to pelt a shop front with stones or start a riot—the party's answer to China's Red Guards.

It was cool in the shade of the tree. A langour came over him and his eyelids drooped. He saw as in a haze, a flurry at the gate as guards presented arms and waved a car through, a BMW three litres that was as well known in the capital as the President's ceremonial chariot. The boys of the Dropout Brigade were galvanized into action and rushed to make a human ring around the car as it came to a halt near the veranda steps.

In the car sat Swami Rajguru, whose name had become a household word in the capital, a living legend. The preacher of yoga to the highest in the land, a philosopher and philanthropist who ran a clinic as well as an ashram; a man who was endowed with inexhaustible virility, and who, even though he was believed to be in his eighties, looked no more than forty. His shoulder-length hair which was without a streak of grey shone like a lion's mane, a symbol of purity, of maleness; a man above all, who possessed strangely hypnotic powers and who preached salvation through the full enjoyment of sensual pleasures.

The Swami had always intrigued Visram; half village Sadhu, half faith healer, with shades of Rasputin and Don Juan. He shook himself awake and went close to the car, wondering if the Swami's arrival had anything to do with why he had been kept waiting. Was Rajguru the man who was going to decide if a further explanation was required from him? Was he also the man who was sitting beside Pashupat the previous night?

There was a stir among the men who had been waiting in the veranda. A portly man shambled down the steps with two bewhiskered younger men who were obviously his aides or, in the jargon of the times, chamchas. Visram recognized the man as the film producer, Dalpat Rao. As the door of the car opened, all three were standing with folded hands.

A woman rushed up with a basket and took out from it a marigold garland. Rajguru grinned and bent forward so that she could put the garland round his neck.

The film magnate and his chamchas looked on helplessly, having been one-upped by some village crone who had had the presence of mind to come equipped with an extra garland, just in case. Someone whispered a word in Dalpat Rao's ears. He thrust a hand deep into a side pocket and brought out a wad of currency notes. His face aglow with devotion, he bent forward to deposit his offering at the Swami's feet, but recoiled as he saw the Swami's lips curl in abhorrence and his legs jerk back as through to avoid the touch of his fingers.

That was when the man sitting beside the driver spoke. 'No, no! No money, please! Only fruit and flowers. Swamiji is very strict. Those who have donations to make must bring them to the ashram, where they will be given a proper receipt. The money will be used to heal bodies and to foster spiritual learning. Please take your money away.'

There was a murmur of approval from the small crowd, as shamefacedly, Dalpat Rao picked up the bundle of notes. 'I shall present myself at the ashram,' he said as the Swami got out of the car.

He dashed straight through the veranda and into the interior of the house, like a doctor on his rounds, a man above protocol. He was wearing nothing but a white muslin dhoti, one end of which was draped around his powerful shoulders. The hair on his chest was matted like a bear's fur.

He must outrank even the Cabinet ministers, Visram remembered thinking as he strolled back to his tree. He leaned against the bole. Soon his eyes closed and his head drooped.

A little before one o'clock, an Inspector in plain clothes came and woke him up. 'Mr Kaul said to tell you, sir, that you need not wait any longer.'

Visram noticed that the BMW had gone. The dropouts were playing cards under a tree. The film magnate who had tried to ingratiate himself with Rajguru was still waiting.

His own 1971 model Fiat was parked well away from the gate. He drove straight to his office which was nearly empty for the lunch hour. He sent for sandwiches and coffee and read through the day's mail. At two, his secretary came. From then on till six, he dictated and signed letters, and passed orders on the dozen or so files which bore red IMMEDIATE labels.

At six he was finished for the day, but reluctant to go home in case he discovered that his flat had not been searched, and that his carefully laid out clues were exactly as he had left them.

He drove to the Delhi Sports Club, parked his car, and went for a walk. He needed time to sort out his thoughts. He had a queer feeling that he was following in the footsteps of another man who had been racked by the same doubts: Deputy Superintendent Om Prakash Agarwal, ranged against criminals who had the fullest cooperation of the politicians and officials who wielded the real power in the land.

He tramped the silent streets; Safdar Jung, Aurangzeb, Prithviraj, Mansingh, Akbar, and the loops and lanes that went behind them. At the end of the hour he was back at the car park of his club, still undecided on his course of action.

He needed guidance; advice from someone he trusted, looked up to.

And again he was struck by the similarity of his predicament with that of the man who had come to him for advice and whom he had rebuffed. He wondered if the man he was going to for advice would prove equally unsympathetic.

He ate a quick meal at the Kwality restaurant and drove to his flat.

~

A purely professional safety precaution prevented him from going in to the bedroom to look if the brandy and the other stuff was still there. He first examined the outer room. Only because two of the six pamphlets and catalogues which he had always taken care to put upside down in his book cases had been righted, did he know that his flat had been searched. After that he knew that the brandy and the watch and the foreign money would have gone. They had. But the waste-paper basket in which he had tipped the remains of the book he had burnt, looked undisturbed.

Unless they had taken away only a sample of the ashes and one or two bits of the charred cover. He looked again, very carefully, but could not be sure.

Whoever had carried out the search, obviously knew his job, and that made him a doubly dangerous man to contend with.

~

The penthouse of Sarang Tower was the highest habitation in Delhi; it was believed to be also the most private, because it could be reached only by a special lift which remained on the penthouse floor and was sent down only after a caller had identified himself over the house telephone.

This was Swami Rajguru's retreat from the world. The million lights of the great city winked below, like a starlit sky mirrored and magnified. The large, central room opened on to a veranda and a roof garden.

Ekanti Ma had put on a Ravi Shankar-Chatur Lal record on the player. Soft music filled the air. Rajguru lay sprawled on a long, padded chair covered in red leather which had come from France. The folds of muslin which draped his body helped to enhance its perfection, and the champagne coloured lampshades gave his skin a golden glow. But his face wore a deep frown. 'That silly fool will just have to go,' he said, speaking casually, as though he was discussing the weather.

His visitor sat forward in his chair and shook his head. He was a tall, powerfully built man with a ruggedly handsome face and cruel, heavy-lidded eyes. He was dressed in a brown raw silk safari suit. 'If he has read the diary, then certainly, Swamiji.'

'How can he not have read it, if he went to the trouble of burning it?'

'I'm not sure, but I'll know in a day or two. Meanwhile, there are other ways of killing a cat. Perfectly...er, within the framework of the law. Remove a thorn with a thorn, as they say. We policemen have our own ways.'

The Swami stifled a yawn but did not say anything.

'You see, the bastard thinks he's very clever. He knew his flat was...' he checked himself mid-sentence.

Two young maids walked in, bearing trays held like temple offerings. They were dressed in brief, plunging cholis and see-through saris. The Swami would not permit male servants to work in his rooftop temple, was served by a staff of young women hand-picked by Ekanti Ma who had also trained them in their duties.

One of the maids had brought drinks—premium whisky and old brandy and soda and ice, and a glass of pale lemon grass tea—and the other had brought hot canapes and nuts. They deposited the trays on a serving table and were about to serve the drinks when Ekanti Ma stopped them with a gesture and shooed them away. As the two girls shuffled off, swaying their hips seductively, Rajguru asked his guest, 'You were saying, Surbinder?'

Surbinder had been watching the posteriors of the two girls with evident appreciation, but quickly turned to his host. 'As I said, Visram must have expected that his flat would be searched. He decided to play a trick on us—sort of, turn the tables. He planted false clues, knowing that if we made a case against him, he could easily prove them to be false and thus show that someone was trying to frame him. Oh, it stuck out a mile! A newfangled watch, foreign money...the lot. A neat little ambush.'

'Dangerous man,' Swami Rajguru commented.

Ekanti Ma handed them their glasses. Lemon grass tea for the Swami and Black Label on the rocks for Surbinder.

Surbinder smiled his thanks and went on. 'So I decided to catch him in his own trap. You see I am not making a regular case of it.'

'No?'

'No Swamiji. I am making a confidential complaint to his chief. The Chief of Investigations is a man called Chopra. One of these dried-up koi-hais. Old school tie, honour, all that bullshit. An officer must not only be uncorrupt, but must be seen to be uncorrupt. As I said, I made a report to him, confidential. I told him we had to search Lal's flat because of a reliable tip and that we were horrified to discover a whole lot of stuff which he could not have obtained by legal means. I have passed the evidence on to him.'

Rajguru sipped his tea. 'And you think he will play?'

'He was like a tiger roused. Scandal is what he hates most. He as good as told me he's going to ask Lal to resign—for the good name of the service. Let the COI have his way over this. No one can point a finger at me.' Surbinder gave a triumphant grin and took a large gulp of whisky.

A jetliner flashed overhead with a great roar, winking green and red lights and gaining height.

'I suppose it is much the best way,' Swamiji admitted. 'Still, if Lal has read the diary, then he is really dangerous.'

'In that case he will have to be put out of harm's way, Swamiji. But that should pose no problem. Thanks,' he said to Ekanti Ma who was holding before him a silver dish with hot canapes: prawns in batter and oysters on bits of flaky pastry and little squares of cheese on toast.

CHAPTER 5

VISRAM had not felt so excited for years; the sort of feeling that came over you before a crucial tennis match when you knew you were playing at the peak of your form, he told himself. You could hardly wait for the game to begin.

As he wrote out his message, he was more than ever conscious that he was imitating Om Prakash.

Must see you urgently where we can be sure no one is listening. But please play the tape before meeting me.

The man he was going to see, A.B. Chopra, was the same man to whom Surbinder of the Delhi police had complained about the smuggled articles discovered in Superintendent Lal's flat.

A.B. Chopra, familiarly known in the service as ABC was the Chief of Investigations in the Special Branch of the Police Department, which dealt with foreign intelligence agents in the country. He was therefore someone who could be presumed to be immune from being spied upon by a sister service, the Research and Analysis Wing, or RAW, which had become a sinister word, like the Gestapo or the KGB. But then one could never be sure. It was the general belief that, since the Emergency had been declared, there was no office in the capital where you could be absolutely certain that someone was not either listening to or recording what was being said.

The police bugged the telephones of the Generals and the Admirals and planted recording devices in their homes and offices, and the Army signals performed a similar service in respect of the ministers and the officials of the secretariat. Then there were the Directorate of Intelligence Bureau and RAW which, between them, spied on the spies. It was RAW which was believed to possess the most advanced and sophisticated snooping devices.

Visram Lal put the note into his pocket along with the tape of his talk with Agarwal and Pashupat. He then drove to a coffee shop in the outer circle in Connaught Place and rang the Duty Officer at the Bureau of Investigations.

'I want to see ABC,' he told the Duty Officer. 'As soon as possible.'

'Mr Lal,' the DO said excitedly. 'The COI has been trying to get hold of you, sir. We even traced your car in the club car park but you were not in the building—or the premises. I'll just check and ring you back. Five minutes.'

'Don't bother,' Lal told him. 'I'll ring you in five minutes.'

~

It was nearly half past nine when Visram reached the bungalow in Duplex Lane. ABC had just finished dinner. Normally Visram would have been asked to join him at coffee. Not today. An orderly showed him into a study, saluted and left.

Mr Chopra came within minutes, looking glum. He answered Visram's greeting gruffly and took out from his drawer two sealed plastic envelopes containing the watch and the foreign currency. Then Visram noticed the canvas sack on the floor which also bore a seal and which must have contained the bottles of brandy.

'You might as well sit down, Lal,' the COI said very coldly.

Visram Lal had known Chopra since his very first year on probation, and five years earlier, they had both worked together in the drive against the sopan-margi terrorists and been awarded President's medals. The service knew Chopra as something of a leftover from the Raj, an upright and hardworking officer whom none of the Chief Ministers seemed to want in their states because he was not sufficiently committed to their political ideology or their ethics. He was close to retirement anyhow and had been found a sinecure which had little, to do with everyday problems of law and order.

It was Visram Lal and a handful of others who had worked under Chopra as young men, who knew him as a warm and civilized human being, exceptionally shrewd and professionally brilliant. A man to go to for advice in a crisis, a man to depend on. If he knew you were straight, he was on your side.

'I was astonished,' ABC said, pointing to the two envelopes. 'Shocked!'

His eyes fell on the note Visram was holding out. As he read it, his expression did not change, and his voice was still sternly disapproving.

'What have you got to say?'

'What is there to say, sir?' Visram said in a penitent voice, and held out the envelope containing the tape.

Chopra took the envelope and pushed it under a file. Then he scribbled something on a paper and passed it to Visram. He said, 'It has pained me greatly. I wish I had been spared this unpleasant duty. But I cannot shirk it either. If the case takes its normal course, the scandal will be...'

The COI paused. Visram did not say anything; he did not want to say anything that would have gone against the line ABC had decided to take.

'There is a less unsavoury alternative. And for this we have to thank the officer who had to perform this disagreeable duty against a fellow officer. He could not have been more considerate. Instead of putting up the case through official channels, he thought of coming to see me.'

'I would abide by your advice, sir.'

'Oh, no. This has nothing to do with me. The decision must be yours. I can only set out the implications. If a case is made, why, there might be some technicality of law which might get you off the hook. But that does not mean that you will still have a future in the service. Oh, no! And the scandal! So the...the sensible thing to do might be to...you know, choose the lesser evil, the quieter exit.'

'As you say, Mr Chopra.'

'Damn it. I don't say anything. It is your choice.'

'All right, sir. I will...take the quieter exit.'

There was nearly a minute's silence. 'I think that would be

the best way. This will naturally take a little time. A week, maybe. There is a procedure...meanwhile you should consider yourself to be on leave.'

There followed another awkward silence, and the COI said. 'I am sorry it had to end this way. Such a promising career.' He did not shake hands.

It was only after he had driven as far as the circle around India Gate that Visram stopped the car under a street light and opened Chopra's note. He read, *Six thirty a.m. tomorrow, Lodhi Gardens main gate.*

The air, untouched by the day's sun, unpolluted by the day's petrol fumes, was cool and fresh. The trees dripped with dew. The two men sitting with their backs resting against a crumbling grave, might have been thieves discussing plans for their next robbery. In the early morning light, Sikandar Lodhi's tomb looked as if it was made of frosted glass.

'You were lucky to have got those bits on tape,' ABC told Visram Lal as he handed him the brown envelope. 'You knew they would come for the diary and wanted them to believe that you had burned it. Right? That's why you went to the trouble of planting those other things—to give them a case which you could prove to be false.'

'I had to think of something in a hurry.'

'Because you didn't want the girl, Om's sister, to be harassed?'

That's part of it.'

'Well, frankly I don't know that they will fall for it. Surbinder is nobody's fool. He must be only waiting for the laboratory report on the burned bits. Meanwhile, he has pushed the thing into my lap, just to show how above board everything is. You get the picture now?'

'What's Surbinder up to, sir?'

'My post, for starts,' the COI said.

'I'd heard rumours. But then there must be a dozen others between him and you.'

'Oh, they'll jump him up; no doubt about that. He's proved himself to be committed, has he not?—as someone who'll not jib at soiling his hands to order? Seniority means nothing—not even for the highest judges in the land. Anyway, there it is. I don't think it will be long before they cotton on and come cracking down on you.'

'But then, if we don't play it this way, I see no other way of going about it, sir. Do you?' Visram asked.,

ABC squinted against the sunlight and shook his head. 'I don't. At the same time, it's a great risk. For what? Om is dead. His sister?—she just has to surrender the diary and she has nothing to worry about.'

'For the same thing as Om died, shall we say, sir. To find the truth.'

The COI shrugged, then threw up his hands. 'Well, you keep that tape safe. With that and whatever other evidence you have up your sleeve, they can't make a case stand. I can do my part by holding back your papers. Meanwhile, see what you can achieve by working from the outside—playing against the bank, as it were.'

'I suppose there's no way of laying hands on the diary somehow.'

'None at all.'

'And the moment they discover that it was not burnt, they'll raid the Surana Offices, grill Om's sister...'

'You bet. They're desperate men, remember. And the official machinery will be working for them. And Surbinder, much as I detest the man, there's one thing I will say; he does get results.'

'That means I shall have to start where Om started,' Visram Lal pointed out. 'By trying to get Dorabji to tell me his story and then tying it up with whatever other evidence I am able to dig up. The trouble is, where to begin?—with Dorabji in custody and classified as a maximum security prisoner.'

'No.' Chopra shook his head and hand at the same time. 'Things are a little different right now. Dorabji has been admitted to the Sukhija hospital, for observation and tests. Stomach ulcer, I believe. It should not be difficult to make contact with him there. The problem will be to get him to talk. Remember he's terrified. Knows he has powerful enemies—and Om's death must have shaken him.' The COI looked at his watch. 'Sorry I cannot be more helpful.'

Visram Lal had come for sympathy and advice; he was getting encouragement and even cooperation. 'How do I get in touch with you?' he asked.

'All been thought of,' Chopra said breezily. 'But only if you must. Ring the Duty Officer. He has instructions to pass on messages exactly as they come. Say, "Is that the Willingdon Hospital?" if it is urgent. I will meet you in the car park at Sangli mess within the hour. Or say "Is that the Irwin nursing home?" and I shall meet you the next morning—same place. Each time we meet, we shall decide on a new place for the next meeting. Okay?'

Visram's breath quickened. This was something he had not hoped for. Did this mean that the Chief of Investigations was actually batting on his side? He asked, 'The way you…er, fell in with my suggestions and even had the signals for our next meeting ready…does that mean that there are others also who are…playing against the bank, and that you're coordinating their work?'

Mr Chopra shook his head and looked stern. 'You just go ahead on your own, Lal. If I hear of anything that I think would be useful to you, I'll pass it on. Meanwhile, secrecy is absolutely vital. Well, I can tell you that you are not alone.' Mr Chopra gave the impression that he had already said too much. He sprang to his feet, brushed the dust off his olive-green velvet corduroy trousers, and dashed off energetically to complete his morning walk.

Visram Lal gave him five minutes and then strolled out of the dark tomb and into the real world. He heard the clatter of hoofbeats. A big-made man in polo boots and cloth cap riding on a big chestnut horse cantered past and then turned for a second look at him and waved.

Deputy Inspector General Surbinder Singh was taking his morning ride on the grassy slopes surrounding the tombs of the Lodhi dynasty.

~

Manekji Hormusji Dorabji squatted on a pink rubber sheet on a steel bench in a small room in the X-ray department of the Sukhija hospital, and he was shivering because the only covering he had on was a hospital towel.

They had made him fast the whole of the previous day, filled his stomach with a gooey white liquid, and had taken several X-ray photographs, and because he was a prisoner who could not be allowed to mix with the other patients or staff, had told him to wait in the Resident Medical Officer's room while the RMO was doing his rounds. 'Someone will come and see you in half an hour,' the matron had told him.

When Dorabji had first started having stomach cramps, he had put them down to the jail diet. But, as the cramps had continued and worsened, he had reported to the visiting doctor who had recommended that he should undergo tests for a stomach ulcer.

The tests were going on. Soon he would be told what was wrong with him. After that they would begin the treatment.

He wondered if they would keep him in the hospital or send him back to jail. He was indifferent; they were both alike. At the moment, all he wanted was a cigarette.

The door opened and a man walked in. Dorabji adjusted the towel around his waist. The man pulled up a stool close to his bench and perched himself on it. He took out a packet of Gold Flake and said, 'You can smoke. I've checked with your doctor.'

Dorabji accepted a cigarette but held it between his fingers. 'That means you're not a doctor. It follows that you're a policeman.' His face wore a scowl.

His visitor grinned. 'As it happens, you're right. I am a policeman. The name is Lal—Superintendent. I want to talk to you.'

Dorabji gave a hollow laugh, stuck his cigarette between his lips and bent forward for a light. He took a puff and said, 'You think I'm mad?'

'I'm a friend of Deputy Superintendent Agarwal.'

'Of the late Mr Agarwal, you mean. They bumped him off, didn't they?' And Dorabji pointed his cigarette accusingly at the door of the room. 'Not that he was an angel. The bastard tricked me into signing a confession. All he wanted was that I should mention no names. *Just say you did it on your own and we'll guarantee we'll get you off. Might even get you a part of the money as a reward.* Four of your bigshot officers were there when he made that promise, nodding their heads off. Balls! But lately he'd begun to realize what a shit he had been—at least he said so. Now they've bumped him off and instead of a Deputy SP, I find they've put a full SP in charge of my case. I can read the signs. What do you want? Another confession?'

'Look,' Visram said sternly, 'you know very well that Agarwal died because he was trying to discover who the people were who got you into this scrape and what they were up to. Let me tell you that I am a Senior SP, and under a cloud for befriending Agarwal. And who knows, I too may be risking my life.'

Dorabji gave a rude laugh. 'For me, Superintendent?'

'No bloody fear! For Om Prakash, who was my friend. Wait.' Visram took out the little recorder from his pocket and switched it on. 'Listen to this. I'm sure you will recognize Om's voice.'

'*Would you like a drink, Om? Or are you still a TT?*'

'*Still TT, Mr Lal. How well you remember. No, never touch the stuff.*'

Then, after a pause. '*I've come for advice, Mr Lal. Didn't know who else to turn to. It's about the Dorabji case.*'

Visram Lal ran the tape through the early part of Om Prakash's talk with him which ended by Om saying, '*Because you're the only man in the service whom I trust, Mr Lal.*'

Visram switched off the recorder and said, 'Okay?'

Dorabji who was listening with bent head, nodded, but he was frowning. He said, 'How can one tell? You people have so many tricks up your sleeve.' He smoked in silence for a few seconds and went on. 'And yet, someone should be told, shouldn't he? Now that Agarwal is dead.'

'You're talking sense.'

'It's a long story, Mr Lal.'

'Listen, we certainly won't have time for the full story today. Just answer a few questions—truthfully. Then we'll have another go, tomorrow. I've arranged to have you brought here again. Same time. I'll be waiting here, Okay?'

'You've thought of everything, haven't you, Mr Lal. Even taken my cooperation for granted.' He shrugged and made a helpless gesture with his hands. 'Can I have another cigarette?'

Visram passed the cigarettes and matches to him. 'Let's begin at the beginning, shall we?' he said, 'by recapitulating what came out in the papers. Someone ordered the manager of the Vishal Bharat bank to take out seventy lakh rupees from the bank's vaults, put the money in a trunk, and drive over to the gate of the Race Course where a man would be waiting for him: you. Both of you were given code signals to identify each other with. After establishing that you were the right person, he was to drive you to a taxi stand, help you transfer the box with the money into a taxi and go away. The box weighed nearly seventy kilogrammes. You were to transfer the money into two suitcases which you had brought along with you. You were to deliver the suitcases to someone else. Okay, so far?'

Dorabji who had kept puffing nervously at his cigarette and looking resentfully at the tape recorder on the bench, hopped up and put away the recorder in the farthest corner of the room, and draped the rubber sheet from his bench over it. He sat down again and said irritably, 'Yes, all that came in the papers.'

That was when Lal fired a question in the hope of catching Dorabji off his guard. 'Whose money was it?'

'I don't know. Some hush-hush fund of the Government or of the party—may be even of the bank. It must run into millions—oh, billions! What matters is that they knew it was there, for the taking; and that it could be drawn out by merely making a telephone call and saying the right word.'

'Who's they?'

Dorabji stiffened and shook his head. 'If I answer that, I'll have burned my boats, won't I. I don't know how much I should tell—I want time to think.'

'How were you chosen, to get the money from the bank?'

'I had done jobs for them before.'

'Similar jobs? Taken money from someone and passed it on to someone else?'

Dorabji nodded. 'Bloody stooge, that's what I was. Damn it! How could I have known the code unless someone had given it to me? How could I have discovered what the signals were? Tell me? I was merely the servant; paid to do a job—same as you. Be the front man and collect your remuneration; twenty-five thousand. You think that's good money, for just a morning's work. But something goes wrong and they drop you in the shit—and you're finished for life.' His face had become flushed and his chest heaved.

'Something did go wrong,' Visram Lal prompted, very softly.

'You bet it did! If that fat swine at the bank hadn't taken two hours to bring the cash, if only that bitch hadn't got cold feet and run away, I wouldn't be in jail, would I?—but sitting pretty…' he stopped because his voice broke. The cigarette shook in his hand.

'So the woman you were supposed to pass the money to wasn't there,' Visram said. This was going better than he had hoped for and he was keeping his fingers crossed.

'Y'ah. I was to meet her at noon. That gave me an hour to get the money. The man at the bank took more than two hours to bring it. She had gone.'

'You didn't think of going to her house?'

'Don't be daft. If I had known where she lived I wouldn't be wandering all over Delhi like a lost soul, with seven million rupees on my back, would I?'

'You mean you didn't know the woman?'

'Oh, we had…done business before. I had seen her, she had seen me. But even then we had to use code words. Every time there were new code words. They're clever, those buggers. Think of everything.'

'What was the code?'

'I had to say, "*Behenji, aap kis fouj ki neta hain?*" and she had to answer "*Mein mukti bahini ki neta hun.*"'

'But surely, you must have discovered who she was, later on?' Visram asked sounding very casual.

Dorabji gave him a resentful look and shook his head. 'No.'

Liar, Lal thought to himself and asked, 'Where was the money going?'

Dorabji dragged on his cigarette and again shook his head. 'Surely you don't think I knew that?'

'Oh, come off it,' Visram snapped with impatience. 'Of course I do. Your entire case depended on your knowing, damn it! Agarwal must have found out—talked things over with you.'

Dorabji gave him a foxy look and squinted his eyes. 'Never.'

Visram sprang up from his seat. 'You bloody fool! No wonder you find yourself in jail when all you were was a messenger boy. But you deserve no better. Don't you realize that this is your very last chance of revealing what you know so that we can bring the real culprits to book? And you have not told me a thing that was not in the papers. Go to hell then; screw yourself! I'm not coming again.'

He got up and turned to go and turned again as Dorabji said, 'All right. Mauritius.'

'How?'

'Ekanti Ma was taking it.'

'Who's she?' Visram asked, and sat down again.

'Oh, come off it, Superintendent,' Dorabji retorted. 'Call yourself a police officer and you don't know who Ekanti Ma is?'

'Rajguru Swami's chief disciple?'

'His procuress, according to Om Prakash Agarwal.'

'Was she the person who was to take over the money from you?'

'Yes, the leader of the Mukti Bahini—bitch!' Dorabji said with anger. 'But I didn't know who she was at the time. Agarwal found out. She went abroad every month or so, with suitcases stuffed with money.'

'What about the customs? They often check unaccompanied baggage.'

Dorabji gave one of his hoarse laughs. 'Customs checks! What antiquated ideas you suffer from, Mr Lal. Don't you know that those two thugs who guard the Kremlin portals just have to pass the word that someone is not to be checked and you could take a dead horse out of the country—leave alone cash.'

'Pashupat and Kaul?' Visram asked. 'Are they a part of this set up?'

Dorabji put out his tongue and cursed himself. 'Smart, aren't you, Superintendent. Dangerous! You needled me into telling you things which I have not even told my lawyer. All right, enough! Way I look at it—they were things discovered by Agarwal anyhow: who the woman was, where she was going. But who engaged me, gave me my orders—well, that's different.'

'But the Owl and the Pussycat are somehow in it, are they not?' Visram persisted.

'That's something I won't say either yes or no to. You policemen are all the same. Who can trust you?'

'You have to trust somebody.'

'I know that, damn it. But once they discover how much I know—they'll kill me. Why do you think I refused to accept bail?' He demanded in an anguished tone. 'Why?' He glared at Lal and then, very purposefully got up and retrieved the rubber sheet and spread it on his bench. Then he lay down, folding his hands over his chest, and shut his eyes.

Visram watched him, feeling helpless. Then he leaned over and patted his shoulder. Dorabji grasped his hand, trustingly and, after a few seconds sat up again. 'Okay, I'll tell you. If Agarwal could trust you, that's good enough for me.'

That was when the door opened. A man in a long white coat walked in, followed by the Matron who was complaining in an agitated voice, 'But the police have no business to go barging into a patient's room, Dr Chand. How can my…' she checked herself mid-sentence.

'You will come back, tomorrow, Mr Lal, won't you?' Dorabji whispered, again clutching his hand.

As Visram walked down the tiled corridor smelling of disinfectants, he was conscious of a sense of guilt. After all, the Matron was quite right to complain. He had no business to be worrying her patients.

It was only after he had got into his car that he remembered that the room he had been in was not the patient's room. She was obviously talking about some other room, some other policeman.

~

Visram caught himself humming, and laughed out aloud. For the first time in months, he was conscious of being stretched to the peak of his mental and physical abilities. From being one of the super clerks who sat in an office all day, passing files up and down, he was engaged in work for which he had been trained and in which he revelled. He was investigating a case which the police force of the capital had been precluded from probing.

He drove at crawling speed past the rubble around Peeli Masjid Like a field that had been ploughed over, he reflected. Only a couple of weeks earlier, many thousands of people had lived here. All of them had been uprooted overnight, herded like cattle, taken to the countryside and left in the middle of nowhere to make new lives for themselves.

A blot on the face of the city had been removed, so they said. The way the members of his service had stood by with batons and tear gas shells and loaded stenguns while the bulldozers flattened the houses, had made people like himself hang their heads in shame. That was one of the things that had made the name of his service a dirty word. A splendid force had been transformed into an immense, dehumanized machine of mass terror.

And adding insult to injury, were the Thirty-Point hoardings, left standing in the middle of the devastation—like something out of 1984, he reflected, a barrage of slogans pounded at the proles to keep them under massive sedation.

He drove away these unpleasant thoughts, reminding himself how well his session with Dorabji had gone. Another meeting and he might be within sight of the solution.

This had been a good day for him. Why not follow his luck and see if he could talk that stupid girl Netra Agarwal into giving him her brother's diary?

~

The street-level door was open. Visram Lal rang the bell and then went up the stairs. The door at the landing was opened by an elderly maid, who kept it on the chain and waited for him to tell her who he was. Then she smiled and let him come in. She showed him into a small sitting room that led from the entrance alcove.

He looked round the room. It was tidy enough. At least there were no traces of the upheaval it had been subjected to only two days earlier. After that he stood facing the window which overlooked the front lawn and the main road beyond and, in the distance, the shimmering white eminence of Sarang Tower.

The sound of a door opening made him turn. Netra came in, wearing a white sari which may or may not have signified that she was in mourning, her face bearing the scrubbed, chiselled look that sorrow or fasting imparts to a woman's face. And for the first time Visram Lal caught himself thinking what a beautiful woman she was.

'I suppose you have come about the diary, Mr Lal,' she said.

That was precisely what he had come for. But he shook his head and said, 'No. I just looked in to see how you were after...the assault of the other night.'

'Oh, that. I'd almost forgotten. Death somehow makes other troubles look small.'

'I also wanted to say how shocked I was and sorry. Om was a friend.'

She gave him a hard look. 'He too thought so, Mr Lal—until an hour before he died. Do sit down.'

'Your brother was a deeply disturbed man, Miss Agarwal. When one is in that sort of a state, it is difficult to think clearly; realize who is your friend, who isn't.'

'You are not a doctor, are you, Mr Lal?'

He could see there was no point in lingering. He would have liked to warn her that she should remove the diary from wherever she had hidden it because it was quite certain that the Surana offices would be turned inside out by the tax raiders and that the company's bank lockers would be seized.

'I was told by the police that Om had had a lot to drink—that it had been established beyond doubt.' Her voice had gone trembly and her eyes were bright. 'That a friend whom he had been to see that night had testified that he had drunk nearly a bottle. You knew that he never drank, didn't you, Mr Lal?'

'Of course, I did. I told you we had known each other well.'

There was a silence while he looked away, at the view through the window, knowing that she was wiping her eyes. She blew her nose and asked, 'Was there anything else, Mr Lal?'

He had not thought of it before, but he found himself saying: 'As a matter of fact, there was. It is just that, any time you feel the need...I mean, in case there is a threat or something, I want you to give me a ring. I was a friend of Om's; I want you to know that I am your friend too.'

She peered at him uncomprehendingly. 'What was it that you said just now: if one is emotionally disturbed, one cannot decide who is one's friend, who is not. Well, I must be in that sort of state of aberration, Mr Lal.'

God, he was being put in his place, he thought. 'It is only a precaution, Miss Agarwal. I'll leave my number, just in case.'

'If you must. Please write it down. There's a pad near the telephone.'

He shrugged, feeling helpless in the face of feminine obduracy. He got up and went over to the telephone desk and wrote down his name and number on a tear-sheet pad. That was when he noticed some writing on the same page.

El-Taj Mori Gate. 8.30.

'Well, good day, Mr Lal. I suppose I ought to say, thank you for coming, and in my turn, ask how you are after being hit on the head.' She got up and turned to go, but he stopped her with a gesture.

'Oh, Miss Agarwal. El-Taj. You have not been to the place before, have you?'

Her eyes narrowed as though the question had upset her. 'No, why?'

'Well, it is not the sort of place where—where people like yourself go.'

'Really? Immoral? Crawling with call girls and pimps? Or merely non-you?'

'It is what they call a pot-joint. Offbeat and well, coarse.'

'What a lot you know, Mr Lal, about disreputable joints?'

'It is my business to know; if only to be able to warn decent girls from venturing into them.'

'That is kind of you, Mr. Lal, to be concerned about my morals. But one gets sort of...unshockable, after learning that policemen tape the conversations of their trusted friends...'

'I wasn't thinking of your morals, Miss Agarwal,' he retorted.

'I am told that things often get a little rough at the El-Taj. You know, free-for-alls between rival gangs of toughs. The Dropout Brigade has recently adopted the place...and they have rivals.' He paused and added. 'If you are going to this place for some reason... well, I could take you there, you know.'

'To look after me?' she asked with a mocking smile. 'But how kind of you, Mr Lal, to be concerned about my safety as well as my reputation. As it happen, I'm quite capable of looking after myself. I took a course of judo at Berkley. Qualified to be an instructor, in fact.'

'You? A judo instructor?'

'Yes, Mr Lal. I think I will be able to handle whatever kind of roughhouse the El-Taj specializes in. If I ever go there, that is. And now I will say it. Thank you for coming. And goodbye.'

The door closed behind him with a sharp click.

CHAPTER 6

Two miles beyond Palam airport, almost lost in the vast concourse of nondescript sheds and hangars that belong to the Indian Air Force, was Swami Rajguru's ashram, a six-acre wooded plot containing half a dozen snow-white bungalows of different sizes, designed by the German architect, Rainer Storch.

The frontage was protected by a nine-foot high wall topped with three strands of barbed wire, and the other three sides by the Air Force's picket and barbed wire fencing. To be sure, the neat, ornamental gate in the wall that ran alongside the main road was open day and night, but it was guarded by teams of alert Gurkha guards.

Swami Rajguru made something of a boast of the fact that his guards were recruited from among ex-commandoes, and were thus professionally trained to kill their opponents without weapons of any kind, and with as little fuss and noise as possible. But an Air Force officer who had once strayed into the gate after a party in the Palam mess, swore that the guard who had barred his way had aimed at him a sporting rifle fitted with a scope-sight as well as an attachment at the end of the barrel to deaden the sound of the report. But then no one else had seen any of the guards carrying weapons.

The only two cars which could go in and out freely were known by sight to the guards. One was the Swami's own black BMW. The other was a tiny, one-of-a-kind vehicle fitted with scooter wheels. It had been painstakingly hand-assembled in a small garage in Mehrauli by a team of mechanics led by Ambika Das, who was a skilled electric welder. At least a dozen cars of different makes from Europe and Japan had been dismantled so that their parts could be used to build this wonder vehicle. The car was owned by the son of the Great Leader, Kalas Kak, who was known to his friends as Kakji. No one but Kakji or Ambika Das was allowed to drive it.

All other cars had to be parked outside, in the space especially provided by the municipal authorities who had taken it away from land that had been set aside for an artificial limb centre. An undersecretary in the Health Ministry who had pointed out in his noting on the file that the land had been earmarked for another purpose was summarily dismissed and was later sent to prison on a charge of being anti-government. And with that the lesson had gone home that Swami Rajguru was a highly privileged person, that any favour done to him by officials would not go unrewarded, and that anyone whom the Swami found uncooperative be shown no mercy. It was openly said in Delhi that the Customs authorities had gone overboard in trying to help the Swami, and had not only waived the duty on a new radiator that had been imported for the BMW, but had had the crate delivered at the Swami's door in their own van.

Even that pampered service, the Air Force, much to the amusement of its sister services, came off the loser in a toe-to-toe confrontation with the Swami. It had set up a howl of protest that an ashram should be located in the midst of their operational establishments. In particular, they said that their special weapons testing range could be actually overlooked from the ashram which adjoined it, and thus constituted a grave security risk. After a career Air Commodore had found himself passed for promotion, the Air Force had quietly withdrawn its complaint and proceeded to build a high wall between the ashram and their range.

After that it had been the Swami's turn to take the offensive. He charged that the special weapons testing range being situated next-door to his ashram disturbed its inmates in their studies and prayers and caused a setback to the health of his patients. Upon this, the Air Force, only after a token protest, had agreed to shift their establishment to a distant part of their estate as soon as the necessary facilities could be constructed. Meanwhile, they would take good care to arrange their range practices in such a way as to cause the least disturbance to the inmates of the ashram.

Swami Rajguru was generally accepted to be the foremost exponent of yoga in the land of yoga, and the best proof of that of course, was his body which, for all its eighty-odd years, was as firm, supple, and healthy, as that of any man in the prime of his life; it possessed a glow like that of seasoned teakwood, which, his devotees swore, was an unmistakable sign of spiritual eminence.

To be sure there were scoffers. With Swami Rajguru's recent dizzy rise as the spiritual guide and yoga teacher of the Great Leader and the closest buddy of the Great Leader's son, discontented politicians in the ranks of the Opposition had begun to ask a lot of awkward questions. What about the Swami's well-known aversion to being touched by male hands?—they asked. Was that not the reason why he did not permit his male devotees to put garlands round his neck or even to touch his feet? Did it not betray a streak of some deep-seated psychoneurosis? Then again, it was whispered that the Swami had undergone circumcision. How could that fit in with his pretension to being a holy Hindu?

'And if the man says he's nearly ninety years old, where was he hiding his light during the first fifty years of his life?' they asked.

Whenever anyone had the temerity to voice these doubts in the hearing of the Swami, the answers had been perplexingly oracular. 'Who can be made to see if he keeps his eyes firmly shut?' he would say. Or: 'The tongue of a skeptic is like a runaway horse.'

But only a few months earlier, an enterprising interviewer for a BBC television programme, Ronald Black, had, by his needling questions, managed to extract less imprecise answers from the Swami.

'To say that I have a...dislike of being touched by male hands, is a despicable lie,' Rajguru had answered with great emphasis, and looking directly into the lense of the camera. 'Possibly its origin lies in the fact that I am an upasak...you know, a devotee, of the Goddess Durga in her avatar as Shakti, power. To me Shakti represents the perfect human form. But of course I have among my students, many eminent men too from all over the world who will testify...'

At this stage, the interviewer had made as if to adjust the ribbon of the microphone around the Swami's neck, and both his cameramen had caught the reflexive recoil of the Swami's body, and the look of abhorrence that had come over the Swami's face.

'And those who cast doubts on my Hinduism, cast doubts on the Hinduism of Swami Shraddhanand himself,' Rajguru had gone on. 'And on the programme of shuddhi, or readmittance into the religion, that was initiated by that greatest Hindu of this century, Shraddhanand, and taken up after him by Savarkar and others. I was born in the little village of Inayat Kila, in what was the Northwest Frontier Province. In an Afridi raid on the village, all the other members of my family were killed and I was taken away, converted to Islam and circumcised. At the age of ten, I ran away and made my way to Swami Shraddhanand's ashram. This must have been around the year 1885 or 1886. Shraddhanand who knew my parents, reconverted me and adopted me. It was he who sent me to the Tashi-lunpo monastery in the Gilgit Himalayas.'

'And that is where you spent the next fifty years?' Ronald Black had asked, with a straight face.

'Yes, sir. I lived among holy men, learning what little I know about the secret of life—of existence. That is where I would have been today, if your countrymen who were commanding the Maharaja of Kashmir's Gilgit garrison had not betrayed their salt and surrendered the province to Pakistan.'

'And what did you learn, in those fifty years?' Ronald Black had asked.

'That the human body was not created to perish within the Christian span of three-score and ten, sir. That is one of the things which I learned which your viewers will understand. In the monastery I daily conferred with those who had fought in what you call the Mutiny, and had been boys together with Tilak and Ram Mohun Roy.'

'And yoga is the key to your longevity, Rajguruji?'

'It is the key to life itself.'

Predictably, the edited version of the interview shown on Indian Television did not show the whole of the BBC film. But from what was shown the Indian viewers generally agreed that Rajguru had scored heavily over his interviewer.

That interview had boosted up his popularity and prestige. The sales of his book on yoga, which was already translated into eighteen languages had gone into hundreds of thousands. At that Swami Rajguru was not like other yoga experts who, when they became well-known, trained others to teach yoga and set up schools all over the country. He still taught yoga himself; yoga and, to a chosen few, tantra.

To be able to afford the prices of yoga lessons at the ashram, you had to be either very rich or very influential; to be able to afford the treatment in the ashram's clinic, you had to be a beautiful woman, and it did not matter if you were not rich. His specialities were the indeterminate ailments which women suffered from before entering middle age, as well as weight problems and childlessness. He was no believer in medicines, and his treatment consisted of special exercises, massage, baths and meditation and what was believed to be the hypnotic influence of being in the vicinity of the Swami.

Through the gate, even a passing traveller could get a glimpse of the bungalows among the trees at the end of the curving drive. Four of the bungalows were open to those who came to take yoga lessons. They were on four corners of an immaculate lawn and joined by gravelled paths. One was the yoga centre, the other had facilities for the oil and herbal massage and steam baths. The third was the administration and recreation building, and the fourth, the meditation pavilion, whose main hall had a marble statue of the goddess Shakti, especially sculpted by the French artist, Alphonso Oger.

Separated from this area by a belt of shady trees and another gate were the two remaining bungalows. One of these was the clinic, and the other contained Swamiji's private office and a consulting room, and, at the back, an inner sanctum which was a room with no windows and a steel door like that of a bank's vault, with the air coming through half a dozen small air conditioner grills fitted low into the walls. Even the inmates of the ashram had no idea what this room contained, but believed that it was a tantric shrine, reserved exclusively for the use of the Swami and his chief disciples.

Swami Rajguru had just finished his day's chores at the ashram, by participating in the sunset prayer of its inmates. The prayer was a simple affair, a communal meditation with eyes glued on the image of Shakti, and it did not take quite fifteen minutes.

From the meditation pavilion Rajguru walked brisky to the

private office. He walked through the waiting room, ignoring the salutation of the ashram's new secretary, Vanita Dave, who had risen to her feet and folded her hands in a namaskar, but, nevertheless, thinking to himself what an inspired choice Vanita had proved to be.

Ekanti Ma must have interviewed a hundred girls, some of whom had been to charm schools in Europe and had worked in multinational firms, before she selected Vanita who had not even applied for the job. The choice was particularly difficult because Vanita's predecessor, a smart Anglo-Indian girl who had earlier served as an air hostess, had died in somewhat mysterious circumstances. Her sari was believed to have caught fire, and she had burned to death in a locked room. Even though the emergency newspapers had not been allowed to report the girl's death, there had been rumours of suicide following a sex scandal involving some big names among the Swami's cronies, and it was his great and good friend, Kalas Kak who had rushed to his aid and worked his magic to hush up the affair.

But in the public mind, the ashram was fast acquiring an image of being a school for the teaching of Kama Sutra to the rich and the glamorous, and to counter this image, it was thought essential that the new secretary had to be someone who, even though endowed with more than average good looks, had to conform to the Hindu ideal of womanhood, of purity of mind and body, of obedience and housewifely virtues; a girl who did not paint her nails or use eyeshadow or lipstick and wore flowers in her hair and a tika on her forehead, but who, all the same spoke English well and had been to college.

Vanita Dave's father had been a subeditor of Mahatma Gandhi's newspaper in Vardha, and Vanita herself had been brought up in an orthodox Hindu family and in an atmosphere of Gandhian simplicity. When Ekanti Ma saw her, she had been employed as an assistant librarian in the Ramjas Teachers' College. Since she was supporting her mother and an aged uncle, it had not been difficult to lure her away by offering her a thousand rupees a month, which was twice her salary as the assistant librarian.

Within a minute of Rajguru entering his office, Vanita took in his glass of pale lemon grass tea, and the file of the week's newspaper clippings about himself, each clipping pasted onto yellow copy paper bearing the ashram's crest which was a black Nandi bull over the motto: *Through yoga to full enjoyment of life.*

'Am I doing anything this evening?' Rajguru asked.

'You said to say yes to a showing of a cultural film at the Chinese Embassy. Eight-thirty p.m.'

Maoism and the adulation for the Red Guards was not Rajguru's idea of culture, and all films bored him in any case. But then he had accepted the invitation at Ekanti Ma's instance. She was the one who was on a first-name basis with the Chinese diplomats, and he was anxious to maintain their friendship. Useful people too, because they had once sent out a message for Ekanti Ma on their network. 'Oh, yes...'

'And there's an invitation to a birthday party,' Vanita Dave went on. 'From Ambika Das.'

'What's that?' Rajguru asked.

'Came this morning, by hand. It is RSVP.'

Rajguru suppressed a curse. The nerve of the man!—just because he had become the bosom companion of Kalas Kak. A couple of months earlier he was one of the slogan-shouters of the spontaneous rallies; now his position as chauffeur-companion to the heir apparent had gone to his head. Like a sepoy inviting the colonel of the regiment to some low dive, Rajguru thought to himself. 'Where is it?' he asked.

'Place called El-Taj, in Mori Gate.'

'Never heard of it!' Rajguru shook his head in disgust and pursed his lips. 'No, no; can't see myself in that sort of place...men's room horseplay and giggling girls,' he muttered almost to himself. 'Just forget about it, Vanita. No need to answer the RSVP. Anything else?'

'No, Swamiji.'

'Tell my chauffeur not to wait. I'll drive myself. Eight-thirty, you said.'

But as Vanita turned to go, he suddenly had second thoughts. It was not good policy to antagonize someone who was so close to Kalas Kak. He said, 'Oh, wait. On second thoughts, Vanita, ring the Ashoka flower shop to send roses to the El-Taj, with a card. You write on it, Happy Birthday or something, will you. Two dozen—not more.'

She went out, demure as ever, her head bent slightly. He could see the full circle of yellow flowers around the bun of hair, like a target receding. His eyes caressed the understated posterior and his fingers fluttered restlessly over the green baize of the table. He ran his tongue over his lips and smiled to himself. It was odd how this girl who had not even looked him in the face and treated him as some kind of a family elder had the capacity to make him mad with desire.

It was a minute or two before he could compose himself sufficiently to turn to routine matters, such as his weekly scanning of the press-cuttings file. He read them with the expression of a man reading a letter from a close friend. From time to time he took a sip of his tea.

GRATEFUL FILM STAR
DONATES SWIMMING POOL

'RAJGURU HAS GIVEN ME NEW LIFE'

> Constance June, famous Hollywood star whose heavy dependence on sleeping pills was driving her out of her mind...had noticed during her stay in the ashram that it lacked a heated indoor swimming pool for winter bathing...

He turned the page. There was a picture of himself standing in his muslin dhoti beside a gleaming new aeroplane and in company with two foreigners in overcoats and earmuffs. The headline said:

GATWICK AIRCRAFT COMPANY PRESENTS EXECUTIVE PLANE

Rajguru turned to another page and frowned as he read:

CANADIAN LUMBER MAGNATE DONATES
HUNDRED THOUSAND DOLLARS

He pressed the intercom switch and said, 'Vanita, what is this about this Candian roughneck who came here? Hundred thousand? I thought it was to be a million.'

'I checked, Guruji. It seems they made a mistake. Mr Hartman had said a million rupees, not dollars...'

'Oh, you have checked. I was surprised. Anyway, that must affect our running total of foreign receipts...yes, please.'

'I've got it in front of me, Rajguru. Taking the rupee as a tenth of the dollar. Well, it is three million eight hundred and thirty nine thousand three hundred dollars.'

'That should be about right. Naturally I had assumed we had passed the four million mark. Thanks, Vanita,' and the holy man who was believed to be in his eighties switched off the intercom.

~

Ten miles away, in an office in the heart of downtown New Delhi, another man was studying precisely the same set of clippings, even if this lot were all pinned together and not pasted on different sheets. He too was drinking tea, but it was in a thick cup from the police canteen.

'What do you make the running total to be?' he asked the man who had brought the file.

'Nearing three million, sir. Dollars, that is,' the man answered. 'But then, we may not have covered everything.'

'Also we didn't start the file till a few months ago. So it would be safe to add another million, you think?'

'Oh, absolutely, sir.'

'Fantastic!' the Chief of Investigations said to his confidential clerk. 'Four million dollars. How can one believe it. And yet, it is all there. Coming from abroad, clean, through banks. Everything above board, even well advertised.'

Mr A.B. Chopra, shook his head again and picked up his cup of tea. It had gone cold and a skin of powdered milk had formed on top. He pushed the cup away in disgust.

CHAPTER 7

VISRAM parked his Fiat on Circular Road and walked.

Eight-thirty, Netra Agarwal had put down on her pad. He wanted to get there well before that.

El-Taj was close to the moat. Outside the door was a yellow and red sign which said OUT OF BOUNDS TO DEFENCE PERSONNEL. A doorman in nondescript clothes leaned against a bicycle-stand in the shadows behind the signpost, his hands thrust deep into his trouser pockets.

Only after he had climbed the three steps and gone in did it strike Visram that the man did not look like a doorman. He had seemed to cringe as Visram passed, as though to make himself inconspicuous. On an impulse he went out to take a second look, but the man had gone. He could see him walking towards Mori Gate, walking with a peculiar hunched gait as though he suffered from some physical infirmity.

Visram went back into the dimness and the stale air spiked with the reek of ganja, unless his policeman's nose had caught the scent of trouble brewing.

He chose a table well towards the back of the long room, in a nook formed by a pillar and a potted palm, and from which he could observe the entrance door. He called a waiter and ordered a beer.

His eyes grew accustomed to the gloom. About a dozen long-haired young men and perhaps half that many girls who looked indistinguishable from their escorts sat at a table occupying one side of the small dance floor. At least half of the men wore the costume that had come to be identified with the Dropout Brigade, knee-length orange kurta, loose white pyjamas, and Kolhapuri chappals; and the girls either wore salwar kameezes or jeans and shirts. A cigarette was being passed from hand to hand. One of the girls made a face and refused it, but was prevailed upon by the others to take a puff.

He saw Netra come in and being shown to a table on the other side of the dance floor. She ordered something from the waiter, then took out a book and began to read. Visram noticed that she was wearing steel-rimmed glasses.

Three young men, all wearing floppy pyjamas and orange shirts came in and among boisterous greetings, joined the party. Another table was dragged to make extra room and there was a hunt for chairs. The young men and girls rose and redistributed themselves. Three of the men who found themselves without girls on either side, began to talk animatedly and kept turning their heads in Netra's direction. She glanced at her watch and then at the door and turned to her book.

A small boy in a red and white uniform and a red pillbox cap came in, carrying a basket of red roses wrapped in cellophane. He walked self-importantly to one of the young men in saffron kurtas, saluted, and handed him the flowers. The man glanced at the card, beckoned to a waiter, and told him to take away the flowers, making it clear to his companions that the gift was not welcome. If the boy who brought them was expecting a tip, he did not get it. He saluted and went away, this time looking even smaller.

The man for whom the flowers were meant watched the small boy go out. Then he got up and sauntered across the floor to Netra's table and leaned over. He said something to her which made Netra shake her head and point a hand towards the door. As the young man returned to his table, some of his companions gave a muted hiss and made faces at him which prompted him to turn scowling in Netra's direction, make a V sign with his fingers, and say something which Visram could not hear, but which made her cheeks redden.

Visram called a waiter and ordered another beer. It was well past eight-thirty. 'Why don't you throw out that man?' he said to the waiter.

'He is Ambika Das,' the waiter said in a hushed whisper as though it explained everything.

Visram looked again. He had heard of Ambika Das, the chief lieutenant of the Marshal of the Dropout Brigade, an unlettered electric welder who had been made a city councillor and was now recognized as a powerful political boss in the capital.

A moustache and a lot of hair, overfull lips and flaring nostrils, an unrefined face on a frame that was squat and square and bulged at the hips.

'It is his birthday,' the waiter was saying. 'They are expecting the big ones to join. The Begum, Ekanti Ma, the Rajguru, even Kakji—excuse me!'

He scuttled as though diving for shelter.

Visram saw that Ambika Das had again waddled across to Netra's table and was saying something which made her look up in annoyance. She closed her book and took off her glasses and put them into her bag and rose as though to go along with him, and then she said something that had made him whip round with anger. That was when Ambika Das grabbed her by the wrist and pulled her away from her table.

'Swine!' Visram said to himself and sprang to his feet, and then checked himself.

Miss Netra Agarwal could certainly look after herself; what she had told him about being a judo instructor was no idle boast. Instead of pulling away, she had lurched forward in Ambika Das's direction, and then, catching him off balance, had hooked her foot behind his right knee. Whatever she then did with both hands had had the effect of sending Ambika Das slithering clean across the dance floor, holding up his hands as though for protection.

For a moment or two, everyone had remained frozen in the positions they were in, and then Ambika Das had uttered a foul oath and lunged forward, scowling, doubling his fists.

That was when the lights went out, and someone screamed.

Visram knew that the most prudent thing to do when there was free-for-all in pitch darkness was to stand with one's back to the wall. But there was no sound in the room except that of heavy breathing. Someone was coming from the service door, holding a pencil torch. Visram pounced and grabbed hold of the torch and wrenched it away. Then, flashing it on and off, he made for the table where Netra had been sitting. He flashed the light briefly at her face, said, 'It's me, Visram Lal. Come on, let's get out of here before they wreck the place. Hold on to my arm.'

She grabbed his arm and they made for the door. They had come out into the streets when the lights came on behind them. And then they heard the police whistles and the sirens of a squad car racing somewhere on the other side of Mori Gate.

They were in Visram's car, skirting Kashmere Gate. So far, neither of them had said a word. 'I suppose you were at the El-Taj in line of duty,' Netra asked.

'Well, no; I thought I'd just...you know, be around—in case there was trouble.'

'Which there was.'

'But then I didn't know that...that you really could handle that sort of trouble. Pity you tangled into Ambika Das, though.'

'Is that who he was?'

'Yes. You have made powerful enemies, Miss Agarwal. The Dropout Brigade itself.'

It was good to hear her laugh. 'You mean not even my friends in the police can help?'

'God, no! The police take orders from...from those who run the Brigade.' He hesitated and went on, 'And let me clear one misunderstanding. I am not in this professionally. In fact, I don't even know whether I am in the police force still.'

'Then why are you so...interested in this case, Mr Lal?'

'You may not believe my reasons. I'm really on a sort of private mission; to discover whatever Om wanted to tell me—what he had put down in his diary.'

'I thought we'd come to that, sooner or later,' Netra Agarwal commented as if she was speaking to herself. Then she asked, 'Where are we going?'

'I'm hungry,' he told her. 'And so should you be. I thought we'd go and eat somewhere—unless you have any strong objections.'

'No strong objections,' she told him. 'But only if you promise not to go on pumping me about the diary.'

It was as he was turning the car into the drive of Maiden's hotel that he asked, 'You don't normally wear glasses, do you, Miss Agarwal?'

'No. They were a sort of...defence.'

'Defence?'

'On the principle that men usually don't make passes at girls who wear glasses.'

'Not girls like you. Glasses are not going to be much protection,' he told her very seriously, as though he was weighing his words carefully.

The car park was not full. All the same, he drove to the side of the main building where the residents were allowed to park their cars in the drive fronting their block.

~

When they came out of the hotel, it was nearly eleven. After the cold and filtered air of the restaurant, it was like stepping into a steam bath. The night was heavy with the scents of summer, and the light patchy. As they walked through the ornate garden with its fishponds and bricked paths, Netra took Visram's arm. Two chauffeurs who had been lounging behind the only other car parked in the drive, stopped chatting and turned their heads to look at them. It was only later that Visram thought it odd that there should be two chauffeurs when there was only one car.

Kashmere Gate, twin arches left over from a fort wall. It somehow belonged more to the British who had stormed it than to the Moguls who had built it. Delhi's own Sphinx. It had always held a special fascination for him.

He held himself to his promise till they were well past the gate. Then he asked, 'Now can I say something about the diary?'

'Must you, Mr Lal? I was beginning to enjoy the drive.'

'You see, my surmise is that you've hidden it in one of the Company's safes, or in a bank locker.'

'Wherever it is, it is quite safe.'

'I don't think so, Miss Agarwal. In fact, if it is in the Company's premises, the sooner you put it away somewhere else, the better.'

She turned to look at him. 'So that whoever is keeping a watch on my movements will know where I've put it. Is that the idea?'

He laughed and shook his head. 'I don't know how to convince you that I am not speaking as a policeman but—as a friend. You see, it was something I had done that had given them the impression that Om had given the diary to me and that I had burned it. The moment they discover that he never gave it to me, they will organize a raid on the obvious places—even open bank lockers.'

'You mean an income tax raid?' she asked. 'I don't think so, Mr Lal. Perhaps you know that Vinay Surana is...well, one of the *in* people, that he always gives handsomely to party funds. What you may not know is that he is in charge of collecting donations from business houses all over the Punjab and Rajasthan. And I don't need to tell you that donations to a political party are illegal. They're not going to raid his offices.'

'The diary is far more important to the people who matter, than Surana's goodwill, I can assure you, Miss Agarwal. But I hope you're right. Now I promise not to say anything more about it.'

She was silent for a while and then said. 'You sound very convincing, Mr Lal. But then Om rang me just to warn me that you were...well, not to be trusted. I'm sorry.'

They were about to turn into Sikandar road when he suddenly swerved and turned into a bylane. After driving for a couple of hundred yards, he stopped the car to one side.

'What's the matter?' Netra Agarwal asked.

'What I told you. They're raiding the Surana offices.'

'How do you know?'

'Didn't you see the police jeeps and the lorry in the corner bungalow? One of the Suranas lives there, doesn't he?'

'That's right, Ashok, the nephew. But...but does that mean...'

'Yes, Miss Agarwal. All the Surana houses, offices, godowns—a raid must be going on now.'

'Oh, my god!' she gasped. 'And he's not even here, but in Jaipur...on their work—trying to raise money...'

He threw the car into gear and began to drive. 'Likely as not there is a police party keeping a watch on your flat too,' he said. 'But I shouldn't worry. After all, they know your premises were gone over the other day.'

'You mean—those thugs with masks, were there on police business?'

'I wouldn't say that, Miss Agarwal. It is just that those thugs with the masks were sent by more powerful people who give the police their orders.'

He drove past the retail shop owned by the Suranas in the Lodhi Market. Right enough, a raid was in progress.

'So you were...you were telling me the truth!' she gasped.

He made no answer but drove on. As they were passing the Golf Course, she touched his shoulder and said, 'Could you please go to Parliament Street. I want to see if...if they're there too.'

He did not ask her if that was where she had kept Om's diary, but turned the car. There was a police cordon around the office building of the Surana Refrigeration and Air Conditioning division, and three police vans were parked near the entrance. Inside the building, all the lights seemed to be on.

He took a U-turn on the empty road and began to drive towards Great Place when she spoke again. 'Could you stop the car somewhere, please. There are one or two things that I ought to tell you.'

He drove on as if he had not heard, but turned into Rajpath and slowed down. He brought the car to a halt near the edge of the Boat Club lawn.

'One thing I do want to know,' he said. 'And I want an honest answer. Have you read the diary, Miss Agarwal?—All that your brother had written?'

'No. He told me it was a secret document. In fact he gave it to me sealed in an envelope. That's what I had kept in the safe there, in the Parliament Street office.'

'That's bad,' he said. 'I was hoping you had read it, and could have told me what was there. Now...now I doubt if we'll ever know.'

For a minute or two, neither of them spoke. Visram stared at the strip of stale water. In the faint light it looked dark and sinister.

'My word, you do look angry!' Netra remarked.

Visram Lal who was conscious of a mounting sense of frustration, shrugged and lit a cigarette.

'Look, Mr Lal,' she said. 'When Om gave me that diary to keep, he told me it was dynamite, and that they might even kill him to try and get it back. At the time I didn't believe him.'

'Did he say who they were?'

'No. I asked, but he didn't want to...to involve me more than he already had.'

'How much had you become involved?'

'He sent me to the airport to photograph a woman who was going to Mauritius. You see he didn't trust his...his colleagues not to betray him. He gave me one of those tiny cameras.'

'Minox. Did you get any photographs?'

'I aimed the camera and made three exposures. Then I returned the camera to him.'

'Do you know who the woman was?'

'No, Mr Lal. Om had described her, and also said she might be accompanied by a police or customs officer. But I would recognize her if I saw her again. Also, I'm sure we could find out from the passenger list, couldn't we?'

He gave her a surprised glance. She was looking at an aeroplane flying overhead. 'What else? Miss Agarwal?'

'Well, you know how it is. He was very secretive, and yet one couldn't help knowing something of what he was up to. After all he was investigating the bank fraud case. Everyone knows that some really big names are involved...' she stopped and looked at him, and, since he did not say anything, went on. 'Well, from what Om said from time to time, I got the impression that the diary would tell the full story of the bank fraud case—who the people were, what they were up to, and all that. But that it was not going to be of much help for settling scores with Mr Big. That's what he used to say.'

'Really?'

'He set far more store by this other thing that he had sent Sartaj to find for him. My winning trick, he used to call it.'

'What name did you say?'

'Sartaj Puri, the man I was to meet at the El-Taj this evening. He's an ex-policeman, and Om thought very highly of him. They were chasing the Chambal dacoits together when this man got a bullet through his shoulder. He was discharged, on a pension. He often did jobs for Om which he...wanted no one to know about.'

Visram's breath quickened as he waited for her to go on.

'Well, he didn't show up.'

'Damn!' Visram cursed. 'And I don't suppose you have any idea what this man looks like or...'

'Oh, but I do, Mr Lal. I once gave him some money on Om's

behalf. He came to the flat. Little dried up looking man with a pinched face, slouching to one side because of that bullet in his shoulder. Nervous as a mouse.'

'But why the El-Taj for God's sake?' he asked with irritation. 'Why not go to your flat?'

She turned to him in surprise. 'But, Mr Lal! Remember he is an ex-policeman. He knows how you people worked. Must have known that the flat would be kept under watch.'

'But surely the stupid fool must have known that, if the flat was being watched, the phone would be bugged too, wouldn't it?'

'He's not all that stupid, Mr Lal. He had thought of a way of getting round that. He would not tell me his name over the phone, but identified himself as the man to whom I had once given a hundred and fifty rupees. Then he told me to open the telephone book where it gives the list of restaurants, and look for a place which had half his name. We agreed on a time: an hour after he had visited my flat. I know it must all seem childish to you but...I thought it was quite foolproof.'

'And then you went and put it down on your pad.'

'That was stupid of me, wasn't it. But I did ensure that I was not followed. Took an office car to Connaught Place, then walked in and out of shops, took a taxi, doubled back in a bus and finally an autorickshaw...all that.'

'Any idea why he didn't turn up?'

'None at all,' she answered. 'None at all, unless...well, he had hinted that he'd keep some sort of a watch to see if I was being followed. At least he told me that, if he did not show up, I was to conclude that someone from your lot had come snooping. May be he saw you going in, Mr Lal.'

Visram remembered the man he had seen lurking in the shadows near the El-Taj door, sidling away as he passed, and then walking like a crab towards Mori Gate.

The realization dawned upon him that, but for his interference, Netra Agarwal might even now have been in possession of what Om had called his winning trick. And the way she was staring at him, he realized that she too felt the same.

CHAPTER 8

THAT Saturday morning, the offices of the Surana companies all over India had opened for business as usual, but no work was done. Clerks huddled in groups, whispering, and executives sat glumly, pretending that everything was normal.

The emergency newspapers, emasculated and precensored, and with half their space filled with the doings and pronouncements of the Great Leader and of the Great Leader's family members, and the other half with advertisements of the Thirty-Point programme and warmed-over sports news, had at last found something they could get their teeth into.

Most of the papers had merely reproduced the handouts of the official news agency, Varta, which was a replica of the New China News agency. But the *Times* and the *Chronicle*, which were party-approved papers, had gone to town and made up their own stories.

SURANA OFFICES RAIDED, screamed the headlines. The raids, from all accounts, had been as well organized as those on the Mahindra companies' premises. 'An amazing job of coordination and synchronization for which the alert officials of the revenue intelligence service deserve the country's gratitude,' the *Chronicle* gushed. In Delhi, Calcutta, Bombay, and a dozen other towns, what the *Times* described as the 'storm troopers of the enforcement directorate' had 'gone over the top' at precisely eleven minutes past eleven p.m. A total of nine hundred officers were said to have participated in the 'operation'.

Incriminating documents were said to have been recovered. No one knew what they were. There were rumours going round that Vinay Surana had been marched off to Tihar jail, even that he had shot himself.

No one had seen him since eight o'clock that morning, and the last person to see him was his private secretary, Miss Netra Agarwal.

And she was not answering telephone calls and had given instructions to the durban at the gate not to let in any newspaper reporters or photographers.

Netra had come to the office half an hour earlier than her usual time, just to see if there was anything she could do before the Chairman came in. He was due to return from Jaipur by the early morning flight and would be driven from Palam straight to the office, because he had two meetings scheduled for the morning. One was with the Demag people who were going to discuss a collaboration deal for a plastic industry, and the other was with the trustees of the Surana charities.

Her own office was exactly as she had left it. From a cursory glance, she would have said that they had not subjected it to even a token search. Then she had noticed the light in the Chairman's office and opened the connecting door.

Vinay Surana sat slumped on the carpet in front of the steel filing cabinet, and all around him were strewn files and envelopes which he had obviously taken out of the cabinet. He turned and stared at her in annoyance. Then he licked his lips and said, 'Ah, Miss Agarwal. Will you please see if my chauffeur has arrived?'

'He hadn't when I came up,' she told him. She could see that whatever he had found missing from the filing cabinet had given him a severe jolt. 'I drove straight back from Jaipur, when I heard,' he mumbled, and suddenly realizing that he was squatting on the floor, heaved himself into the chair behind his desk.

'Shall I get you something, Mr Surana?' Netra asked. 'A glass of water…or a cup of tea?'

'No, no; just see if my car…I sent it home with Mrs Surana. Perhaps you could ring for a taxi.'

'Certainly, Mr Surana.'

Even as she was going out, she heard the toot from the driver. The car had come. Surana got up from the chair and shot past her as though he was running away from something. He had not even bothered to put away any of his private papers. Netra gathered up the files and the share certificates and the legal looking envelopes tied round with green tape, and put them back into the drawers. They could not have needed to call in one of their specialists to pick the lock, she reflected as she turned the key.

~

Atmaram Satham was dressed in a grubby singlet and shorts which, years earlier, had begun life as a pair of trousers but been snipped off at the knees. He wore rubber chappals and a three-day beard. He had not seen the papers because he did not believe in buying papers which he could read free in his office later in the day.

At the moment he was engaged in his favourite morning chore, which was spraying insecticide over his rose plants. He watched a yellow caterpillar shrivel and then looked up in annoyance as a car turned into his drive. He was mouthing words of effusive greeting even before his scowl had changed into an expansive smile. The third richest man in India had come to visit him.

Vinay Surana looked like a scruffy and short-sighted bear that had been chased by a swarm of bees. The smile on Satham's face froze as he went forward to greet him. He dropped his spray gun and whisked his visitor indoors.

Frantic telephone calls must have been made. The first car arrived in seven minutes. In another eighteen, nine cars were lined nose-to-all behind Surana's Imperial Chrysler, filling the short drive of the class II bungalow on Rose Avenue which, during British days, was allotted to Grade I clerks and office Superintendents.

Mr Atmaram Satham was the Chief Honorary Treasurer of the National Democratic Front party. The eight others who had been summoned by him were either members of his subcommittee or party executives. All of them were small men who had risen to middle-order positions in the party's hierarchy because of their unquestioning subservience to the leadership of the moment and their ability to change their allegiance whenever the leadership changed. Their strength lay in their being professional yes-men who had amply proved their incapacity either to think for themselves or to take any independent action. Their special talent was their ability to get worked up to order—into a mood of angry denunciation or exuberant approval—at a signal from the leader of the moment. They were perfect specimens of what the Americans called log-rollers.

They were altogether benumbed by the crisis, and for a time all they could do was to scowl at Vinay Surana who had brought about their predicament.

A three-page document, which Surana had kept in his filing cabinet, had been taken away by those who had raided his office. It was vital to the interests of the party that even the men who had conducted the raid must be prevented from reading the document.

'But where else was I to keep it?' Surana kept asking. 'In any case, they opened all my safes—even bank lockers.'

'But how could they even think of raiding your premises?' Satham asked. 'Knowing that...well, you are one of us. You have not...not done anything to offend the Great Leader, have you?'

'Don't be absurd!' Surana snapped. 'You know very well we had a meeting only three days ago, and that the Great Leader directed that I should go to Jaipur and put the bite again on the Rajmata. That was where...'

'Yes, yes, of course!' Satham stopped him from revealing anything further. There was no need for the small-timers to know the real nature of Surana's mission to Jaipur. 'And I take it that you have not done anything to upset Kalas Kak, either?'

'Upset? I sent him a lakh rupees only the other day because they had no money to pay the factory labour.'

'It is a cunning plot on the part of the CIA,' one of the others suggested, on the principle that any trouble that the party encountered could be safely attributed to the machinations of the CIA.

'Diabolical plot,' someone else echoed.

They had known all along that the Great Leader would have to be informed before any real damage was done. The anger and venom of the Great Leader was a byword by now. Heads would roll. The point was, if they delayed passing the information to the top and the contents of the documents became known to the Opposition parties, all of them would certainly find themselves out of job and possibly in a prison cell. Each of them tried to take Surana into a corner and pump him about whether his own name figured in the document. Surana's answer was a forbidding scowl.

He was fuming at the topsy-turviness of things, at what he was sure was a colossal bit of bungling on someone's part. It was unthinkable to him that anyone in his senses would order a raid on his premises.

That he was entrusted with the delicate task of raising money for the party from fellow-businessmen and the more vulnerable ex-princes, was not known to outsiders; and even the eight party hacks who sat squirming and sweating in Satham's sitting room had no idea that he was the party's slush fund operator. To them as to most outsiders, his palpable credentials for recognition as the most favoured industrialist in the country, a shining contrast to the Tatas and the Mahindras, was his recent title of Padma Vibhushan and his even more recent appointment as a director of the mammoth industrial complex set up near the capital by the heir apparent, Kalas Kak. Surely, anyone who had the authority to order a tax raid must be aware how friendly he was with the top leadership?

That his offices and premises should have been subjected to a raid was a humiliation he would never get over. But the loss of the document was not his problem. Whoever had ordered the raid would have to take the consequences of what fell into the hands of the tax-enforcement people as a result of the raid.

And serve him right too. 'Are you not going to inform the Great Leader?' he asked Satham.

Satham's hand shook as he picked up the receiver. His colleagues watched him like street urchins eyeing one of their number doing something daring, ready to scatter if anything went wrong. Surana went into the veranda and picked up the extension.

'What is it, Satham-bhai,' he heard the Pussycat ask. 'The Surana raid? I cannot see what is so confidential about it that you want to speak personally to...I mean it is all in the papers, Mr Satham—as you will see when you reach your office and get to read the papers.'

'But how could they raid...'

'No one is above the law of the land, Satham bhai,' Pashupat pronounced prompously. 'However rich, however influential. Black money is the curse of this country.'

The way he said it made Surana suspect that it was Pashupat who had either ordered the raid, or that he knew who had ordered it and why.

Satham was speaking in a whine. The eight white-clothed men wriggled round him in a tight scrum as they tried to listen to what was being said. Surana heard the Pussycat's loud curse. 'What? Oh, my God! The stupid fool. How could he have kept such a thing in his file cupboard. Yes, yes, you'd better come over. I cannot tell you when you will be called in—may take hours. God, what a mess! What? Certainly. Bring Surana too. I want to give the chap a piece of my mind...putting all of us in this predicament—the ass!'

Vinay Surana felt hot with anger. Barely four years earlier, Pashupat had applied for a supervisor's job in his plant in Kotah, and had been turned down by the Assistant Manager who had interviewed him. Surana himself had not even known about it till a few months earlier, when Pashupat had called upon him to dismiss the Assistant Manager.

CHAPTER 9

THE first rainfall of the year has a scent of its own, subtle and refreshing, like that of an expensive cologne. But it did not penetrate the corridors of the hospital.

The RMO was in his room, peering at an X-ray photograph clipped against a lighted frame with the sort of instant concentration that only doctors can switch on and off at will. He turned his head and said, 'I'm afraid you cannot see your patient, Mr Lal. He's in the ICU. And the Registrar said to send you to him when you came.'

The muscles of his stomach constricted and a shiver ran over his skin before the meaning of what the man in the white coat was telling him registered. 'The intensive care unit? Does that mean he's very ill?'

'You go and see the Registrar, Mr Lal,' the Duty MO said. Then he returned to his X-ray and switched on his concentration.

The Registrar, Dr P.A. Taneja, sat behind a vast desk in a corner room of the administrative block. A doctor who had turned his back on the hazards of professionalism to become an office hack, he was a daily bridge-player and weekend golfer who, by sheer dint of making the right friends and influencing the right people, had managed to get himself put on the invitation lists of half of the capital's embassies. He was a plump, round-faced man with thick, wavy hair, and an air of smugness that professional doctors seldom achieved, and a smile that was believed to be virtually ineradicable.

But he was not smiling as he hopped up from his swivel chair to intercept Visram Lal at the door of the room. 'Ah, Mr Lal. Let's go out into the fresh air for a breather, shall we. Hot here, after that storm.' He grabbed hold of Visram's hand and led him to the back of the building and down into a central quadrangle of grass and shrubs that was set aside for the use of the hospital staff. 'I say,' he asked in a confidential whisper. 'What are you chaps up to?'

'I don't know what you're talking about,' Visram told him.

'That prisoner you asked to see yesterday. He's dying.'

'Oh, my God!'

'Please, Mr Lal. I know you police people have all sorts of special reasons to ask us to break hospital rules. But...but when things go wrong, it's chaps like me who will get it in the neck.'

Visram knew that he was talking about Dorabji, and asked, 'What went wrong with Dorabji so suddenly? His ulcer?'

'Ulcer, hell. He began retching and lost control over his bowels and went into a coma. We rushed him into the ICU and pumped out his stomach. He's still unconscious.'

'Was it something he ate, Dr Taneja?'

Taneja reacted with an accusing stare. 'So you do know. Stands out a mile. The symptoms are of poisoning. And yet there was no poison that they could identify...at least not without involved laboratory tests that would take days. The PMO called a conference, which I, naturally, attended. You know what the concensus was? The possibility of one of the newfangled toxins being introduced into the blood-stream, cannot be ruled out.'

'What do you mean, newfangled toxin?' Visram asked, his voice betraying his helpless anger.

'Such as they've developed at the Halfkine for experimental purposes. Someone told me that a spoonful in a bucket of water can kill a bull in minutes—and no taste and smell to speak of.'

'But who could have got hold of such a poison, doctor?' Visram asked, very patiently.

'The only people who were given a few grains each were the defence services intelligence and your own secret service...'

'And who could have given it to Dorabji?'

Taneja cocked his neck and assumed his disbelieving stare. 'It could be you—it could be the other chap.'

'What other chap, for God's sake?'

'The man your people said to let into the man's room with those magazines and things...'

'Who rang you, doctor? From what office? As to myself, I came and saw you personally about having a talk with Dorabji.'

'Well, Mr Lal. I cannot be expected to know every man in your organization. It is enough for me if I get a call saying please hold the line for the Chief Superintendent...'

'Is that what happened?'

'Of course...and I sent word to the Matron to let the man go into the security ward...' He stopped abruptly and whispered, 'So that's over.'

He was looking at two white-coated young men who were walking briskly towards a door marked COFFEE SHOP, STAFF ONLY. They walked in silence and with lowered heads.

'They're the two interns who had been attending to Dorabji, in the ICU,' Taneja explained. 'And their coming out together for coffee can only mean one thing.'

Somewhere a bell peeled. The breeze suddenly freshened and dried the moisture that had beaded Visram's face. 'Does that mean the man's dead?' he asked.

Dr Taneja pursed his lips and nodded. He took out a packet of cigarettes and held it before Visram.

Visram remembered how he had given Dorabji cigarettes, and how, at the end of their interview, the man who had no friend in the world had suddenly clutched his hand and pressed it as though to seek comfort.

And then he asked himself if Dorabji would have died if he had not come to ask him questions in the RMO's room.

~

There was no delay. Surana and Satham were whisked indoors. The eight others who had accompanied them in the hope that they might later be able to say that they had been consulted by the Great Leader, were made to wait in the veranda. Even the two watchmen did not consider it necessary to exchange a word of greeting with them.

The interview, conducted in a soundproofed room, did not last quite ten minutes. At the end of it, the two men came out looking like schoolboys who had had a session with the Headmaster. Surana had been told that he had just lost his collaboration deal with Demag; Satham that he would not get a party ticket for the next election.

As he walked through the outer office, Satham looked a stricken man. His step faltered, sweat poured out of his body, and his head buzzed. God, was he coming in for a stroke?—he wondered. But Surana was already calculating how much more money he would have to pump into the business follies of the Great Leader's son and which no investor in his senses would have touched, to get back into favour. Whatever the price, he had made up his mind not to put off the Demag people. The deal would go through.

Even as the two men slunk out, the Pussycat made two telephone calls. His voice was known to his listeners and all he told them was, 'Bullawa hai.'

Bullawa hai, a phrase of peasant Hindi, means simply, 'there's a summons.' It had become a part of the mystique of the Emergency. The listener had to drop everything and report to the residence of the Great Leader. Nothing else was to be said on the telephone on either side.

The first to arrive was the Minister of Inland Revenue, Hemraj Alkush. He was told to ensure that all the documents taken away from Surana's safe were to be put into a bag unread, and the bag sealed and delivered to Alkush, who was to open it himself and burn the two lists. The remaining documents and articles were to be returned to Surana.

Not a word was wasted. The orders were crisp, clear, businesslike. Meanwhile, another minister who had come in answer to the summons, the Minister of Publicity Media, Gyan Sharan, was having coffee and biscuits in the drawing room with the members of the Great Leader's family. He was shown into the soundproofed room the minute Alkush was dismissed.

'See that the newspapers make no further mention of the Surana raids,' the Great Leader told him.

'Shall I issue a denial that there was any raid?' Gyan Sharan, always ready to bend over backwards, asked.

'No, no,' The voice was impatient, schoolmasterish. 'I just want to see no more mention of the raid—anywhere.'

By now the ministers had become accustomed to the Great Leader's methods. There would be no written orders. Everything was by word of mouth. Houses would be bulldozed, people sent to jails, air services cancelled, electric connections to offices and printing presses would be stopped without so much as a signed order. To be sure this method of getting things done had not trickled down to some of the middle-level officials; but that was because they were plodders, unable to rise above the requirements of procedure. And it was up to the ministers to give short shrift to such officials as chose to ask for written orders. They had ample authority to deal with indiscipline without bothering the top leadership.

As it happened, the Enforcement Directorate Officer who was in charge of the Surana raid made the mistake of asking for a receipt for the sealed bag with the contents of Surana's office safe. He was told to call for it later in the day. The order he got that afternoon was to the effect that he had been posted to Nagaland and must report to his new superior within twenty-four hours. Three weeks later, he was arrested on the charge that he was seen at a gathering of Phizo's followers, and imprisoned under MISA for indulging in treasonable activities.

The Officials of the Ministry of Publicity Media, however, acted with a proper sense of responsibility. No one thought of asking for orders in writing. The Chief Censor ordered his deputies, who ordered the newspaper editors: Kill the Surana raids.

On the following morning, the officials of the Revenue Enforcement department took back all the documents and articles they had impounded from the Surana Companies' premises. Vinay Surana had given instructions that they were to be treated to elaborate luncheons in the executive lunch rooms, and that no one was to make a fuss if it was found that some of the papers taken were not returned. But the superintendents in charge of all the establishments sent round a note to the Chairman, certifying that nothing was missing.

Which, as far as it went, was quite true. The small sealed envelope which the Chairman's secretary had deposited in the filing cabinet in the Parliament Street office, was not a company document, and, in any case, the superintendent had no knowledge that Miss Agarwal had hidden it there.

As to what was missing from the papers that had been taken away from the Chairman's private filing cabinet in his office, it was of course not known to any of the officers of the company.

~

First, Om. Then Dorabji. Both because they had known too much. Who was next on the list? Visram Lal? Netra Agarwal?

No. Now that they must have discovered that Om's case diary was intact in its sealed envelope, it was unlikely that they would bother any longer about Miss Agarwal.

That left himself, heading the queue. By now they must know that he was on the trail and had talked to both Om and Dorabji. It was unlikely that they would know how little he had been told by either of them.

The trouble was that they did not know how much, or how little, he knew. He was someone who constituted a danger. Even if they did not send some hired killer to finish him off, they could always have him arrested and locked up under MISA. The thought of the cockroaches and bedbugs in Tihar jail, the filth of its communal lavatories, made his skin crawl.

One thing stood out. His official flat in Arjun Singh Park would be ceaselessly watched, and all his telephone conversations taped. The moment he made a false step, they would move in. The initiative was wholly in their hands. To be able to proceed with his investigations, he had to be a free agent. The one thing he could not afford was to be under surveillance.

He pulled out from the recess above his clothes cupboard, a suitcase which he normally took when travelling by air. He dusted it and began to pack.

Before I go away, I must report to ABC, he told himself, but, even as he picked up the receiver, felt a twinge of shame. He was giving in to a weakness which servicemen all over the world suffered from: the craving to take orders. After all, it was not as though he could not get in touch with ABC any time there was need to do so—if he had something to report.

That was just it. He had nothing to report; nothing except the fact that Dorabji had died. And that would be in the evening papers.

It was the realization that he would only be reporting his failure to make any headway, as much as the shame of showing himself as being incapable of carrying on on his own in a tough situation, that deterred him from making the call.

Stripping for action, he told himself as he packed. It meant getting rid of all non-essential gear. When it came to a push, one really needed so little. The car would be left in a garage, to be available on call. He did not himself know where he was going. Perhaps it would be better to absent himself from Delhi for a few days. At least it would not look odd. After all he was supposed to be under suspension. What was more natural than that he should go away somewhere to avoid embarrassing his friends and acquaintances?

What happened to his position in the service, the progress of the case of his supposed request for retirement, did not bother him in the least. He had the fullest confidence in his chief, and knew that his interests would not suffer.

The Beretta with a full magazine and three spare clips, the Vienna police helmet, and the little leather bag of special tools that contained the most sophisticated housebreaking impliments and a torch, were the professional items. Half a dozen shirts and four pairs of trousers, wash-and-wear underclothes, a battery-operated shaver, toilet things, spare socks and handkerchiefs, and a zipper windcheater, two paperback anthologies. He could not think of anything else.

He snapped the suitcase shut. He was ready to go. The suitcase could not have weighed the regulation twenty kilograms that they let you take on Indian Airlines. How little one needed.

He gave an all round look and slumped into his favourite chair. He lit a cigarette and again thought how he ought to tell someone that he was not going to be found in his usual haunts.

This time he almost gave in. It was the need to hear a friendly and encouraging voice as much as for any professional reason that he could think of that prompted him to dial the number: 4003001. There was a single burr before someone picked up the instrument and said, 'Special Branch.'

He put back the receiver almost without meaning to, like someone hastily setting right a misdemeanour before he was discovered. He stubbed the cigarette angrily, picked up his bag, and made for the door.

He had already opened the door when the telephone began to ring.

He whipped round and stood scowling at the instrument for a few seconds before he realized how nervous he was acting. He put down his suitcase and ran across and picked up the receiver. 'Hello?' he said.

'Is that the Willingdon Hospital?' a male voice asked.

'Wrong number,' Visram said and put down the receiver. His fingers had left a wet mark on the handset and his heart was thumping.

Sangli Mess. A huddle of shabby barracks that had outlived their natural span of life and resembled a rundown labour camp in a mining town. But the trees which had been planted when the mess was built, thirty years earlier, had now come of age and created a dense shade around the car park which sweated tar. A dog lay fast asleep under one of the trees.

The car in which they sat radiated heat. 'I just had to see you,' ABC told Visram. 'Before you did your vanishing trick.' He looked a worried man, or like a man who was conscious that he was doing something underhand, Visram thought.

'How did you know I was thinking of vanishing?'

'Only sensible. After what happened to Dorabji.'

'What did happen actually, sir? They won't know till after the autopsy, will they?'

ABC shook his head. 'No autopsy. The body has already been disposed of—cremated, I believe.'

'But the Parsis don't cremate! There must have been relatives to...to claim the body—take it to the tower of silence.'

'Apparently not. Anyway, that's the position. The doctors certified natural causes.'

'Damn!' Visram cursed. 'That Registrar chap was sure it wasn't... natural causes. As good as accused me of murdering the man.'

'That's one reason why you should thank your stars that the verdict was what it was. Otherwise by now you'd have been arrested as suspect number one.'

Visram had not thought of that particular possibility. For a few seconds he fought off the idea of giving up his mission and resuming his normal life. How remote it seemed.

'But that's not what I called you here for,' ABC was saying impatiently. 'And I haven't much time. I'm between two meetings, and hope I shan't be missed for a while. Here.' He produced some sheets from his pocket and gave them to Visram. 'It's the only copy we have, and I don't want to have any copies made for the simple reason that no one must suspect that we have seen these papers.'

A harmonium started playing scales in one of the mess quarters and a woman's voice joined in, squeakily singing out: sa, re, ga, ma, pa... The dog under the tree woke up, shook itself and trotted off purposefully in the direction of the music. ABC made a face, glanced at his watch, and went on, 'Remember your asking me if I had someone else doing some private snooping? Well. I have. And one of them was in the party which raided Surana's office. They found these papers there, and the man was able to have a copy made before passing them on to the Director—must have sat up all night. Just take a look, will you. I...I want a reaction.'

Visram spread out the sheets on his knee, holding them well down so that anyone who happened to be passing should not notice that he was reading them. No one passed.

There were two lists. The first contained fifty-eight names, the second nineteen. Each name had a sum of rupees shown against it. At least half the names in the first list were known to Visram because they were either some of the country's leading industrialists, or ex-ruling Princes or their wives. But none of the names on the second list was familiar to him.

'The first is a list of donations, is it, sir?' he asked.

ABC nodded.

'And donations to party funds by industrial concerns are illegal,' Visram continued. 'Might get the donors prison terms.'

'That, of course, but what else?' ABC was frowning. He again glanced at his watch.

'The total is a formidable sum, isn't it,' Visram said, lamely, feeling that this was not the answer the other wanted. 'Only a little under five million rupees. Staggering.'

'And the other list?' ABC asked, looking into the distance as though to give his companion a better chance to concentrate his thoughts. 'Oh, come on,' he said irritably. 'Surely there are some names on that other list which you've heard of before.'

Visram went over the shorter list once again. 'Ram Tanay Jha?' he asked.

'What about him?'

'MLA from Padmakoshal, isn't he? Oh, wait a minute! But how stupid of me! Wasn't he the chap who changed over to the ruling party last year, and with him...oh, God!...brought eighteen others. They crossed the floor and toppled the government...God, what a stink this would make!'

The figures against the names ranged from Rs 25,000 to Rs 90,000. More than a million rupees had been distributed.

'So that's how they got power in Padmakoshal. By buying up these nineteen legislators! And the money was paid to them by Vinay Surana.'

ABC was nodding in agreement even as he was wiping his neck with a handkerchief which was already ringing wet. 'There's something else that occurred to me,' he said. 'I have been keeping a file on the Swami! Not officially, God, no! Just a private record, as it were, of the money he receives from abroad. I have always wondered if there was not some sort of a connection between these vast sums collected for the party which being illegal, are not subjected to any audit...and...'

ABC stopped, giving the impression that he had already said more than he had intended to. 'And the sort of sum involved in the Dorabji case?—is that what you mean, sir?' Visram asked.

Mr Chopra pursed his lips and cocked his head as though to listen to the lady who was learning to sing. She was now voicing the opening notes of a raga, but was finding it difficult to follow herself on the harmonium. Ga-ga-sa-ga-ma-pa-ga-ma-ni-dha...

'I don't want to influence your thinking,' ABC said at last. 'It's vital to keep our brains clear. Now I'm afraid I must scram.'

They arranged the next rendezvous. 'The same signals,' ABC said, 'But we'll meet in the grounds of the Birla Temple. You know, where the concrete animals are. My duty telephone is manned day and night.'

Mr Chopra had not bargained for the fact that a time might come when he may not be in a position to enjoy the privileges of his position, such as a telephone which was manned day and night.

Visram gave the papers back to ABC and slid out of the car and strolled in the direction of the mess office. After giving him a couple of minutes, ABC started his car and drove off.

Vanita Dave picked up the tray of lemon grass tea and waited for the second hand on her HMT watch with the cracked plastic strap to complete its circle. Of late she had begun to experience a sense of pleasurable nervousness whenever she and her employer were alone together. She had several times caught him staring at her with those lustful eyes of his as though he was trying to read her innermost thoughts.

It was five o'clock. She bit her lip and pushed open the door. 'Mr Surbinder rang, Guruji,' she reported as she placed the tray on the side table. She was conscious that he was watching her every movement, and the look in his eyes made her florid with excitement. 'Said it was urgent, Guruji,' she added.

Rajguru grunted, almost absent-mindedly. Then he said, 'Will you get him then, Vanita?'

After his secretary had shut the heavy, cork-lined door behind her, Rajguru gave a deep sigh and smiled to himself. Then from the waistband of his dhoti, he took out a gold pill box no bigger than a baby's thimble, and shook out a small, gummy-looking grey pill. He dropped it into his tea and waited for it to dissolve.

The telephone rang. 'Ah, Surbinder,' Rajguru said. 'I take it you are on the scrambler. Good. I'm switching on to secret now. Of course I am by myself. The point is, are you, Good!'

Swami Rajguru must have been the only non-official in the country to possess scrambler telephones. He had one in his ashram and another in his penthouse—so that from either place he could speak to those who had similar instruments in absolute secrecy. He flicked the switch of the green telephone, and said, 'Yes, Surbinder?'

He doodled as he listened. 'In the Lodhi Gardens?' He asked. 'At six-thirty? But surely they were not together?' The tablet had now dissolved and he took a sip of his tea.

'No, Guruji,' Surbinder said.

'In that case it could have been no more than a coincidence.'

'That's what I too thought, sir,' Surbinder told him.

Two thin lines appeared on the Swami's forehead, and his fingers began to drum on the table in a slow rhythm, as Surbinder recounted that, just as a precaution, he had decided to have a watch kept on the COI's movements.

'Very sensible,' Rajguru told him. 'And...what did you discover?'

'That they're hand-in-glove, Swamiji; keep in touch, meet...'

'The bhenchods!' Guruji cursed and went on cursing softly, as he heard the other tell him how, Chopra and Lal had met only a couple of hours earlier, in the car park of the Sangli Mess, and that they had been seen sitting in a car for nearly fifteen minutes and talking animatedly. 'Well, there's nothing I can do to foil whatever they're up to, sir. After all, Chopra is miles senior...'

'Of course not,' Rajguru assured him. 'You leave it to me. It'll only mean...' he stopped.

There was nearly a whole minute's silence while Rajguru sipped his tea and took a couple of deep breaths, and, unable to endure the suspense, Surbinder from the other end said, 'Sir, what were you saying, sir?'

Rajguru drained his glass of tea and smacked his lips at the aftertaste created by his opium pill. Then he said, 'It'll mean that you'll have to take over from him much sooner than we had planned for.'

There was a squeaking sound at the other end, and impatiently Rajguru asked. 'What is it, Surbinder? What did you say? Oh, no; it should not take more than a couple of days.'

~

Among those who were rightfully entitled to scrambler telephone in their houses were police officers of the rank of DIG and higher. Surbinder rang his house, and told his wife to get on the secret phone. Then he gave her the good news. He was going to be made the Chief of Investigations.

'No, no; I'm not joking, darling,' he had to assure her. 'Hen ji? Oh, before the week is over, certainly. Hen ji? Oh, absolutely pucca. What about ABC? Darling, why did you have to mention that name at a time like this? ABC will be rolling his bedding—and you will be riding with me in a flag car with two gold stars.'

~

The four people who sat behind the steel doors of the tantric shrine in Swami Rajguru's ashram might have been engaged in some mystic ritual of their cult, if it had not been for the fact that they were looking in the opposite direction from the only object in the room which might have had some conceivable connection with a religious cult.

This was a life-size oil painting of the Goddess Shakti, done by the Polish artist, Janos Rakosi. One of the foremost of the Piccasso school of painters, Rakosi had painted the Goddess in some manifestation that no Hindu devotee would have recognized. There was something in her of an angel as well as of a witch, but more than anything else, she was a woman who had worked herself into a mood of flaming anger and was poised to destroy the world.

The people in the room sat in the dark, staring at a small white screen set up at the far end of the room, saying nothing. They were looking at the microfilmed pages of a secret government file.

Pashupat, who was operating the projector, switched it off with a click, and put on the lights. Rakosi's Shakti once again became visible, looking down upon the room with celestial malevolence. Pashupat extracted the roll of film and passed it to his uncle Kaul, who put it away in its allotted slot in one of the drawers of the two steel cabinets that were kept in the room.

'That's all we seem to have on Chopra,' Pashupat remarked, sounding a trifle disappointed. 'That he has a sister who is married to an American and lives in Vermont.' He got up and helped himself from one of the three bottles kept on a tray.

'Oh, come, Pussycat,' Ekanti Ma protested. 'For that matter I have a sister who married a Frenchman—lives in Avignon.'

'But, madam,' Kaul intervened, speaking thickly because of the paan he had just inserted in his mouth. '*You* don't happen to hold a high position in one of our secret services. Having a sister who is an American citizen makes Chopra a distinct security risk.'

'I suppose we could make out that there is some sort of a CIA connection, with the sister's husband, couldn't we?' Rajguru said.

'Oh, easy,' Kaul answered.

'I assure the members of this august house,' Pashupat said, parodying the voice and speech-rhythms of a Cabinet Minister.

'That it is with profound regret that I have taken this step. But I shall never allow it to be said that the security of this great nation was subordinated to the interests of one person, however high. Never. Never!'

They all laughed. 'I hope you're right,' Ekanti Ma said. 'Padati calls himself a Gandhian. They can be awkward, at times. These Gandhians.'

'Madam, we can make him turn cartwheels,' Pashupat said. 'You only have to see the dossier of this particular Gandhian... juicy is not the word.'

'Let's have a look, shall we?' Rajguru asked.

'I've got it right here, Swamiji,' Kaul answered.

The lights went out again, and the screen became illuminated. The images flashed on the screen. At first only the cover of the file, with a diagonal cross and the 'Top Secret' label, then the registry number and title and cross references to other files. Then followed three pages of biographical information on a man called Vidyadhar Padati. 'Ah, here we are, sir.' Pashupat said as a typed report came on the screen:

> In April 1970, the Warden of Kilachand Orphanage named Shri Padati as the seducer of a teenage girl, Anupa Mehta. Padati thereupon adopted said girl, and found her a job in Swadeshi Emporium. Anupa remained Padati's mistress for more than a year. In February 1971, Mrs Padati (Asha), ran away from Ministerial residence, alleging that her husband had installed Anupa in the servants' quarters. Politically influential people prevailed upon Mrs Padati to return to husband on the promise that Anupa would be evicted from the house. She was forcibly driven out, in a state of advanced pregnancy. She led a vagrant existence and took some medicine to get rid of her child. She died in the public ward of the Cama hospital. She made a dying declaration naming Vidyadhar Padati as the father of her child. Inquiry was quashed by telephone instructions from Chief Minister.'

'Anything more on this?' the Swami asked.

'We have a photostat of the girl's dying declaration,' Pashupat answered. 'Also there is another sex scandal, involving a school mistress. And there's this.'

The screen showed a handwritten letter written on an aerogram. It had obviously been opened by a postal censor and photographed before being despatched.

If you look after Kumar's fees and expenses in London till he qualifies as a Computer Engineer, we can make the necessary adjustments. The total is not likely to exceed £3,000.

'God! Who did the fool write that to?' Rajguru asked.

'The sales Manager of a fertilizer firm. They were trying to get a contract at the time, from his ministry. He was Agriculture then. Oh, there's more of the same...'

'Don't bother. That bit is enough to get him to sack ten Chopras. Isn't it odd how they always get caught out on this foreign exchange business. Sex scandal is...well, more juicy...but so difficult to bring home.'

The lights came on, illuminating the windowless room. Ekanti Ma switched off the air conditioner, and Pashupat picked up the tray of drinks.

'One of you will see to it that the press gets hold of the proper angle, won't you,' the Rajguru said. 'That Chopra was suspected of being too friendly with the CIA to remain as the Chief of Investigations?'

'Certainly, Swamiji,' they both answered. 'Unless you want it pitched stronger. Openly allege that he was a CIA agent.'

'I don't advise that,' Swamiji answered. He had never believed in using a sledgehammer to crush a peanut.

They all trooped out, and Rajguru himself locked the room and turned off the lights.

~

The microfilm library of the secret dossiers of the men and women prominent in the nation's life, had a sinister history of its own, encompassing, aside from the most unprincipled snooping into the ordinary citizen's life, double-cross, blackmail and, some said, even murder.

It had begun life as the brainchild of Shamkant Sen, who,

because of an American college education and a preference for all things American, had come to be known as Uncle Sham. An obscure and lifelong party pack, he had, as a consequence of some barefaced horse-trading among the leaders during a political free-for-all, found himself pitchforked into the position of a junior minister. One of his ministerial jobs was to phase out a high-powered secret agency that had been set up in a hurry during the Chinese war of 1962 to gather border intelligence, but had become redundant for more than ten years.

J. Edgar Hoover had died that year, and the methods by which he had made himself the most feared if not the most powerful man in America were coming out into the open. Uncle Sham took a leaf right out of Hoover's book.

Instead of winding up the intelligence agency, he had channelized the resources of his ministry in such a way as to revitalize it. He had given his star agents a new task: to collect all the scandal they could about his political enemies.

'Power does not come out of the barrel of a gun,' Uncle Sham used to tell his few admirers. 'In democracies it flows from your knowledge of your rivals' secrets.'

His men had gone about it with great gusto. The library had grown in scope as well as size, and with it had grown Uncle Sham's stock as a politician. He had been found a place in the Cabinet, and it was common talk that, after the next election, he would become the Prime Minister. There was nothing to stop him. Except death.

He died only a few weeks before that next election. His jeep had hurtled down a Himalayan valley while he was on a propoganda tour. There were rumours of foul play, but then such rumours always crop up whenever an important politician dies in India.

The person who held temporary charge of Uncle Sham's portfolio during the interlude of the General Election, was Udamrao Maney, a simple-minded peasant from the west coast who was in his mid-seventies. He was also an ardent devote of Swami Rajguru. At one of his weekly visits to the Swami's penthouse, Maney was holding forth about the deviousness of politicians in general and of his predecessor in office in particular. That was when he happened to mention the secret dossiers on prominent people that he had come across in the two Godrej filing cabinets in the little strongroom directly behind his office.

'Quite hair-raising, some of the stuff,' he had commented with a simulated shudder.

Rajguru too had looked mildly shocked, and proceeded to question his visitor closely on the files. Then he had made a quick decision of which the first manifestation was his ordering a bottle of Royal Salute whisky to be brought out.

Since it was well known in the Swami's circles that he served this brand only when Kalas Kak came to visit him, it was but natural that Udamrao Maney should feel greatly flattered. 'What more special friend can one have to serve special whisky to than Bhai Udamrao?' the Swami had said to Ekanti Ma.

So far, the Swami's source of power had been his mysterious influence over the Great Leader. Here was his chance of creating an alternative source that was independent of anyone's patronage. For the next half-hour, he had discoursed ponderously on the philosophy of Chanakya, which distinguished between pure truth and national good, and on the impracticability of the Gandhian approach to ends and means; how, sometimes, it was necessary to have at one's disposal the means to compel people to do things against their inclinations. 'Oh, only once in a long while—but naturally. Still, the power must be there, in the hands of someone who is above self-interest, someone who can be trusted never to abuse it…never!'

Bombarded by esoteric arguments, and mellowed by the whisky and an Upman cigar, Minister Maney had surrendered without resistance. Indeed in later years he was often assailed by a mood of self-congratulation for having prevailed upon the Swami to agree to accept the responsibility of guiding the nation's affairs in moments of crises. The very next day after his visit to the Swami, he had given orders to have the secret files microfilmed.

The work was entrusted to the same people who had collected the information, the intelligence wing of the ministry. But while the ministry employed scores of skilled secret agents, it had only two photographers who could do the microfilming. Working in alternate shifts so that they could operate their unwieldy overhead cameras without coming into each other's way in the constricted space of the ministry's strongroom, it had taken the two men nearly six weeks to have all the files put on film. And after that the Minister himself had taken the spools personally to Rajguru in two large Samsonite suitcases.

It was long after the filming of the documents was over that the two photographers happening to talk about their assignments, began to suspect that each of them had been made to film the entire contents of the secret cabinets, and that between them they might have produced two separate sets of microfilms of the dossiers held in the strongroom. This duplication of labour they put down to a stupid mistake on the part of the Minister, or of their own departmental superior.

They had no means of actually checking up if they really had produced two sets of films, or of knowing why the films had been ordered and what had happened to them.

Swami Rajguru had thus managed to create a parallel record of scandal in high places that was not under the control of a government agency. And not even the two men he had chosen as his henchmen for passing on his orders to ministers and officials, suspected that there might be another set of microfilm spools in existence somewhere.

Udamrao Maney, an easygoing man who was fond of good wine and Havana cigars, happened to lose his seat in the elections. But he was given ample proof that he had done well to have persuaded the Swami to take an interest in the nation's affairs. His fondest hopes were of spending the twilight years of his life in a diplomatic post in one of the sleepier embassies in the heart of Africa. With the blessings of his guru, he had been granted his wish: a forseeable future of duty-free wines and cigars and a tax-free salary.

And even though Pashupat and Kaul were the Swami's most trusted agents, neither of them had been a lowed to see their own dossiers, or been permitted to enter the tantric shrine unless Ekanti Ma or the Swami were present.

CHAPTER 10

VISRAM drove slowly past the golf course. At both roundabouts that he passed, the policemen on duty gave him cracking salutes.

Losing yourself in a land as vast and heavily populated as India was easy enough. He knew that several of the opposition leaders who had gone underground upon the declaration of the Emergency were still at large. But his own problem was different. As a senior police officer who had been in the capital for a couple of years, he was known to most of the city's policemen by sight. One of the disadvantages of the service was that you were always under observation. He would have to wait for the night to make his bid for escape.

He spent the afternoon at his club, first in the reading room and then playing bridge. While in the bridge room, he saw ABC come through the door but stop in his tracks when he saw him. Visram Lal was ostensibly in disgrace—an officer under suspension. ABC had turned right round and gone out.

The summer day dragged on. It was not till seven-thirty that he thought it was time to go, and it was still not dark outiside.

As he came out of the gate, he ran smack into a demonstration by the youth wing of the National Democratic Front. Ambika Das and his men were holding their weekly 'Spontaneous Rally' to give thanks for the leadership.

Visram tried to back the car, but found that two other cars had formed up behind him. And then the crowd parted in the middle as it cleared a lane for a small white car with scooter wheels to pass through. A balding young man with a puffy face and blinking eyes covered with thick lenses in black frames beamed at them and then raised his hands like a boxer who had been declared a winner. The cheering suddenly rose to a crescendo, and drums crashed.

'Our leader!' someone yelled.

'Jai!' the crowd answered.

'The Nation's leader!'

'Jai!'

Jai, jai, jai-jai-jai! And suddenly they were dancing the bhangra, yelling themselves hoarse, throwing up their arms and jumping, beating drums. They then burst into song, 'Our leader; Nation's leader' which had become the national anthem of the Emergency. It was like a tribal orgy from the jungle brought to a traffic roundabout.

And it was sad to see how half a dozen elderly men who had no doubt been caught up in the demonstration were posturing grotesquely in imitation of Ambika Das and his men, and pretending to be enjoying themselves hugely. Visram recognized a respected city father, Shamji Bhanot, fat and grey-haired, puffing and sweating. His glasses had slid down under his nose and one of his chappals had come off. Idly he wondered how long Bhanot would be able to keep up this tempo, and what his wife and children would have to say if they saw him behaving like a clown.

It was said that the members of the Dropout Brigade were paid ten rupees every time they were called out for these spontaneous rallies, but of course that may have been a rumour started by the opposition. At that the dropouts were not much different from their counterpart in Europe and America, where they were said to cause riots and fight the police to be able to touch the flesh of some pop singer or football star. The young had to have an idol, and it was a mercy that these rallies had now been reduced to one or two a week; not so long ago, there used to be as many as half a dozen rallies every day, and several streets were almost permanently closed to traffic.

It was the sight of people like Bhanot, aping the dropouts and dancing the bhangra in the city's streets that filled one with disgust.

And suddenly, the urge to get away hit him like a wave of panic; get away even for a few hours from this city which he had come to love and which had now become the control room of a type of rule that had reversed the definition of democracy and was far more despotic than the Raj in its most repressive days; an Orwellian nightmare in which, to be insufficiently devoted to the Great Leader was an unforgivable sin. To demonstrate a properly venomous hatred for the villians of the opposition or a fervent adoration for the Great Leader and the heir apparent had become a citizen's primary duty.

The crowd had dispersed. A ritual had been performed; the week's exercise to show loyalty was over. The demonstrators broke off in groups, and were suddenly turned into college boys returning from a cricket match, laughing and chatting, their fervour had drained away. A constable came up to his car and saluted.

Visram drove to Lilaram's garage in Panchkuin Road and left his car there for servicing. 'Please get your mechanic to check the brakes and the lights,' he told the attendant. 'I shali be away for a couple of days—maybe more. No, no; I'll ring myself, when I get back, and come for it.'

He waved away the attendant's offer to get him a taxi. His suitcase in his hand, he hailed a scooter rickshaw and asked to be taken to Connaught Place. At the traffic light near the Regal Cinema, he saw a scooter draw up beside the rickshaw, ridden by a man in a green crash helmet. After getting himself dropped at Sahib Singh's shop and buying a tube of mosquito cream which he did not want, he waited just inside the door till he saw a taxi draw up and drop a fare. He scrambled into it and told the driver, 'Just go round the circus, will you? I'm trying to find an address.' About halfway through the circle, he saw the man on the scooter again, this time about fifty yards behind. So they had put a tail on him. Clever of Surbinder, he thought, to have sent a man on a scooter instead of one of those departmental motorcycles which Visram would have recognized even from the sound of their engines.

He got out in Daryaganj and walked purposefully in the midst of the evening throngs. He saw a bus slowing down for a herd of buffaloes which was being coaxed across the road and jumped in. It was a jam-packed mid-town bus and it went winding in and out of streets which he had never seen before. After ensuring that the man in the green helmet was nowhere in sight, he alighted from the bus, walked right through a department store and took another cab, still undecided about his destination. The driver had turned and was looking questioningly at him when he heard the whistle of a train, and said on the spur of the moment, 'New Delhi railway station!'

The Punjab Mail was just steaming in. He had plenty of time to buy his ticket and jump into a first class carriage that had become empty. At Delhi junction, a few minutes before the train was about to start on its onwards journey, he went up to the Conductor and, after making sure that he had an empty coupe to offer, changed to air-conditioned.

It was cool in the train after the oppressive heat, and the air, fresh. But he could breathe freely only after the train had passed the outskirts of the metropolis. He bolted the carriage door and tried to sleep, but the sounds of wild cheering, the sight of a grandfatherly man jumping up and down like a bear kept him awake for hours.

And then the thought struck him that he was like a man running away from a city under seige; not as a refugee but a deserter.

~

At that Kasauli was almost an extention of Delhi's clubland, Visram reflected. Here at least half the summer population was made up by officials from Delhi and their wives.

In fact he was lucky to be given a room in the Kasauli Club's annexe. 'Only till the weekend, Mr Lal,' the Secretary apologized. 'After that, we're booked right through the summer.'

'I want it only for two nights,' he told the secretary. In the event, he occupied the room for only one night.

Visram had read of fictional detectives who, when they were baffled by a case, locked themselves in a room with a bottle of Scotch or bourbon for a few hours to mull over the available evidence. He, Visram, had never resorted to this particular expedient before, but, now that he was on his own and not a part of a vast investigative machine, he thought it would be a good idea to try and think things out, particularly since ABC had made something of a point of not wanting to influence his mind.

The feeling that he had deserted a city under seige still lingered. All the same it would have been a crime to spend what little time he had, being locked up in his room. He did not much care for bourbon, and even though he liked Scotch, more than a couple of ounces of it invariably gave him a headache. He ordered a thermos of coffee and a bottle of water and sandwiches. In the Kasauli bazaar, he bought a stout walking stick and a pound of black Simla cherries. He aimed in the direction of a shady peak on the left of the Sanawar school, and took himself for a day's trek.

It was cold in the shady parts, and the air was stiff with summer scents.

He did not understand big money, and figures always confused him. He had to make a special effort to try and make some sense of the paper ABC had shown him.

So Vinay Surana had collected nearly five million rupees for the party in illegal donations. Surana's franchise was restricted to the Punjab and Rajasthan, and there were at least half a dozen other fundraisers like him in the rest of the country. If they had matched Surana's performance, the party had managed to collect nearly thirty-five million rupees in donations alone.

The middle-level industrialists and the fifty or so major ex-ruling princes were like sitting ducks for the party's cash-hunters. A new excise levy or a party-encouraged strike could put the former out of business, and a new item for expropriation or a tax raid make paupers of the princes. Invariably they paid; the industrialists made up the losses by jacking up prices, the princes by clandestine sales of jewelry and heirlooms...he gave a start.

A blue-grey stone the size of a football on which he was about to step gave a sharp squawk and rocketed off into the valley, and after that three young kalij chicks scuttled among the pine needles.

What was he thinking about? Donations. But then donations formed only a part of the party's funds, which were said to run into hundreds of millions. Someone had actually mentioned the figure of nine hundred million...

Vast sums were collected from traders, steel merchants and sugar merchants, from oil, cloth, grain, cement and fertilizer merchants, by the simple expedient of putting restrictions on sales and then removing the restrictions when the ransom was paid. So much for a bolt of cloth, for a bag of sugar, for a tonne of cement.

Suddenly it would be found that sugar had gone off the market, or cooking oil, or pulses, or kerosene. A month or so later, whatever was off the market would again be available with equal suddenness. But only at greatly enhanced prices. After that ministers made set speeches denouncing hoarders and black marketeers. The traders for their part blamed the politicians. The common man believed that the profits were shared equally.

At that, how could one be sure how much of the money collected by the politicians in office went to the party? Visram asked himself. By their very nature, they were clandestine transactions. To ask for a receipt for whatever you paid was regarded as an affront, and for such a transgression even a minor official could send you to jail under one or the other of the emergency laws.

The bigger industrialists like Surana had found their own answers to these insatiable demands from the party. They readily gave whatever was asked for but demanded special favours in returns. A few industrialists who did not go along with the trend were singled out for chastisement or worse.

The black money in the country was, even according to the government's own assessment, at least as much as the annual budget. But little had been done to unearth the black money because it was believed that by now much of it had been siphoned off by the party or its inner circle of favourites.

Vast purchases were made from foreign countries, of fertilizers, mining equipment, aeroplanes and other items. In every such purchase, the party was believed to insist on a kickback. The Lockheed Aircraft company had revealed at an enquiry that they had lost out to a French rival company because the latter had paid a million dollars to the party fund.

A million dollars! Visram took a deep breath. That itself was nearly nine million rupees. There were said to be similar gifts from other foreign companies. If there were only a hundred such deals, the figure of nine hundred million seemed, if anything a little on the modest side.

There were dozens of other avenues of making money for those in unchallengeable control of all the organs of the government: the threat of income tax raids, of stopping electric power to your factory, of offering protection to the smugglers, of holding up censorship certificates to films...

India made more films than any other country in the world—certainly a hundred films every year. The going rate for a censorship clearance was said to be a lakh of rupees—a hundred thousand.

'And for this, we're made to hang around the corridors in Delhi, as though we're beggars looking for favours,' Nagesh Kumar, the actor-producer had once told him.

They were far from beggars. Each film had cost them on an average forty lakhs to produce; money they would have to write off unless they forked out the extra lakh to be able to exhibit their film.

Visram whistled. A hundred thousand for every film. That itself was ten million a year!

Nine hundred million did not look all that much of an exaggeration...well, give or take. He whistled again.

He had been walking for more than an hour. He sat down on a log and lit a cigarette.

The cigarette had a sobering effect. It was so easy to let one's imagination soar when one was thinking of other people's chicanery. All the same, rejecting all conceivable exaggerations, the party's cash reserves could never be less than ten crores. Of that sum, perhaps no more than a fourth part was in black money.

But that was two and a half crores of rupees; twenty-five million.

Where could the party's leaders store so much money and know that it was safe where it was.

You would need to have a bank under your control, so that you could use its facilities to store your cash.

Visram frowned and shook his head. Perhaps this was some kind of an answer to a puzzle, but not to the puzzle that ABC had put in his lap. How much money the National Front party possessed and how much of it was held in black money and how it was looked after was no concern of his.

He chucked away his cigarette, picked up his shoulder bag, and resumed his walk.

~

For the next hour, his mind ran on a different track. Now it had become hot and his shirt clung to his back. His shoes were caked with dust and his calves ached.

Supposing, he kept asking himself, supposing that I were to be entrusted with a sum of money that was so vast and acquired by such means that no one had an idea of how much it was within a million or two, and supposing I wanted to help myself to as much of it as I safely could, how would I set about it.

A few thousands; yes. But not a million; not even a hundred thousand. The minute you began showing signs of affluence somebody would catch on. The income tax hounds would want to know where you got the money to buy your flat or the foreign car or the Persian carpet and the fat would be in the fire. Taking the money would be easy enough; but how could you ever use it?

He had nearly reached the top of the ridge when he realized that he was heading for a cluster of pink-roofed buildings surrounded by tall trees. Obviously he had reached one of the private estates that were scattered all over these hills. He could see the backyard of the house and a laundry line stretched between two trees; a whole lot of male and female garments were ballooning in the wind. And then a dog began to bark.

He changed direction and headed for a neck of the hill that seemed to lead away from the estate. The moment he had crossed the top, he was in the shade. He lay down on the pine needles and propped his legs against the bole of a tree to reverse the flow of blood. After a couple of minutes he sat up, drank a little water, and opened his packet of cherries.

From where he sat, pleasantly tired and spitting cherrystones all round him, he could still see the bungalow. The dog had stopped barking. The wind had freshened and the garments on the laundry line were fluttering like so many flags.

It was not the most pleasing part of the scenery, but it held his gaze. And then a sigh escaped his lips because he knew it had provided him with the answer to his puzzle.

~

It was a little before sunset when he returned to the club. A game of tennis was in progress on the court on the way to the annex. He heard someone shouting his name, and it was all he could do to prevent himself from whipping round in alarm.

Avinash Batra, the Colonel of the Combat School, was waving a racquet at him. He waved back and proceeded to his room. Batra's gleaming maroon MG was parked in the drive next to his room.

The tin tub in which he bathed must have been a relic from the days of the Raj. As he sloshed water over his body. Visram was conscious how, if you were a senior enough government servant, it was all the more difficult for you to go into hiding. If Surbinder really had put out a find-and-arrest call for him, they must be already on their way.

It was, of course, possible that Surbinder was not even bothering, having concluded that Visram had not read Om Prakash's diary, and that whatever he had gleaned by questioning Dorabji was fairly innoccuous stuff.

Then he suddenly remembered the man on the scooter who had been shadowing him the previous evening.

As he changed into a fresh shirt and trousers, he kept telling himself that there was, for the first time since he had taken over this investigation, something on the credit side too. He had a feeling that he was within sight of the solution to the Dorabji case; that he had discovered for himself much of what Om could have put down in his diary.

But with that he had put himself in the precise predicament that Om had found himself in. Merely solving the riddle was not enough. As a professional enforcer of the law of the land, his mind was unable to come to terms with a crime that would go unpunished. But in this case, there was little that he or anyone else could do to the people who had hired Dorabji to pick up some bundles of currency notes at one place and deliver them at another, and then when things had gone wrong, had abandoned him and even forced him to sign a confession that it was he who was responsible for the whole thing.

Why, they were in a position to thumb their noses at him and to go on helping themselves to more and more cash from the same source as though nothing had happened.

Through the old-fashioned diamond panes, he could see the Gadkhal saddle. He followed the lights of a car coming from the plains below at the same time as he tried to reason out why some of his colleagues were helping the very people whom they should be doing their best to put behind bars.

Surbinder was clearly doing it for return favours. In the service, he was known to have blotted his copybook in some manner and would have been retired as a Superintendent of some obscure district if he had not attached himself to the politicians in power, or better still, those who wielded some sinister influence over the politicians in power. In the case of the customs officials, it could have been because of a direct order given by either the Owl or the Pussycat, as Dorabji had hinted. There were bound to be others working for them whom he did not know, working for even more ignoble motives—or possibly because they were being blackmailed.

Whoever the big operators were, their real strength lay in their powerful political friends, so powerful that they had even succeeded in making a sensational bank fraud case look like some minor escapade—a pickpocket caught red-handed.

The car lights had reached the Gadkhal fork and turned towards Sanawar. A very cold breeze whistled through the slits in the window, and he wished he had thought of bringing a woolly. The twilight had faded and the room was now dark. He sat down in the cane chair with its quilted seat, and put up his feet on another.

So this had been Om's predicament when he had come to seek his advice; a detective who had solved his case but was powerless to bring the culprits to book. In fact it was they who had finished him off.

But that was because poor Om was working all on his own. Visram gave silent thanks that he was not alone. There was ABC behind him, solid as a rock, clever, experienced, a match for the most diabolic of brains. And admitting that ABC was precluded by circumstances from directing the formidable resources of his organization to the case, it was good to know that he had a few handpicked agents who were placed in key positions in the organizations corrupted by the very people whom he and ABC were trying to bring to justice.

~

It was amazing how some people radiated confidence. He had heard of generals who with their mere presence had been instrumental in turning the tide of battles. Visram wondered to himself if he would have persisted with the Dorabji case if he did not have ABC on his side.

It was a good thought to end a thinking session on, he told himself, as he got up and switched on the light. And as though someone had been waiting outside for the light to go on, he heard a knock on the door, but this time did not give a start. It was Avinash Batra who had come to ask him to join him in a drink in his room. 'I've acquired a bottle of Black Dog,' Batra said, 'and don't want to drink alone.'

~

He had come for a reconnaissance. 'To choose a nice little valley between here and Subathu for a paradrop,' he told Visram. 'But was I glad to get away from Gulag, if only for a couple of days. Chin-chin!'

He was wearing dark-brown corduroys, regimental blazer, soft chukka boots, and five years of his army salary could not have paid for the MG sports, standing outside. Somehow it was right that he should be serving premium Scotch; with anyone else it would have looked at best ostentatious, at worst a sure sign of black money.

Visram knew that Avinash belonged to the Batras of Jallandhar; manufacturers of cement and beer and agricultural machinery and god knew what else. Third-generation money and a good school and college, and rugged good looks; the man who had everything. What made him accept the discipline of the army instead of taking it easy as a senior executive in one of the family concerns, Visram wondered, as he raised his glass. 'Chin-chin!'

'How long are you up for?' Batra asked.

'Not for long.'

'Leave?'

'Sort of.'

'I was asking because I'm going down tomorrow, after early breakfast—wondered if you'd have liked a lift.'

'Not tomorrow, thank you. I thought I'd stay another day, having escaped from…'

'Spontaneous demonstrations?' Batra suggested. He waited for a couple of seconds for Visram to say something, and then went on. 'God, I nearly got caught in one the other day. I was the last car, luckily, and some fool ahead of me in the line must have got impatient and tooted. Made the crowd mad! They rushed at him and danced all round and compelled the people in the car to get out and sing out, "Our leader; nation's leader!"' He made a gesture of revulsion and took a large gulp of his drink.

'What did you do?' Visram asked.

'Turned the car and bolted; tail between my legs. Luckily I was the last car.'

On a peg near the entrance door hung a silk-finished raincoat, on the chest of drawers were two tennis racquets and tins of balls, two fishing rods in canvas cases leaned against the book case, on the mantelshelf was a double crocodile-leather frame, a woman on one side and a child on the other.

The club room was neat, sparsely furnished, spotlessly clean. But Batra looked out of place; a rich man putting up with humbler surroundings and doing his best to show that he was fully at home.

Affluence, breeding, an expensive education. Add to that the code that some of the senior officers in the army were said to live by and which was revealed in little things like not wanting to drink alone. Did they combine to build up some sort of immunity against corrupting influences? The way the man had flared up that night in defence of his calling, and perhaps this childish glee at having escaped chastisement at the hands of the Dropout Brigade, were they any indication of that immunity?

Batra would be a good man to have on one's side, he suddenly thought.

But he had trained himself to distrust impulses and changed the subject. 'I didn't know there was any fishing around here?'

Batra talked of the mahseer he had caught that morning, and which was even then being grilled for him in the club kicthen. They had another drink each, and then went across to the dining room.

At the end of dinner, Visram could hardly keep his eyes open. He went to his room while Batra was trying to find someone to give him a game of billiards.

~

At the risk of being considered eccentric, Visram had left instructions that he did not want what was called chota-hazri, or bed tea. He had slept for nine hours. It was not till 8.30, that he opened the outer door.

Batra was sittng on one of the muda chairs in the veranda. 'I thought you'd meant to start early,' Visram said in surprise.

'I decided to wait till you were up...in case...' he began uncomfortably. 'Look, there's something about your Chief in the paper.' He was holding out the morning's *Tribune*, which must have come by special van from Chandigarh. 'Here.' He was pointing to an item on one of the inner pages. A bold, single column headline and a smaller caption, followed by half a dozen lines of print.

INVESTIGATION CHIEF RELIEVED OF OFFICE

> 'Security of country more important than any citizens,' says Minister. In a brief statement, Shri D.A. Padati revealed that, even though he was personally convinced that no impropriety of any sort on the part of the Chief of Investigations had occured, the fact that his brother-in-law is a CIA official has made his continuation in that position inadvisable. Mr K. Surbinder IPS will take over the post of Chief of Investigations, pending permanent arrangements.

'What did you say?' Batra asked.

He had not said anything, and did not answer. Surbinder. He could see him cantering past the Lodhi tombs and waving. Had he seen ABC too? And after that had him trailed?

He was filled with a sense of helplessness. How could they?—he kept thinking to himself, even suspect ABC's loyalty? It was just that they had discovered that he was probing into the ramifications of the Dorabji case and wanted him out of the way.

'Look,' Batra was saying. 'I could easily wait till you've had breakfast. I mean, in case you felt like driving down so that...hold the Chief's hand...'

And suddenly he wanted to leave; not so much because he thought he would be able to do anything about his Chief's predicament, but because of an acute feeling that he was the next in line, and wanted to be doing something instead of waiting for the other side to mount its attack.

'Yes, that might be best,' he told Batra. 'I won't take more than twenty minutes.'

'Take your time; no hurry at all,' Batra said, and then, just as Visram turned to go, added. 'Well, I don't know about that. Perhaps you'd better hurry—if you too were implicated in whatever your Chief has been up to.'

~

Like most people who professed to be agnostics, Mr A.B. Chopra had a private god, and, later in the year, when he ostensibly went on a day's trip to Chakrata, he made a halt at a wayside Shaivite shrine to offer his thanks and a handful of sweets to a shapeless stone image for the extra half hour that he had been granted as the Chief of Investigation.

He had gone to the office as usual, precisely at ten, because he did not want to give the impression that he considered this to be a special day. 'Come at ten-fifteen,' he had told his successor. 'I'll be ready by then.'

He wanted that fifteen minutes because he was anxious not to leave Visram Lal's case to his successor. He wrote on the file that Superintendent Lal's request for retirement was to be disallowed, and that he should be prosecuted in a court of law for being found in possession of smuggled articles.

However harsh the order looked on paper, he knew that no judge would decide against Lal after he had gone into all the evidence—at least not unless he belonged to the new breed of judges in the land who were eager to prove how committed they were to the political philosophy of the moment.

But that was a risk he had to take. At that it was almost certain that, when the department itself knew what cards Visram held up his sleeve, they would realize how foolish they would be made to look in the court and quietly withdraw the prosecution. What he was ensuring at the moment was to take the decision out of his successor's hands, and thereby give Visram some room for manoeuvering.

'Have the file sent to the Home Secretary at once,' he ordered.

For the next couple of minutes, he busied himself gathering his personal belongings. His wife's photograph, a velvet pincushion that his daughter had made for him when she was a child, a small brass horse, a glass paperweight, his Concise Oxford Dictionary which he had bought in his last year at college. He put these in his briefcase and glanced at his watch. Ten fifteen.

He got up and walked across to the window, which gave him a view of the quadrangle below and the corridors of the offices on three sides. The grass looked surprisingly green for midsummer, but the footpaths that criss-crossed it had become wider. Of the four trees that had been planted in the four corners some years age, only two remained, and both were balding in spots. The beehive in the arch of the minister's room looked ready to fall with its own weight and stirred with life as though someone had thrown a pebble at it. A man was going round in the corridor below with a tray of coffee mugs.

His fingers began to drum on the window ledge, a tell-tale sign that he was getting annoyed. He pulled away his hand.

At any other time, he would have been thinking out something caustic to say about a subordinate not turning up on time. Then he remembered that Surbinder had ceased to be a subordinate and become an equal. Why, the way he had been singled out for this promotion may have even given him some sort of a complex that he was entitled to disregard service civilities or even plain good manners.

Somewhere, a clock struck the half hour, making him conscious of the fact that his staff must know that he was being kept waiting by his successor. He watched the beehive, intently. The bees now looked more at peace. He heard the inner door open and turned, frowning. His personal assistant had come in with the day's mail. He waved him away, saying, 'Nothing to do with me; let Surbinder deal with all that.'

'There is one personal letter, sir,' the PA said.

He glanced at the letter in annoyance; a letter with a foreign stamp, and then he recognized his sister's handwriting. 'Thanks,' he said as he took the letter and tore it open. 'But take away the rest of the stuff. Oh, wait; that file I passed orders on. Has it gone?'

'Yes, sir; with a special messenger,' the PA answered before going back to his room.

It was a short letter, and pinned to it was a cutting from some newspaper. His hands shook as he read it. He slipped both back into the envelope and put it into his pocket. He picked up the torn bit of the envelope from his desk and rolled it into a ball and threw it into the waste basket.

What would have happened if Surbinder had come at the appointed time, he wondered. He, Chopra, would have gone before the day's mail was brought in. And in that case, would a man like Surbinder have forwarded his sister's letter to him?

Not a chance, particularly because the sender's name and address were clearly written on the flap: Mrs R. Howard, 3305, Shady Lane, Rumford, Vt.

And Surbinder would have been perfectly justified in opening the letter and reading it, for was not the sender alleged to have some sort of connection with the CIA? At the very least, Surbinder would have had the letter opened and copied before sending it on. After all, the department had special facilities for steaming open letters.

And then it occured to him that Pushpa could not have been more useful to him if her husband Bob really was someone high up in the CIA and had decided to come to his assistance in this investigation.

Surbinder did not come for another ten minutes, and when he did, he was looking as though he was in a tearing hurry. He did not bother to apologize for being late. The handing over was finished within a couple of minutes.

As Chopra shook hands with his successor and strode out of the office of the COI for the last time, he was actually whistling which his successor put down to an affected air of nonchalance: a man who was fired trying desperately to make out that he did not care.

~

Visram Lal left Kasauli on Monday morning. That same afternoon, a worried looking man in an ill-fitting closed-collar coat and a Punjabi turban on his head, called at the Club office to inquire about him. 'Oh, but Mr Lal has left,' the club clerk told him.

The caller frowned and shook his head. 'Couldn't have. I know Mr Lal by sight and I was at Kalka station the whole of yesterday.'

'Went in the morning, by car. With Colonel Batra.'

'Oh!' the man said, looking very disappointed. He fidgetted as though the chair was full of bugs and asked, 'He didn't leave any of his things behind, did he?'

'No.'

'Or a message for someone who might call? A letter? Anything?'

'Not here, in this office.'

A few hours later, they had traced Visram Lal's movements further. He had travelled to Delhi in Colonel Batra's car, but, after a cup of tea at the Colonel's house in Teen-Murti Marg, had gone off in a rikshaw. They were trying hard to trace the rikshaw driver.

Colonel Batra's wife was putting their son to bed when she was told that someone wanted her on the telephone. An educated voice said, 'I'm sorry to trouble you, but I hear that your husband is not in and wanted to find out if you knew anything about where I could find Superintendent Visram Lal.'

'I don't know,' she had answered peevishly. 'He should be in his house, shouldn't he?'

'And where is that?'

'One of these flats in Arjun Singh park, 39 or 49...there's a nine in it.'

'Thanks,' the man said. 'You don't know where I could get in touch with Colonel Batra, do you?'

'No. But he usually plays bridge. Why don't you try the Club?'

'Yes, I'll do that, thanks,' the man had said, and again apologised for bothering her. He did not tell her that he had already made inquiries at the club and discovered that her husband was not there.

~

At about the time that this conversation was taking place, Colonel Batra was driving an army jeep along the road at the rear of the President's estate, and taking special care not to exceed forty kilometres an hour. He saw the man standing under a roadside tree, and dipped his lights twice in recognition, but did not slow down. He drove right till the end of the crescent and made a U-turn. This time he was on the same side as the man under the tree.

When he approached the man, he slowed down to crawling speed. The man scrambled in while the jeep was still in motion. The moment he was in, the jeep regained its cruising speed.

'A dozen times I must have done it in practice,' Visram Lal said. 'Jumping into a running jeep. This is the first time there's not a make-believe situation.'

'I bet you've never done it before lugging a suitcase either,' Batra said 'How did it go?'

'Perfectly, I think.' Visram answered. 'Got myself dropped at the bus stand, dashed to the office and bought a ticket to Meerut. Then managed to lose myself in the scramble. It was getting dark already.'

'How did you come here?'

'Three rickshaws, walks in between.'

'All that sweat just to lose yourself. Trouble with you police officers is that all the city's traffic cops know you by sight.'

Presently they were on the Palam road. 'Didn't you say you were going to put me up somewhere...somewhere not too far off?' Visram asked in surprise.

'I did. But the place I had thought of for you is...well, there are a couple of our boys staying there right now. I checked. I didn't want to risk putting you in with them.'

'Your boys? You mean agents, don't you, from the borders?'

Batra grinned. 'Actually from beyond the borders. You see we keep what we call a crash-pad for them—a place where they can go to whenever any of them comes here. In fact that's where I propose to shift you in a couple of days. They'll have gone.'

'If I survive those couple of days.'

'Oh, you'll be absolutely safe here—dammit, it's part of the commando range. You should be familiar with the atmosphere.'

So that was where they were headed for. 'Gives me the creeps!' Visram commented. 'You're sure none of your own chaps will come snooping round?'

'Too scared to go near the place. They know the house and grounds are booby-trapped like mad. Death house, they call it. Only I know what's there at any given time, and can deactivate the fun and games.'

'What about outsiders?'

'Not allowed in the vicinity. Warning signs all round. Prohibited area, danger, electrified fence. All that.'

'What a lucky break. To be within half an hour of Delhi and safe as houses.'

'I think we've got everything you might need—in the way of provisions.' He pointed to the bamboo basket in the rear, 'There's a table you can use as a bed,'

'Is there a telephone?'

'Only a direct line; from my office. That's for use when we lay on an exercise—to speak to one of my instructors.'

'And you won't be laying on anything for a few days.'

'For two days. Place all yours.'

They arranged signals, and synchronized watches. 'Let's keep it simple,' Batra said. 'Start with what we call the hour-minute schedule. If there's a ring at nine minutes past nine, or ten minutes past ten, it will be mine. Same at eleven past eleven and so on. Clear?'

'Yes, but what's the need of all this when the other end of the line is in your office.'

'Standard operating procedure. In case someone at the top twists the army's arm and gets my General or someone to ring from my office.'

'I get it. Unless the phone rings at the right time, I don't pick up the receiver.'

'Yes. I'll bring you a pocket radio so that you can correct your watch.'

'You do think of everything, don't you.'

Batra grinned. 'We've to send our boys to operate...across the border, you know. After all if you're called the Dirty Dogs; you must know how to guard against other people's dirty tricks.'

They drove in silence after that. Presently the lake appeared over the horizon, and the road gradually veered closer to the water and ran in a smooth curve along what must have been the lake's edge when it was full. They passed a gate where a sentry flashed his torch at Batra's face and slid back into the darkness.

After going for perhaps half a mile, Batra stopped the jeep on a narrow bridge over a dry watercourse. Now they could see the three decrepit bungalows behind clumps of trees. Was it only five days ago when he was last here, dropped by parachute. That time he had been told that the enemy agents he was to take on were in the central bungalow. Now he was to make for the house on the left, the one closest to the lake.

'Well, this is as far as I'm going to take you,' Batra said. 'The nulla goes all the way up, between the two bungalows. Don't use a torch unless you have to.'

Visram scrambled out of the jeep and Batra handed him the basket and his suitcase. Visram turned to him as though to say something, and anticipating him, Batra told him. 'Safe as houses. I was here a whole day last week, with two of the Weapons Directorate chaps, ripping out every single device we'd put in, because we want to introduce a whole lot of new gadgetry. Real James Bond stuff. The point is, there's nothing there now. Nothing is going to explode when you touch it or step on it or set off an alarm. Good luck! I only wish I was here, camping out with you and doing things instead of playing messenger boy.'

He threw in the gear and drove off.

~

By Tuesday morning, they had managed to trace the rickshaw driver, and hauled him in for questioning. He was a smart young Garhwali, and he told the bearded man in the khaki turban who questioned him, that he remembered the gentleman he had picked up in Teen Murti Marg very well, because the policeman on duty at the street corner had given him a smart salute.

'Good,' said the man in the turban encouragingly. 'And where did you take him?'

'UP Roadways station. I dropped him near the main entrance and heard him asking the hamal who had come for his bag, when the next bus to Meerut was due.'

'And?'

'Then I saw both of them running as though the bus was just about to leave, and the man was anxious to get a seat on it. They went into the building, and at the same time, I got another fare. For Daryaganj.'

That's all they could get out of him. An hour or so later, the bearded man reported to the Chief of Investigations that Visram Lal had gone to Meerut.

Surbinder cursed and took out from his drawer another sheet of cyclostyled paper. It was a blank warrant form under the MISA duly signed by a magistrate and he had been given a hundred of them. All he had to do was to fill in the name of whoever he wanted to be arrested.

He had already used two of these forms for Visram Lal. One had been given to the Inspector at Chanakyapuri Station in whose charge Arjun Singh Park fell, and another had been sent to the railway police in Kalka. This third went off to the Senior Superintendent of Police, Meerut.

CHAPTER 11

After Vinay Surana had gone off in a hurry that morning, Netra Agarwal had ordered the switchboard girl not to put through any calls from newspaper reporters. She half expected her escort of the previous evening to ring up to ask if there was something really damaging in the papers that had been confiscated. And then she remembered that Mr Lal's interest was wholly confined to her brother's diary and that he was not likely to be concerned about how the raid had affected the Surana family's business interests and prestige.

If only he had not come butting in into the El-Taj, she would have discovered what it was that her brother had told Sartaj to find out, and whether he had succeeded. She knew that Sartaj was a resourceful man and that somehow he would try and get in touch with her. After that she would decide whether to pass on whatever he had to say to Visram Lal or not.

Around eleven, her telephone rang. It was Vinay Surana. 'Please ring Mr Lindemann at the Intercontinental, and apologise on my behalf. Tell him I'll get in touch with him later in the day. You need not wait, Miss Agarwal. Oh, and please send them flowers. Choose them yourself.'

The Demag people could not have been more understanding. Not by word or shade of intonation did any of them reveal that they had read in the morning's papers about the raids on Surana offices.

On Saturdays, Netra normally finished work at noon. By the time she had chosen the flowers and delivered them at the hotel, it was well past eleven, and there seemed to be no point in going back to the office. She rang up the Chief Clerk and told him to close up. 'Did anyone telephone?' she asked.

No one had. She got the office car to drop her at her flat. Her maid too answered her question in the negative. Nobody had telephoned. But there was a letter for her, which she had left on the table near the telephone.

The letter bore neither stamp nor address. The white envelope was absolutely blank.

'I found it on the floor,' the maid told her. 'Someone must have slipped it under the door. I nearly threw it away, thinking it was one of those obscene letters.'

Even she had heard about obscene letters, which, like obscene telephone calls and what the papers called 'eve-teasing' had proliferated in the capital since the Emergency. Eve-teasing was indulged in by rowdy youths standing in front of women's hostels or colleges and discussing their charms in uninhibited language. Nowadays the papers were forbidden to give news of such depravities because they were believed to be a sort of special dispensation permissible to the Dropout Brigade.

The letter was short and unsigned.

Sorry got scared for nothing yesterday. Please ring 2539542 *from outside phone soonest after* 9.00 *p.m.*

'Is it one of those awful letters?' the maid asked, pretending to be dusting a wood carving.

'What? Oh, no. In fact it is a letter I was expecting,' Netra told her.

'Is it from that nice man, then? The one who came yesterday and wrote down his telephone number?'

'No. It is not from him. And I'm really not sure that he is what you'd call a nice man.'

Soon after nine, she had rung the number. Sartaj answered the telephone and they arranged to meet at ten the next morning on the lawn outside Humayun's Tomb.

~

The monuments the Mughals built had withstood the real test of architectural excellence: that of time. Two air-conditioned buses marked airsea travels had disgorged crocodiles of perspiring camera-hung men and women. She wondered who would ever want to see Yojana Bhavan or the Russian Embassy four hundred years from now.

'Do you mind standing just where you are for a second Miss?' someone said to her. 'It would be such a pity to take the tomb without a pretty girl in a sari. Watch the birdie... ooops! Thanks a million.'

Humayun's tomb was daunting—something to be viewed from a respectful distance. But all around were other structures which invited closer inspection and were artistically far more satisfying; little broken-down mosques or stables or whatever, readymade subjects for amateur painters.

The lawns were hardly crowded, considering it was a Sunday. It was too hot for family picnicking. But the chaat stall was doing good business, and among the half a dozen people awaiting their turn around the hissing frying pan that was the size of a cartwheel, she saw the wizened, lopsided figure, like a stray from Charles Dickens.

She knew better than to accost him. The first move would be made by him, and only after he had made sure that neither of them had been followed. 'He always looked like a stork,' her brother had once told her. 'And that bullet through his shoulder has done him no good. But I'd rather have him as my leg man than anyone else I can think of.'

She sauntered from monument to monument, was photographed once more by an elderly woman wearing hot pants and chappals. She was resting in the shade of a tree when he came and sat beside her.

For nearly half an hour they talked. He told her that he had been to Kashmir and had rung her brother up from Srinagar the day before he was killed. Then he told her what it was that her brother had wanted him to find out and how he had fared.

'When I saw Superintendent Lal going into El-Taj, I was sure he had come to snoop. I didn't want him to see us together. He's sharp, that man. It was later that I began to feel that I might have been mistaken.'

'What gave you that idea?'

'I saw both of you coming out of Maiden's...well, very friendly.'

For no reason she could think of, she felt her cheeks flush. 'Mr Lal tells me he has taken over whatever Om was investigating, and I for one believe him,' she told him.

He shrugged; at least one of his shoulders went up and down. 'I knew they were good friends, Lal and Om; and I suppose we just have to trust someone. Who knows, he might be able to put this information to some use—what I was able to discover in Kashmir.'

He arranged how they were to communicate. She was to ring from an outside line, either at seven in the morning or at seven in the evening. He would try and be at the telephone at least once in a day. 'But remember that the number I give you to ring will not be the correct one; you have to add the date to it to get the correct number.'

'I'm afraid I don't understand.'

'It is quite simple really. I give you a number, 4349372. You add sixteen to it for today's date and get 4349388. That's where I shall be.'

'I get it now. Tomorrow I add seventeen, and so on.'

'You see this way I can ring you at your house or office and tell you where you can reach me. I don't have a telephone myself.'

'And am I to give the number to Mr Lal?'

'I think so. You seem to be sure he is really on the level. I hope so,' he sprang to his feet. 'Give me ten minutes' start.'

'But wait, Sartaj. I should have asked before. Do you need any money? Om had left five hundred with me. I've brought it.'

'I don't need any money right now. Only if I have to go haring off again somewhere. And I don't see why you should pay for that. It was different with Om.'

'Sure you wouldn't like to keep it—just in case.'

He shook his head. 'No. And look after yourself.'

She waited the stipulated ten minutes and then went and found a taxi. She stopped at a teashop and rang Visram's flat. Much to her own surprise, she had no difficulty in recalling the number he had written down for her.

'Mr Lal's residence,' someone answered in English.

'I want to speak to Mr Lal, please.'

'Who is speaking?'

'Miss Agarwal.'

'I am afraid he's not in. Can I…'

'Can you tell me where I can reach him?'

'I'm afraid not. Can I take a message?'

'It's not important, really. I'll ring again, later. Do you think he'll be back by the evening?

'I really couldn't say, Miss Agarwal.'

She had tried to ring Visram Lal again in the afternoon, and on Monday morning from her office. Both times the same voice had answered, and she had quickly put down the receiver.

On Monday evening, she rang the number Sartaj had given her. He picked up the telephone at the very first ring. 'I'm sorry I have not been able to contact Mr Lal,' she told him.

'I'm not surprised,' he had commented. 'I hear there's a warrant out for him.'

'Warrant?' she had gasped. 'But he's…a police officer.'

'At least we can be sure of his credentials now.'

'I was always quite certain he was on our side,' Netra said petulantly. 'That we could tell him everything.'

'We'll have to find him first,' Sartaj had remarked. And then he had proceeded to give his telephone number for the next day.

'Wish I'd thought of laying on champagne,' Batra said. 'This must be quite an occasion. The Chief of Investigations picnicking with a chum who is hiding from the law.'

'Ex-Chief,' ABC corrected him without bitterness.

The warm breeze was full of the smells of summer, mango blossom and dust and nameless insects. The three men sat in the open, well away from the heat given out by the walls of the bungalow, and they were eating tandoori chicken and naans and pickle with their fingers. A ten-day old moon gave just enough light for them to see what they were eating.

'So long as you've brought some coffee,' Visram said. 'I've been dying for a cup since the morning.'

'Two thermoses full. I'll leave you one.'

They were hard-boiled professionals who were brought together by nothing but much as a shared service ethic and trust in each other's integrity and professional skill. A. B. Chopra, who was the seniormost, fell into the role of the leader and did most of the talking.

Visram Lal explained how, six days earlier, Om Prakash Agarwal had come to him and that, because Om had died in an accident that very night, he had taken over the investigation that he had been conducting.

'Right from the start the thing looked far too straightforward to be true. Seven million rupees had been stolen from a bank and were to be sent to Mauritius, but the attempt had failed. The man who took delivery of the money was caught. He confessed and was convicted.'

'The bloody thing stank to high heaven,' Batra pronounced.

'Yes. Several questions remained unanswered. How could the money be withdrawn by a telephone message? Second, whose money was it? And third, why was it being sent out of the country? The whole thing looked cockeyed. That was when we had a...a stroke of luck.'

ABC saw Visram looking expectantly at him and offered to explain. 'Well, one of the men who raided the Surana offices was personally loyal to me. He passed on to me a copy of a certain document. It revealed that Surana had been collecting donations—very large amounts—from business people and ex-princes, on behalf of the party.'

'But wait a sec,' Batra intervened. 'Are not donations from business houses to political parties illegal?'

'That was just it. Because these funds were illegal, they were not deposited in a bank like other money, but merely handed to a bank's custody, as it were. They were not subjected to any process of accounting or audit.'

'Just ring the bank's manager, speak the code word, and get him to bring out the cash,' Batra said. 'Right?'

'Right.'

'That means whoever was supposed to be managing these funds could help himself to a part of them if he chose to.'

'Again right. And that was precisely what was happening,' ABC said as he picked up a wing of chicken.

A jetliner came swooping down, aiming at the main runway

at Palam, winking its lights merrily and making a tremendous din.

ABC stared fixedly at the plane, turning his body as it flew past. Then he licked his fingers, took a gulp from the bottle of lemonade by his side, and went on, 'The more I tried to fathom out the thing, the more confused did I become. At that stage, I discovered that Visram had become involved in the investigation…in a manner of speaking. At least he had got into trouble over it. Well, I passed on what little information I possessed to him and asked him what he made of the whole thing. I did not want to fill his mind with what I was thinking, but just wanted to give him the facts.'

Again Visram took up the story. 'From the outset, it was clear who the principals were: Rajguru and that woman he calls his chief disciple, Ekanti Ma. And they were aided and abetted by Kaul and Pashupat.'

'The bloody Owl and the Pussycat!' Batra said with a guffaw. 'That pair must be at the back of every dirty deal you can think of, the way they can just pick up the telephone and give orders.'

'That was what they did. Picked up the telephone and told the customs chaps to let the bags with the money go through. It is almost certain that influential friends have organized similar facilities at Plaisance airport—the Mauritius end.'

'Where does the new COI fit into this?' Batra asked. 'I thought that he too was neck deep in this.'

Visram politely waited for ABC to answer this question. But he was spreading pickle on a piece of naan with great concentration. He bit off a piece and smacked his lips. 'How carrot can be made to taste so wonderful beats me,' he remarked.

'I don't believe Surbinder is anything more than small fry,' Visram said. 'Do you, sir?'

'Stooge. Lick your boots for bones from the big table,' ABC said savagely, and took another bite of the naan spread over with carrot pickle.

'Well, he got a bloody great bone, didn't he,' Batra remarked. 'Got made Chief of Investigations.'

'What have you got in that paper bag, Batra?' ABC asked.

'Lychees. Are you ready for them, sir?'

'Not yet.'

Visram Lal continued his story. 'Well, there I was, chasing shadows. Vast funds were there, unaccountable, unaudited, waiting to be picked up by those who knew the signals. So what?'

'What do you mean, so what?' Batra asked. 'I'd like somone to hand me a couple of lakhs and I'd gobble them up without so much as a burp.'

'That's just it, Avinash,' Visram told him. 'I dare say that most of us would know what to do if a lakh or two fell into our laps. But the sums involved run into millions—tens of millions!'

'Baap re!' Batra exclaimed.

'Baap re about expresses it. It was at this stage that Mr Chopra showed me a copy of the lists taken from Surana's office, and then told me that he did not want to influence my mind by whatever he was thinking.' Visram gave a hollow laugh before going on. 'That is a sort of standard departmental euphemism to tell a chap that he was being a stupid oaf who could not see what was staring him in the face. So I took myself off to Kasauli to...to sort of look at the thing with a cool head. I went for a long trek. When I stopped for a rest, I could see a laundry line, ruining the view. And suddenly I had the answer.'

'Shabash!' ABC said softly.

'I'm afraid you have lost me, old boy,' Batra confessed.

'Let me explain that bit,' ABC offered. 'You see, when a Marwari finds he has a lot of black money he cannot use, he turns it into white money. He launders it, see—makes it legitimate. After that he is prepared to show it in his account books and pay taxes on it. OK?'

'I'm not sure,' Batra said, shaking his head.

'Supposing you were in a position to send seven million rupees to Mauritius. What earthly good would it be to you unless you meant to go and live there.'

Batra thought for a moment and shook his head. 'None at all.'

'So you send it there to be laundered. Then get it sent right back in the form of dollars, francs, pounds...clean, see, and coming through banks in the form of gifts to yourself or your institute by grateful disciples...?'

Batra sat up. 'Or swimming pools or a BMW three-li. God! What wouldn't I give to lay my hands on that beauty! But Mr

Chopra, is it...is it really possible? I mean will people buy your rupees and give you dollars and marks in return?'

'Certainly. All you have to do is to send the money to the right place where they buy and sell world currencies. The rate of exchange is quoted in every issue of *Newsweek*, and given out over radio stations and financial newspapers. The official rate side by side with what is called the market rate. You sell at a substantial loss, naturally. But what does it matter, when the money is not yours.'

'And what sort of sums are involved, you think?'

'What's your idea, Visram?' ABC asked. 'Of the hush hush fund only, mind you.'

'I was trying to tie it all up, sir, on the evidence of what Surana had collected. My lowest figure of the secret funds worked out to twenty-five million rupees.'

ABC gave a soft chuckle. 'Proper civil service caution,' he commented. 'Myself, I should be inclined to double that figure. I've known people put it as high as a hundred million rupees.' He reached for a lychee, peeled it, and popped it into his mouth.

'Fantastic! Staggering!' Batra said nodding his head in wonder and admiration. 'I take off my hat to Rajguru. Eighty-odd years old and loves the good things of life—women, fast cars, music, food, travel. Real Sybarite—is that the word? And frankly it makes me positively green with envy at the way he has set it all up. Yoga teacher and father confessor to the Great Leader. Naturally he knows all the secrets, including how to get at the hush-hush funds of the party. He keeps drawing off as much of it as the traffic will bear, sends it out, and has it all piped back. And indoor swimming pools and executive aeroplanes sprout as if by magic.'

'Mind you, some of the money may represent genuine contributions from grateful students or patients,' Visram said cautiously. 'The gullibility of the upper rich.'

ABC spat out a lychee seed and cleared his throat. 'I am in a position to add a footnote to that,' he said rather portentously. 'I have a sister in America. The Minister, Padati, mentioned her name in Parliament the other day. He believes that her husband is a CIA agent. So far as I know, he sells bathroom fittings. But all this is beside the point. Well, when Pushpa, my sister, was last here, in

February it was, I had teased her about the especial chink in the armour of the so-called hard-nosed Yankee businessman: his abject surrender to our sadhus and fakirs. And especially I had quoted the example of our Rajguru who had been showered by her husband's compatriots with dollars and gifts.'

He paused as if for breath, or effect, hawked again, and continued, 'Only a few minutes before I gave over as the COI, I got a letter from Pushpa, and with it she had enclosed a cutting from her local paper, the *Rumford Herald*, it is called. It was a report of a shareholders' meeting of the Gatwick Aircraft Company.'

'Whose president presented a six-seater aeroplane to Rajguru?' Batra asked.

'The same. Tom Gatwick. It seems that the Company had declared no dividend for the year, and a few angry shareholders were heckling the president that he should have gifted an aeroplane to some holy man in India at a time when the company had run into losses. Tom Gatwick told them, and I quote: "Gentlemen, I give you my solemn assurance that no plane manufactured by your company was given free to anyone. And the particular machine to which you refer was fully paid for, one hundred and eighty-three thousand U.S. dollars. That means that we did not even allow the usual dealer's discount. Any of you who wishes to, is welcome to refer to the company's books to verify my statement."'

A silence fell over them. Batra got up and opened one of the thermos flasks and poured coffee.

~

They were still thinking about what Chopra had told them when they heard the sound of firing in the distance; half a dozen sharp crumps, one after the other. 'What on earth's that?' ABC asked. 'Pakistan bombing Palam airport?'

'It's the Air Force's special weapons testing range,' Batra explained. 'Adjoins Rajguru's ashram.'

'God, what a racket it must make there!'

'The Air Force is pretty careful when it uses the range, Mr Chopra. Usually between eight and nine.'

'But why these odd hours?' Visram asked.

Batra laughed. 'They time it so that the Swami will have left the ashram, and the inmates will not have gone to bed.'

'Does it last long?'

'No. Hardly a few minutes. They test one weapon at a time. It is...well, experimental more than operational. In any case they'll be shifting the range soon, near Gurgaon. The Swami is after their blood.'

The bangs and crumps ended in less than five minutes, just as abruptly as they had begun. 'More coffee, Mr Chopra?' Batra asked.

'Not for me. Keeps me awake,' ABC said grumpily.

'Has the opposite effect on me, I'm afraid,' Batra said. 'Puts me to sleep.' He passed the flask to Visram and said, 'All yours,' and then, as a thought occured to him, added, 'I say, I know both of you will think I'm a fool for asking. But has anyone checked to see if this man is not one of our well-known crooks—someone with a record of earlier convictions? Or have I said something stupid?'

'No, Colonel Batra,' ABC assured him, and then, in the tones of a teacher exercising patience in the face of obtuseness, proceeded to explain. 'You see, it is almost standard practice. The first thing a policeman asks himself when he encounters a suspected criminal. Has he a previous record? If he has, then the investigation is merely a matter of routine.'

'And you find that out by checking his fingerprints with those in your records?'

'Right. And I cannot tell you what absurd lengths I went to to procure those of Rajguru. You remember the wedding of the Heir Apparent?'

'August, wasn't it?' Visram asked.

'August, last year. A time of the year when the humidity is near saturation point—in the nineties. The function was held in one of those small bungalows in Aurangzeb road, and it was so quiet as to be almost furtive. No lights or buntings outside, no shehnai music, no reception line, no presents...a Gandhian austerity, and I mean the Gandhi who lived on monkey nuts and goat's milk.'

'And fasts,' Batra added.

'Well, there could not have been fifty people in all, and half of those must be family—one side or the other. And the Chief Guest was a man venerated by both sides...'

'Rajguru,' Visram and Batra said together.

'Rajguru. The food and drink were...well, all of a piece with the austerity; coffee and nimbu-pani and nuts, with lemon grass tea for the chief guest. He sipped it while he dispensed blessings. The whole show did not last quite one hour. And when the big guns left, I did a clever thing. I...'

'But what were you doing at such a gathering, Mr Chopra?' Batra asked.

'In charge of security. Came in turns those days. The army, the police, border security, switched round every week or so because of the Great Leader's phobia of being bumped off like Sheik Najib. Saw an assassin under every bush—remember. "My enemies are waiting to stab me in the back!" The Great Leader repeated at every press conference. Nobody was trusted—but nobody. Anyway, what I did was to stand guard over the Swami's lemon tea glass. It was dark by the time the place was empty. I made a roll of newspaper, fat enough to fit snugly into the glass. Then tipped the glass over so that it was resting upside down on the newspaper roll. I carried the glass to the office, called up the fingerprint men and got them to make transparencies of the prints on the glass. Oh, beauties! Well, I had a dozen cards made and sent them to all our fingerprint bureaus. What did you say?'

'Without mentioning whose prints they were,' Batra asked.

'That's right. As I said, I sent them to all the states and to our own library here. Not a trace.'

'That settles one thing,' Batra said with a sheepish grin. 'He's not one of our own super-thugs.'

'I say,' Visram said. 'I do hope you still have a set of those prints with you...no good having them in your office records.'

'I certainly have...after going to all that trouble to get them...' he trailed off as he watched a flight of cranes flying low overhead as they made for the centre of the lake.

Batra lighted a cigarette and asked, 'So where do we go from here?'

'I wish I knew,' Visram said. 'Apparently nowhere.'

'Oh, for God's sake,' Batra protested. 'You have uncovered a racket, haven't you? Found out they've made away with more money than the great train robbery chaps ever got in England. They're flaunting it before our eyes in this land of austerity. And you...'

'Visram is quite right, Batra,' ABC said. 'All right, granting that we do know what is happening, what can we do about it?'

'Damn it, you should know. You're policemen.'

'That's just it. Being policemen, we know how helpless we are. For one thing there is no complaint that any money has been found missing. There will never be a complaint for the simple reason that the NDF is not going to advertise that it keeps secret funds for dirty work.'

'What sort of dirty work?' Batra asked.

'Why, toppling, for instance; buying legislators. One of the documents found in the Surana raid was a list of cash distributed by Surana to the legislators in Padmakoshal to defect. Eighteen of them...no, nineteen, just crossed the floor and the government fell.'

'God, what crooks rule us!'

'Secondly, the time factor. Admitting that all three of us are experts at dodging pursuit. How long can we go on? I don't give Visram another two days. Remember that they're experts too and they've got the whole machinery of the government working for them. Once they cotton on to what we're up to, we'll probably find that they have stopped my pension on some trumped up charge, and slung you out of the army or posted you to some punishment station.'

Batra laughed irreverently and shook his head. 'The more I hear about the man, the more am I convinced that he must be some sort of a genius. What a man! And to think that I nearly had tea with him...'

'And yet I feel pretty sure that Om Prakash Agarwal had found a way of getting even with Rajguru—his winning trick, he used to call it. If we could only get hold of...'

ABC was sitting up. 'What were you saying, Batra?' he asked, with sudden interest.

'That it is my considered opinion that the man is a genius.'

'No. Something about your drinking tea with him.'

'Oh, that. It was not long after the Bangladesh war. We had those series of meetings with the Pakistani officers, both here and in Rawalpindi. Oh, at all levels, from the Chiefs downward. Well, I was leading one lot who had come here. They're clever, the Pakistanis, far more clued up than our chaps. They had made up their teams in such a way that they always had one or two old India hands. As you know we went in a big way for bhaibandi in those days. Slap-up meals and plenty of Scotch. And this particular team had one of their hot-shot officers heading it. He has just been made an army commander, but he was a brigadier then, Director of Personnel. We had kept a day free for them in Delhi. That was when they asked to go and see the Rajguru.'

'How did they set about it?' ABC asked. 'I mean, how did the name crop up?'

'There was something about the Swami in the papers, just about then, complete with photographs. Oh, yes, that actress, Shirley something… Now what was her name?'

'Shirley Maclaine?' Visram suggested. 'Shirley Temple?'

'Sheriden—that's right. Shirley Sheriden. She had come to take yoga lessons.'

'I see,' ABC said very softly. To Visram he seemed to be peering intently into the distance. 'And who made the suggestion?'

'Anwar Hussain. He was their Military Attache at the time. I must say I was peeved. You see, we had treated them to dinner at the Defence Club and explained what we had laid on for the next day. They had especially asked to see the film, Bobby, and I had gone to a good deal of trouble to get hold of a print and lay on the little theatre in front of South Block. That would have taken us through to lunch, which was at the Ashoka. In the afternoon there was a visit to the Rajrif centre. In the evening, they were giving us dinner.'

'Full day,' ABC commented dryly.

'And then Anwar rings me early in the morning—before seven—to say, could they go and visit Rajguru.'

'What did you do?'

'What could I do, but grin sheepishly and bustle about trying to make arrangements for them to see the Swami.'

'How does one get to see the Swami?' Visram asked. 'I suppose the telephones are unlisted.'

'Only the penthouse telephone is unlisted,' ABC told him. 'But that does not mean that either the army Intelligence or the Police don't have it. In any case the ashram phone is in the book. That's where Batra must have...'

'I did,' Batra said. 'A girl answered the ring, and I said could I go and see her? Always better to go and talk things over, isn't it—makes things so much easier. Oh, smashing looking thing... he certainly knows how to pick them. But a little giggly and...you know, breathless.'

'Vanita Dave?' Visram asked.

'No, some other name. Poor thing committed suicide a few months later, I remember. The Swami was in the Meditation Pavilion, she told me. The door to the inner office was open, and I could see the Swami's desk and chair and part of the room. Like a Hollywood set. Wall to wall carpet, pictures that might have been Hussains and Almelkars...style laid on with a trowel and to hell with the expense...what did you say?'

'Like Bobby Cooka's office in the Air India tower,' Visram mumbled.

'Yes, now that you mention it. Well, the girl gave me a dazzling smile and a cigarette and opened her appointments book. One of those things divided into quarter-hour blocks that dentists use. I told her who I was and that I was taking round seven military officers from a foreign country and that they had expressed a wish to see the Swami. She seemed thrilled. I got the impression that Rajguru was never averse to receiving foreign visitors. "Particularly if they're Americans or Germans," the girl said. I explained that they were not Americans or Germans and left it at that. "So tea instead of cokes," she mumbled to herself and wrote down the appointment. Ten thirty, for half an hour. I told her it would be fine. "Seven plus, you, right?" she said. "Anyway, please don't bring more than ten, because it upsets the tea arrangements". I said I wouldn't, thanked her, and drove to the Intercontinental where we had put them up. I gave Anwar Hussain the glad tidings and I was just going to cancel Bobby when I was told that my office was trying to reach me. It was my girl friend, wanting to know the names of the visitors. Told me to hold the line and came back and said sorry, but the whole thing was off. Just like that.'

'What did you do?' ABC asked.

'I was hopping mad. I tried to ring back, but could not get the number. So I drove down all the way to Palam. The Gurkhas at the gate had orders not to let me in.'

'And that was as near as you came to meeting the Swami?'

Batra grinned. 'I'm afraid so.'

'You don't remember the seven names, do you?'

'No. But I could find out. Of course, I remember Anwar, the MA, and the leader of the delegation, Brigadier Jamal Din.'

'That's the one you said had become an Army Commander?'

'That's right. Lieutenant General. Tipped to be the next chief.'

A jetliner came screaming over the trees, rose high in a steep curve, and became a moving star which all of them followed with their eyes. The silence that ensued after the disappearance of the star had a sobering effect on them. Batra said bitterly. 'Makes one sick to think of it, but it seems that all that Rajguru and his buddies have to do is take a brief holiday from robbing the kitty till both of you are put out of harm's way, and then resume where they had left off.'

'Which should not take more than a couple of days at the most,' Visram said.

'In that case, why not down tools right now, instead of committing harakiri?'

They both looked at ABC for a response. He said, 'But we can do something. Put a fire under their arses—make the bastards jump.'

Frustration often showed itself in coarseness, Visram reflected.

'Look at it this way,' ABC continued. 'They hold all the cards. They're sitting pretty. Time is on their side. All they have to do is to sit back in their trenches while their comrades mop us up. OK. Then the thing for us to do is to get them to come screaming out.'

'And how do we do that, sir?' Batra asked.

'Smoke the bastards out, that's how. Get them hopping mad!'

A stony silence met this revelation. Batra and Visram looked into the distance while ABC peered at their faces in turn. Then he went on, sounding very earnest, 'But I really mean it. What I think we should do is to go and beard the man—tell him all that we have found out. Get the swine rattled. Then wait for him to make his move. At least we shall have deprived him of his principal weapon: inaction. Don't you see? We must make him act, come out into the open.'

It was by the exercise of self-discipline that Batra prevented himself from coming out with something rude, but he could not conceal the tremor of sarcasam in his voice when he said, 'And who, may I ask, does the bearding of the lion—in his den?'

'I am afraid we don't have much choice there, do we. It'll have to be Visram. We're awfully thin on the ground, aren't we?'

'Do you really mean that, Mr Chopra?' Batra asked accusingly. 'Do you honestly believe that Visram Lal can walk into Rajguru's penthouse, tell him that he is a fake and a swindler, and be suffered to come back and make a report to you about what he was given with his lemon tea?'

'There are risks in all operations,' ABC protested with a shade of petulance. 'All that one can ensure is to provide against foreseeable risks. Very well. I believe I have a plan that will at least give us a fighting chance. I want to put it to you. Only if both of you agree that it is worth a try, will we go ahead. Now listen.'

They listened, but not as professional intelligence men or even as thinking individuals, knowing that they were already too deeply committed to back out.

ABC did not take quite ten minutes to explain his plan. After that they discussed its pros and cons for another ten. At one stage in the discussion, Batra gave out a long, low whistle, and taunted ABC, 'And you call us the Dirty Tricks boys! The way your minds work, you policemen would put the KGB to shame.'

'Are you surprised?' ABC retorted. 'Don't forget that we're often called upon to match wits with our own RAW. And our boast is that RAW would make the KGB look like boy scouts.'

~

Rajguru was standing on his head, his feet rigid, his toes pointing straight up. And he was fast asleep. He had often told interviewers that he had mastered the art of willing himself to sleep any time he wished to ('Oh, yes, even while I am taking a walk—when I was still a young monk in the Tashi Lunpo monastery near the Nanga Parbat, at the turn of the century.') And he had demonstrated again and again to his disciples that they could set a clock by the time of his coming awake.

In the entrance lobby of the penthouse, the telephone rang. Ekanti Ma who took the call, glanced at the electric clock and said, 'Ring back in six minutes, please. I'll put you through.'

Exactly six minutes later, Rajguru had come out of his sleep or trance. He sprang out of the shirshasan in a clean, athletic roll, and stood straight up dressed only in his katch or exercise briefs. That was when the extension in the exercise alcove gave a discreet burr. One of the two girls who were in attendance brought the instrument to him.

'Yes, Surbinder,' Rajguru said. 'Don't tell me you're still all at sea.'

Surbinder was apologetic. 'I'm afraid we are, Swamiji. No trace in Meerut. My guess is he never went there.'

'What good is a guess?'

'Well, sir. If he is here, it should be only a matter of hours before we arrest him. Every station house in the capital has been told that he is to be arrested at sight. All the station officers know him in any case. He cannot escape. The moment he emerges from his hiding place he will be caught.'

'I hope so. What else?'

'The girl doesn't know, either. Keeps ringing him up. This afternoon she drove up to his flat to enquire. Sent the driver up. She herself remained in the car.'

'Why is she so anxious to see him, you think? Has she some... additional knowledge?'

'It is a mystery. After we found the diary, I had taken off the men watching her flat, even though of course, we listen in to both her telephones. But she made one or two calls from outside telephones, and on Sunday morning she had gone out for nearly two hours. I have put back the men to keep her under watch.'

'You think she's up to some mischief?'

'I don't think so. After all she never read the diary. I'm keeping a watch, all the same.'

'What about the man who drove him down from Kasauli? Who is he?'

'Army chap. Heads the Special Effects squad—what they call the Dirty Dozen. Hush-hush job. The point is, it gives him lots of opportunities to be missing from the scene. Accountable only to the DMI. Yesterday he was out playing bridge—at least when we located the house where he was supposed to be playing, he was there. But that was well past nine. What is disturbing is that he is missing again, this evening, and we have checked his usual haunts.'

'Not there?'

'I'm afraid not, Swamiji.'

'I don't like this at all, Surbinder,' the Swami said almost as though he was offering a blessing. 'Not at all,' he added a little less unctuously, and put down the receiver.

He resumed his workout, by going straight into a mayurasan, first on his right leg, and then shifting to his left; a rigid figure that might have been made of wood, his eyes wide open but unseeing. After that, he performed a series of quick exercises intended to tone up his stomach muscles, then drove out all the air from his lungs very slowly, and for more than two minutes stopped breathing altogether.

His body was like that of a colt. It had no visible muscles, and yet it was hard, supple, springy; and its skin shone like that of a trout seen in shallow water.

The workout completed, he shed his katch, and lay face down on a hard wooden bench covered with a thin, palm-leaf mat. That was when the two girls, both of whom were from a temple in Tellichery, began to give his body its daily massage with herbal oils. They went about their jobs with skill and energy, rubbing and kneading and pounding the muscles with the heels of their palms. Within twenty minutes, they were both panting hard and perspiring freely.

After that, came the bath. Rajguru's own version of a health-bath. Jets of steaming hot water alternated with a needle-sharp spray of ice-cold water. He came out of the bath and stood on a weighing scale as droplets trickled down on the marble floor.

From the wall that was made of mirrors, his face smiled back at him, a man conscious that he had never looked better, never felt fitter.

Then in the misted mirror he saw Ekanti Ma who had brought him his glass of steaming hot lemon grass tea.

CHAPTER 12

AT first, the man who asked to speak to Ekanti Ma, would not give his name. 'Please tell Mataji it is something to do with the Mukti Bahini,' he had said, giving the code name she had used with Dorabji.

But the girl who took the call insisted on knowing his name. 'Otherwise I cannot give her your message,' she told the caller.

'The name is Girja Shankar.'

'And what do you want?'

'Look', the man said as though he was making an effort to be patient. 'I am a Sevasangh M.P. from Amraoti, and when some of us held a demonstrations before Parliament last month, we were put into Tihar jail. I was released last evening, on parole. You'll find my name in the paper—as one of those who were arrested.'

'I've got all that down,' the girl at the other end said. 'But what do you want to see…'

'Mataji will understand, say I must speak to her, and that it is about the Mukti Bahini. She will understand.'

It did not take Ekanti Ma more than a minute to come to the telephone. 'Yes, Mr Girja Shankar,' she said without any preliminaries. 'What do you want to speak to me about?'

'I was in Tihar jail for four weeks. Manekji Dorabji and I were in the same squad, for work as well as exercise.'

'How did you find this telephone number?'

'Dorabji gave it to me.'

A pause, and then, 'Oh, I see. And what do you want?'

'Well, Mataji. I'm a very poor man. I thought we could come to...to some sort of working arrangement...'

'You mean you want money, don't you?'

The man coughed nervously before he said. 'That was my idea—but please understand, Madam, that considering the—the information that has come my way...my demands are very modest. I'm not a grasping man...but one thing.'

'Yes?'

'For reasons which...which I'd much rather not speak of over the telephone, it is absolutely vital that I see you without delay.'

Ekanti Ma heard a soft sound behind her, and put a hand on the receiver. Rajguru, who had been listening on the extension in the sitting room, was standing in the open doorway, and nodding. 'All right, you'd better come here ...what time? Oh...let me see...er...' she had raised her eyebrows and was looking at Rajguru, who held up both hands with one finger folded. 'Why not come right away?' she said to the caller. 'Nine o'clock. I'll send the lift down. You give your name to the lift man and he'll bring you up, Mr Girja Shankar.'

~

In the records maintained in the Estates Office of the CPWD, the last C-2 type bungalow in Motibagh, in the cul-de-sac bordering the green belt, was shown as being in occupation by the officers of the Public Audit Committee, and the residents of the neighbouring bungalows who were service officers and their families, had become used to its occupants being out on tour for weeks at a time.

'Living off the unfortunate clerks and superintendents of whatever office they're auditing,' one of the naval officers had said indignantly. 'And salting away their TA and DA...you know what blood-suckers auditors are.'

That particular accusation had gained currency. Whenever a car or jeep was seen outside the bungalow or lights in the windows, they knew that the auditors had returned to base for a few days. 'But the buggers will be off again,' someone usually commented. 'Eating and drinking free and being paid allowances.'

In actual fact, the bungalow, 238 Motibagh, was used by the Inter-services Special Effects Section, or ISPEC, for lodging its informers who found it expedient to come without notice, and had to be given accommodation. Its telephone was unlisted.

The call was made from what would have been the drawing room of the downstairs flat if one of the auditors had lived there, and from its wide window, they could see Sarang Towers about half a mile away, a jet-age Qutub Minar of white cement and glass. ABC had parted the yellow hessian curtains brought from the ISPEC imprest accounts, and had trained his binoculars on the penthouse. All he could see was a part of the wall and a trellis on which an alamanda vine had been trained.

Batra, who had been listening on an extension while Visram was doing the talking, put down the receiver and uttered a theatrical sigh. He shrugged his shoulders and said. 'God! It was like listening to a cobra spitting.'

'Do cobras spit?' Visram asked. He was trying out a broad-brimmed, floppy jungle hat which Batra had provided.

'This one does,' Batra said. 'Girja Shankar came in handy, didn't he. I only hope the woman doesn't ring back the real Girja Shankar to...'

'Not here,' ABC reassured him. 'Gone back to Amraoti. I checked.'

'Pull the brim a little more down,' Batra told Visram.

ABC cleared his throat and said, 'This is the point where we can still stop, gentlemen. Once we've taken the plunge, we'll be too deeply committed to...'

For answer, Visram glanced at his watch. He got up and opened the door and walked out. From the window they watched him striding towards the main road and saw him hail a rickshaw from the stand at the crossing.

Chopra was licking his lips. 'I don't think they'll do anything till they've talked to him and found out what he's after,' he told Batra. 'That's the margin we have to work in. This bit of luck we deserve.'

After that they sat in silence. Batra took out his cigarette case and they both lit cigarettes. The silence had an eerie quality, like the silence before a countdown. Then they heard a childish voice shouting a word of abuse in the street outside, and for some reason which neither could have explained, they both laughed. Then Batra said, 'Five minutes past nine.'

ABC nodded, picked up the telephone, and again dialled the number of Rajguru's apartment. 'This is the Chanakyapuri Police Thana,' he said. 'I'm the Station officer, Inspector Kohli, speaking. I must speak to the Swamiji, please—yes, yes—please hurry.'

~

The lift was waiting, and after he had given his name, its uniformed attendant gave him a military salute and stood aside for him to enter. It was an express lift, the sort that shoots up at great speed and has to slow down before stopping. As the door slid open, he found himself shoved violently from behind and into the arms of a man who stood crouching. He was pinned down in a vice-like grip while the lift man came from behind and began to search him for weapons.

Luckily he had anticipated some such procedure, which was the only reason why he was able to fight back the countermoves that should have come into play automatically, as a reflexive response: the sudden contracting of his body and slipping out of the clutch by dropping to the floor, then diving at his assailant's legs. But then he was Girja Shankar, a Sevasangh agitator, not someone who had earned the coveted grading of 'Instructor-Proficiency' at the Army's school of Combat.

The thought crossed his mind that the two men who were searching him had also been trained in some school for unarmed combat. They were very thorough, very professional; they even examined his wallet to see if it contained a razor blade.

The lift man went back into the lift first, then the other man released his grip and followed him. As the lift went down with an electric hum, he saw a door behind him open and Ekanti Ma come in. 'Ah, there you are, Mr Girja Shankar,' she said effusively. 'Exactly on time. Sorry you were subjected to a search. But one never knows, these days, does one? And it was a little...I mean you did sound a little intimidating on the phone.'

He simpered and mumbled a greeting and folded his hands, his green hat still jammed on his head. He followed her through a long passage and into an enormous patio that was half garden and half boudoir, and then to a small corner room that looked like a study and music room combined. It was air-conditioned and its windows overlooked Mogul Delhi: Jama Masjid and the Red Fort and the river. He had an idea that he had been brought to this room so that he could be kept under observation, because there was a dull mirror fitted into one wall. He had heard of see-through mirrors but had not seen one before. He had no doubt in his mind that someone would be listening in to whatever he had to say to Ekanti Ma.

'We can talk privately here,' Ekanti Ma told him.

Politely, he waited for her to sit down, and then himself sat down, nervously, on the edge of the chair. He said: 'You may have read in the papers about the Sevasangh Morcha last month—before the Parliament building. It was lathi charged and...'

'Yes, and some of the leaders were arrested.'

'That's right. I was one of them.'

'From Amraoti, you said.'

'How well you remember.'

He told her that in Tihar jail he had met Manekji Dorabji, and since he had heard so much about the Dorabji case, had tried to pump him for information. Over the next few days, he and Dorabji had become friends, and Dorabji had told him things which he said he had not told anyone else.

'What sort of things, Mr Girja Shankar?'

'For instance that he had run similar errands before; as a courier, taken money from the bank manager before and passed it to you; how the code signals were changed every time, and also the place of meetings.'

'What else?'

'That he helped you to transfer the money into suitcases which you had brought, and after that you travelled with the money to the airport. That at the airport...'

Somewhere in the house, a telephone rang. Ekanti Ma excused herself and went to answer it. Visram glanced at his watch. It was exactly five minutes since he had arrived. Once again he thought to himself what a wonderful thing it was to have brilliant professionals like ABC and Batra working for you. He got up and went to the window. You could see right into the Red Fort, and the silver curve of the Jamuna winding round it.

He heard a soft footfall and turned very quickly, and the look he caught in Ekanti Ma's eyes made his heart beat faster. 'What a stupendous view,' he said, conversationally.

She sat down in her chair, and pulled her sari primly over her ankles. 'Where were we?' she said. 'Oh, yes. Your friend Dorabji told you that I took the money to the airport.'

Was there a tremor in her voice? he asked himself. The suggestion of fear? Only a few minutes earlier, she had been so poised, the dignified, elegant woman with the well-preserved figure and finely chiselled features—like a retired film actress. Now there were patches of white on both sides of her nose. She dabbed her upper lip with a handkerchief and asked, 'I took the money to the airport to go where, Mr Girja Shankar?'

'Mauritius.'

She raised her eyebrows and frowned. 'Mauri...oh, yes. French, wasn't it? An island? And what else?'

'That the customs let your bags go through without checking?'

'Really? Why would they do that, did he say?'

She was playing it very well, he thought, but not really succeeding; subtlety never came easy to these actresses, he remembered. He said, 'Because the customs officials were given instructions by...by certain highly placed men who pass orders in the name of the Great Leader.'

'Is the Great Leader involved in this, too, then?' she asked.

'He didn't know.'

'I see. You asked, did you? Please go ahead. I hope it is not going to take very long.'

He told her how Dorabji believed that similar arrangements had been made at Plaisance in Mauritius to let the suitcases go through unexamined; how the money was laundered through financiers in Mauritius by paying them handsome discounts; then brought back to India in the form of donations, or gifts.

'How interesting. And Mr Dorabji told you all this?'

He made a nervous gesture with his hands and picked up his hat which he had put down on the floor beside him. 'Remember, I was there for nearly a month. We had a lot of...leisure. We talked.'

She had recovered her poise. Oddly enough it made him feel a little more confident that the plan devised by ABC might succeed.

'What a vivid imagination this man Dorabji must have had—or is it you who suffer from it Mr...Mr Girja Shankar?'

He shook his head and ran his tongue over his lips. 'May I smoke?'

'Please do. Oh, and you never told me the...the purpose of your visit. Some arrangement, you were saying.'

He had taken out his packet of cigarettes, but put it back into his pocket. 'I thought I would offer my services in Dorabji's place... as a courier, since...'

'Since he's dead?' she prompted.

He found that he had to clear his throat before he could bring himself to answer. 'That too, but...but since I have come to know so much.'

There was a faint smile on Ekanti Ma's face now. 'And what do you hope to get by...by acting as a courier?'

'What Dorabji was getting?'

'What *was* he getting?'

'Twenty-five thousand every time...a fixed fee.' He glanced at his watch. It was fifteen minutes since he had come. He said, 'I'm sure you will want time to consider my proposal. You might... that is, there must be others to consult. I could ring you back, this evening...or later. Would you prefer that? Now, if you will excuse me...you have been most kind.' He rose to his feet. The hat slipped out of his hand. As he picked it up, he could see that Ekanti Ma was smiling indulgently and with narrowed eyes. And then he realized that she was looking over his shoulders, at someone else who had come into the room.

He turned and saw Rajguru, dressed in his usual muslin dhoti with one end of it draped over his shoulder. Visram shuffled his feet and bowed.

'I hope you're not in a tearing hurry, Mr Shankar,' Rajguru said. 'Could you give me just a few minutes, you think? Ten, say? Oh, good!' The voice was that of a priest, exuding confidence, inviting—a cat inviting a mouse for a game, Visram thought. He had heard the voice before, over the telephone, when Pashupat had first called him. Rajguru made a gesture with his hands, and again he was reminded of a priest conferring blessings on a temple visitor.

Ekanti Ma rose to her feet, gave Visram an almost pitying look, and went out of the room, mumbling something. 'Do sit down,' Rajguru was saying. 'And please smoke, if you want to.'

Visram flopped down into his chair and took out his packet of cigarettes. His hands shook as he lighted one.

'I think I should explain that I have heard most of what you say Dorabji told you,' Rajguru went on. 'Does that surprise you?'

'It does. I thought I was speaking in confidence.'

There was an artless smile on the Rajguru's face, like that of a child which had done something mildly naughty... 'You see there's a little gadget planted in this room—very efficient. I heard you very clearly. What a lot you seem to know of what was going on. And to think that I had always regarded Dorabji as being rather stupid—bovine. One never knows does one?' He waited as though he expected Visram to say something and went on. 'I am really interested in the proposal you have made. But will you give me a little time to—to think it over? I mean, there are so many angles. Meantime, I have been dying to ask one or two questions. Tell me, what sort of feeling came over you when Dorabji told you whatever he had to?'

'Feeling—I really don't understand.'

'Were you shocked—saddened, made happy?

'Well, shocked certainly. I mean at the sheer enormity of the thing. Why, the money ran into tens of millions...'

'Are you a...a possionate supporter of the NDF, Mr...Mr Shankar?'

'How can I be? I belong to the Sevasangh—the Opposition.'

'And yet you were not secretly delighted that some people were eating away at the vitals of the NDF, as it were, by helping themselves to the party's secret funds?'

Like a clever lawyer opening a line of interrogation for cornering a star witness, Visram thought. 'I fail to see what connection there can be, Swamiji,' he began lamely. 'Between—excuse my frankness, Swamiji—between someone robbing the till and the country's politics.'

Again Rajguru raised his hands in a gesture of benediction. It was difficult not to be swayed by the man's sheer presence, not to go on staring at his virile body that was nearly naked, its golden skin shining through the thin muslin of his dhoti. How could one talk as an equal to someone who was accepted as a sort of High Priest by the great and the famous and the glamourous?

'Do you concern yourself with abstract problems of right and wrong, Mr Shankar?'

'I don't even know what you mean, sir,' Visram confessed.

'Do you think of actions in terms of ends and means?—for instance?'

This time Visram did not make an answer, feeling within himself that this was Rajguru's way of playing cat-and-mouse with him. After a pause, Rajguru went on, 'If it is your aim somehow to bring down the one-person rule of the Great Leader, to restore the independence of the judiciary, the freedom of the press, the rights of the individual, the functions of democracy, should you not applaud the people who are doing your work far more effectively—by sabotaging your opponents, even if it is by...by robbing the till, as you describe it?'

'I suppose there is something in what you say, Swamiji. Perhaps the detractors of the Great Leader should thank you for...your efforts on behalf of democracy.'

But High Priests are immune to sarcasm. The Rajguru beamed as at a compliment. 'I'm glad you see it in the...the right perspective.' The Swami gave his schoolboy grin, and went on. 'Supposing, just supposing, that what Dorabji told you is actually happening. It should hardly affect the ordinary citizen. But anyone who is at all politically mature should treat these—these robbers of the till, as you described them—as some kind of national heroes, should he not, instead of as villains?'

Visram gave a confused look but made no answer.

'Luckily it is not—not as though you're an officer of the law—someone who can think of life only as a ding-dong battle between the law and the breakers of the law, but a seasoned politician—a man of the world who can take the broad view. What's that?'

'I was saying that there is nothing that even an officer of the law can object to, because it is not as though there is a complaint. I mean, even the NDF party has not complained that any funds are missing.'

'Precisely, Mr Girja Shankar. I like your frankness...oh, yes. So your purpose in wanting to speak to Ekanti Ma was, er, dictated by no other motive than...a desire to cut yourself into the game, eh?'

It was not easy to face that benign stare. 'Yes, Swamiji.'

'Good. I always suspect noble motives, don't you—particularly among others, Ah, that finishes our ten minutes.'

It was uncanny. He wore no watch, and there was no clock in the room. Visram's wristwatch was covered by the cuff of his bush-shirt. He pulled his sleeve and glanced at his watch; precisely ten minutes since they had begun to talk.

'As I said, I shall have to think hard about your proposal—consider what terms would be fair. Will you give me a ring in the evening, then?—about five, shall we say?'

'Of course, Swamiji,' Visram said eagerly. 'You will be at the ashram, I take it. Certainly I shall ring.'

'There can be nothing certain in this world, alas, Mr...Mr Girja Shankar,' Rajguru said, ruefully. He rose and said, 'Come, let me show you the way out. No, no; no trouble at all.'

He felt small, a schoolboy being shown out of his study by the Head, as he followed the Swami through the patio and the long corridor. Rajguru stopped in front of the heavily carved rosewood door and motioned him to go through. The hooded eyes were watching him, and they had a sinister glint. Like that of a lizard watching some insect, Visram thought, as he opened the door.

Three men were standing in the lobby. One of them who wore the uniform of in Inspector, stood stiffly at attention and saluted. 'Good morning, sir,' he said, and then went on. 'Superintendent Lal, it is my duty to serve this paper on you, sir. It is a warrant of arrest under the Maintenance of Internal Security Act. I have also to take you into custody.'

With one hand on the doorknob, Visram turned to look behind, and saw the holy face made common by whatever common thoughts were passing through the Swami's head. The lips curled, the nostrils flared, the eyes screwed into slits.

'Don't fail to give me a ring at five, Mr Visram Lal,' Swamiji said, very softly.

'I hope you will not make it necessary for us to put handcuffs on you, sir,' the Inspector said, very sternly, balancing skillfully on a tightrope between duty and respect to a senior officer.

'Oh, he's not carrying any weapons, Inspector,' Rajguru assured him.

Flanked by the two plain-clothed constables and followed closely by the Inspector, Visram entered the waiting lift.

~

Both the lift man and the man who had assisted him in frisking Visram Lal watched the proceedings with interest. A black Ambassador had been drawn right up to the entrance steps of Sarang Towers. Its driver had opened the rear door but was sitting rigidly at the wheel, and had the engine running. The inspector and his men all but frogmarched their victim out of the lift and bundled him into the rear of the car. The two men jumped in and sat flanking him. The inspector himself took the seat beside the driver but sat sideways so that he could keep an eye on his prisoner. 'Chanakyapuri thana,' he ordered the driver, and the car sped away.

Before it had gone half a mile, one of the men in the rear seat had changed seats with Visram Lal and put on his green jungle hat. At the corner of Malcha Marg, the car slowed down for a couple of seconds. Visram Lal who was now sitting on the side, jumped out and scrambled into a waiting Fiat, while a man lounging beside the Fiat took his place in the Ambassador. After that, both cars went in different directions. The Ambassador wheeled back in the first traffic circle and headed towards the Ashoka Hotel and then for the Mathura Road. The Fiat turned right and got on to the Ring Road.

Colonel Batra, who was at the wheel of the Fiat wiped his face and the back of his neck with a handkerchief. 'God, you gave me a fright!' he said, 'Ten minutes behind schedule.'

'The holy man kept talking about ends and means,' Visram explained.

'I thought the whole bloody scheme had gone om-phuss.'

'Seems to have worked so far. What happens now?'

'We lie low till the evening, and then throw another fistful of chilli powder under their tails...'

'God, what language!' Visram protested. 'After being subjected to holy talk about ends and means.'

'The idea is to make them mad, and then keep them hopping so that they just have to do something drastic to neutralize us instead of...of waiting till all of us are sent to prison under MISA. Let the bastards come out into the open—so that we can give them battle on nearly equal terms.' Batra waited for a second or two and added, more soberly, 'That's the scenario written by ABC. The point is, will it work?'

'It just has to, doesn't it?' Visram pointed out.

'You mean, if it doesn't we've as good as landed ourselves in Tihar unless they shoot us out of hand,'

'I have great faith in ABC's abilities—when he is on the warpath.'

'Is he on the warpath? He acts so cool.'

'Isn't he, just! When he looks cool and talks in riddles—that's the danger signal. I bet he's itching to eat them raw. And with good reason too—imagine being turfed out under a shadow just to make room for a yes-dog like Surbinder—everyone in the force must be secretly rooting for ABC.'

'And some actually working for him. Right?'

'Only natural, dammit. Thirty years' service—one makes friends too, not just enemies. Where is he now?'

'Told me he had more important things to do,' Batra answered, and then went on in a confidential tone. 'I say, there's something you should know. Chopra gave me a number to ring, which I was to use only if our venture had misfired and you failed to return. As it happened, the number was familiar to me. It is a sort of panic number to ring—you know, in case there is a bombing attack or some emergency of that nature. It is the Defence Minister's private telephone, unlisted. Shook me.'

Visram too felt a chill pass over his body. 'Are you sure?'

'Absolutely. Do you think the old boy is playing a deeper game than both of us realize?'

If he was, it was too late to worry about it, Visram thought. 'Whatever he is doing, I can guarantee you that he is playing on the same side as both of us. And that is enough for me.'

'I hope you're right. But still. To hobnob with the Defence Minister right now—you know it's suicide, don't you?'

'Best not to think about it, then; let ABC do the worrying,' Visram said. 'Where are we headed for?'

'Just cruising round to make sure there's no tail. Then we'll find a cab for you, but not at a rank. You're to make your way to the crash-pad in Motibagh and stay put. In the evening, make your call. Remember we have to keep you under wraps. At least there's no warrant against Chopra and me, so far as I know. Not yet.'

'They keep blank warrants signed by magistrates,' Visram pointed out. 'Surbinder has stacks of them. Only has to fill in your name.

Batra grinned. 'That's why I'm going to spend a full day at the office—build myself a strong alibi, so that the DMI can display proper indignation if someone suggests that I have been hobnobbing with treasonable characters.'

'So now we wait for the Swami to make the next move. Any guess what they'll do?'

'I asked Chopra that. He's quite certain that first they'll go into a huddle—all four of them; ABC says they'll hold a council in that shrine at the ashram. Does anyone really know what happens there? Do you? Does ABC?'

'I certainly don't,' Visram confessed. 'It is possible that ABC has a fairly accurate idea—not that he has given me a hint.'

Batra shook his head. 'How can he? So far as I know, no one other than the four has even seen the inside of the place.'

'I must confess there is something about the man that is a little uncanny,' Visram said. 'I've seen it time and again. A sort of mental antenna which is able to reject false scents…besides, when you've been in the service as long as he has and gained his kind of reputation for fairness and efficiency, it is amazing how people who have worked with you on cases sometime in the past pass on useful tips. I suppose it must sound naive but I have sort of learned to take ABC on trust.'

But it was clear that Batra was not prepared to take anyone's omniscience on trust. He pursed his lips and mumbled, 'Teacher knows best.'

'I say,' Visram asked. 'You Dirty Tricks blokes don't have a gadget that you can plant there, do you?'

'In Rajguru's shrine? Alas, no; not without one of our voodoo boys being allowed the freedom of the place for an hour or so; then we could plant a bug that would enable us to hear every word that was being said there, now, as we are driving in this car. It's really amazing the devices they've come up with. The Russians can put a bug in a strip of wall paint—did that in the American embassy in Moscow. But as things are—no can do. ABC tells me that Rajguru himself keeps the key.'

'I suppose we could break open the door.'

'Oh, easy,' Batra smirked. 'All you'd need is a crowbar and a couple of hefty chaps like you and me. Or better still, a mini-torpedo. Won't need a minute, if we can get as far as the door. If. Perhaps it would be easier to blow up a part of the wall. Masonry is easier to bust than steel...if it's a steel door. You'd be adding housebreaking to your list of felonies.'

'I suppose ABC will find some way,' Visram said. From the expression on Batra's face, he thought that he was trying to prevent himself from saying something rude.

'Ah, there's a cab,' Batra said. 'Do you?'

'Fine.'

'Oh, just one thing. Remember not to bolt the door from inside. One of our own boys might want to use the place.'

'I suppose they have latchkeys.'

'No, oh, no! We can't have them toting keys. It's a simple lock. Tumblers worked with piano keys. They all know the combination. I don't really expect anyone to come though.'

'What do I do if some one does?' Visram asked.

'Keep mum and stay in your corner. They won't want to talk to you either. That's the drill. It does happen once in a while. At one time we had three men there and none of them knew who the other two were. Taxi! Taxi!'

'God! I'd be scared to death,' Visram said. 'Why couldn't I have gone back to that bungalow on the range?'

'Because ABC wants you on hand, that's why. He has plans which, of course, he has not cared to divulge. Anyway, not to worry. If someone does turn up he'll be just as upset to see you planted in his bed,' he waved a hand and drove off.

'Drive towards West End Road, will you?' Visram told the taxi driver. 'I'll tell you when to stop.'

As the taxi was passing the last lot of West End houses with their fussy gardens and minute lawns, Visram's eye was caught by a blaze of shimmering yellow. He turned to look at the laburnum in full bloom. That was when a man passing on a scooter happened to see him.

The man slowed down, knowing that he had no hope of going after the taxi on the open road without being observed by its passenger. He watched till it all but went out of his view, and he cursed softly. Then he saw the taxi come to a stop. He put on a burst of speed to catch up.

From the main road he could see the lane on both sides of which were the neat double-storied, government bungalows. The man who had got out of the taxi was going through the gate of the end house.

That evening, when Netra rang the number Sartaj had given her, a girl's voice answered, 'Netherlands' Embassy, can I help you?'

'Sorry, wrong number,' she apologised. This had never happened before. Sartaj was always where he said he was going to be. She fished out her diary in which she had put down the number the previous evening. It was the correct number. And then she bit her tongue and laughed to herself as she realized her mistake. She had added the figure of today's date to it. She took out the correct change and dialled again. This time it was Sartaj who answered.

'Where are you speaking from?' he asked.

'From the pay telephone in Janpath, in front of the National Archives.'

'I've found him...'

'What!...You have! What did he have to say?'

'I haven't talked to him yet. I just know where he is staying. I mean to go and see him later tonight...around ten. But after making sure that the coast is clear. I'll tell him to contact you somehow... if he wants to check my credentials. I'll find a way, not to worry.'

CHAPTER 13

SWAMI Rajguru was in the Meditation Pavilion, rounding off his morning's tour of the ashram with a short question-and-answer session. He was seated on a low marble bench placed strategically at the feet of Oger's Shakti so that, in the eyes of the congregation, both the Swami and the goddess should form a part of the same dual image, white and marbled with golden shadows; a fountainhead of wisdom, part-earthy, part-celestial.

And at his feet squatted a group consisting of nineteen women and four men, gazing at him open-mouthed, some taking careful notes of his sayings; at least half a dozen had their eyes shut and were swaying gently as though they were listening to a concert of classical music.

'Certainly, salvation can be achieved through the fullest enjoyment of the senses,' Rajguru pronounced with emphasis. 'For mankind, it is the natural path, the ordained path. Kama, carnal lust, must be recognized as a divine force, the light of all sciences, the essence of all religion, a force to be brought to perfection through yoga.'

He frowned as he spied a shadow appear in one of the arches. He had been told that he needed glasses, but knew that wearing them would damage his image as a man who, even though he was nearly ninety years old, was still at the peak of his form.

He saw that it was Vanita Dave, looking helpless and flustered, and trying to catch his eye, and, he thought with a sudden tingling sensation, sexier than ever. He knew that she would not have interrupted his routine unless there was some really pressing reason. It was almost certain that the Great Leader desired his presence; that either Kaul or Pashupat had rung to say that there was a bullawa for him—the Great Leader, or the son, Kalas Kak, for some nefarious purpose of his own.

He nodded and waved Vanita away with a flick of his fingers, and he made a mental note to tell Ekanti Ma how the girl had the ability to turn him on with a mere look. He must ask Ekanti to make a more determined effort to get her to work in the penthouse.

It was a special and assiduously developed trait in Rajguru that he could go on spouting abstract pronouncements while a part of his mind was busy with its own thoughts. For the next five minutes, as he discoursed on the distinction between dharma and adharma, he was also thinking how some girls, even though they came from low-income families, seemed to be immune to the lure of money or clothes, both of which Ekanti had dangled before Vanita to entice her to come and work in the Swami's house. At the moment he wanted Vanita more than anything else in the world. Perhaps her Gandhian upbringing might not be proof against other lures. What? A little car of her own? A trip to New York? How delightful to spend a week at the Plaza, bringing Vanita up to date on the variations of the sexual act.

The half a dozen elderly women who formed the first circle found themselves almost blushing at the looks the Swami was giving them.

He brought the session to a close, suffered the ladies of the first circle to kiss his hand with rubbery wet smacks, and hurried to his office.

He was considerably annoyed to be told that it was Surbinder who had been trying to get hold of him, and had insisted on Vanita calling him to the telephone. He stood beside her as she dialled the number and rested his hand gently on her shoulder. The way she had squirmed in her chair and all but brushed off his hand had pained him. She handed him the telephone and got up from her chair. 'Will you take the call here, Guruji?'

He shook his head and went into his own office. 'Yes, Surbinder?' he demanded curtly.

'Swamiji, I need your help, desperately.'

'Surely you don't need my help to deal with a rat like Superintendent Lal?' Rajguru asked angrily.

'Well, sir. It is about Lal that I am ringing. I am glad to say I have narrowed down the search, and know who his accomplices are. I can promise you an arrest this very evening, but only if...'

'Are you out of your mind, Surbinder?'

'Guruji, I am stuck, and appealing for help. Unless the army co-operates, we're unable to apprehend Lal. But a word...'

'You fool! Do you mean to tell me that your Chanakyapuri man, Inspector Kohli, has not reported to you that he arrested Lal in my house this morning?'

'Sir...I don't know what you—Swamiji, I am sorry, but all the station officers are with me at this moment, in the outer room, including Kohli from the Chanakya...'

Rajguru could only splutter. His hand shook with anger and his eyes fogged. He sounded almost incoherent as he tried to explain to Surbinder what had happened. How a man who called himself Girja Shankar had come to see Ekanti Ma, and how, while he was there, Inspector Kohli had rung to say that one of his men who had been shadowing Lal had spotted him going into his lift and to keep him there till he came. He had come with two constables and a car and taken him away.

He was too disconcerted to listen to what Surbinder wanted. He ended his story in a renewed outburst of anger. 'Come and see me at the ashram at five in the evening,' he told Surbinder. 'Don't waste my time now.'

He was still breathing hard and sweat ran over his arms and chest. It had happened before; anger had aroused a sexual urge that demanded instant fulfilment. All the while he had been talking to that stupid lout, a part of his mind had been engaged in weaving fantasies around a girl sitting mousily in the outer office.

He rang the bell, and when she came in, pad and pencil in hand, he asked her very casually, 'Vanita, how do you come to work?'

'How do I—oh... By bus as far as the hospital. Then I walk.'

'I was thinking we should buy a car for you. Wouldn't you like that? A little mini of your own to run around in?'

'I don't know how to drive a car, Guruji; and I don't think my mother will agree to let me drive about on my own.'

'Oh, well, it was just a thought. What? No, there is nothing else.'

~

'It is the same man who drove him down from Kasauli, Swamiji.'

'And you have evidence that he is still hiding him somewhere?'

'Not evidence. But he certainly has the facilities. He heads a hush-hush section called the Dirty Dogs. He can hide people, give them false papers, disguises, all that. He has a house maintained by the army intelligence where his secret agents are put up when they come for briefings.'

'And where is this house, Surbinder?'

'That's just it, sir. I don't know. There are secrets that the army will not divulge to outsiders. That is why I wanted your intervention; you know, at a much higher level. Either the Great Leader or...'

'Surely either Pashupat or Kaul could have handled this simple thing for you?' Swami Rajguru pointed out, sounding a little impatient.

'They tried, sir. Mr Pashupat failed to elicit...'

'Don't talk rubbish! I know that nobody, but nobody, can afford to say no to that pair. I have seen ministers quaking, and a Lieutenant Governor standing on his head to do their bidding. Surely, even the toughest general will come running with his tail between his legs when he is told that his promotion would be withheld or that his son would never pass his university examination?'

Surbinder shook his head and made a helpless gesture. 'This is a little different, Swamiji; a sort of club within a club; with people backstopping for one another. And they're experts in deception. Batra's superiors and colleagues would swear to all sorts of lies to back him up and...'

Whatever else he was going to say was prevented by the ringing of the telephone. Rajguru snatched the receiver with impatience. 'Yes, what is it?' he snapped at Vanita, and then made frantic gestures to Surbinder to go and listen in on the extension in the outer office. Then he said into the mouthpiece, 'What name did you say?'

'Lal. Visram Lal. You told me to ring at five.'

Rajguru found that he had to clear his throat before he was able to say, 'Oh, yes, I did.'

'I want to know what you have decided about my proposal.'

'Your...well, Mr Lal. I have been extremely busy, and I have only just got down to...to discussing the proposal with a colleague. Could I ring you back, say, in half an hour?'

'You want my telephone number?'

'Yes, I could then...'

'You must think I'm mad, Rajguru,' Visram Lal had answered. 'Or as stupid as your colleague.' There was a burst of rude laughter, and after that the line had gone dead.

Rajguru's heart thumped painfully and his eyes blurred at the sheer audacity of the caller. He had to resort to a spell of pranayam, or stopping his breathing and willing himself into a state of unconsciousness. When he came out of his trance, his eyes fell on Surbinder who had come back into the room, looking shaken and shamefaced. Surbinder was saying something. 'What did you say?'

'Swamiji, all you have to do is to help me find out where the hiding place is. I promise to arrest the man within half an hour.'

'Arrest, did you say?' Rajguru said with venom. It was clear that his trance had not succeeded in enabling him to overcome his fit of anger. 'Is that all your mind can think of? I want to see the man grovel, writhe in pain...howl...beg for mercy...' he stopped, his chest heaving, unable to go on.

He took a few deep breaths and was able to continue. 'I shall find the address, Surbinder,' he said with contempt. 'And then I shall myself do whatever is necessary. I shall not trouble you again, Surbinder.'

The words sent a chill through Surbinder. Suddenly he was reminded that his promotion as the COI was still provisional, and that, in the department itself, he did not have many friends. 'Swamiji, please listen,' he pleaded. 'I promise to get you your man if only...'

'Get out!' the holy man ordered.

Surbinder cowered. As he slunk out of the ashram, his mind was filled with dark forebodings. How was he going to explain to his wife that the car with a flag bearing two gold stars was not going to materialize.

Rajguru asked Vanita Dave to ring the Great Leader's house and get him either Kaul or Pashupat on the telephone. It was Kaul who answered, and he told him to come to the ashram at seven in the evening, and to bring Pashupat with him.

After that he dialled an unlisted number which his secretary did not know, and which, he knew, was equipped with a scrambling device. He was a little put out when Ambika Das's voice answered. Ambika Das had not thanked him for the roses.

'Can I speak to Kakji, please?'

'I'll see if he is free,' Ambika Das said sullenly.

A minute passed. He tried to make out from the background noises what sort of activity was in progress. He thought it was a little too early for a blue film, or for the other orgies that were associated with the hierarchy of the Dropout Brigade. But then it was never too early, he reflected—or too late. And for no reason at all, he thought of Vanita Dave.

The earpiece crackled. It was Ambika Das again. 'Kakji will speak to you in a minute. Meanwhile, he wants to know if it is girl trouble.'

Rajguru had never permitted any of Kakji's cronies to become familiar with him, and fumed at the impertinence. 'Yes, it is,' he countered. 'I went and stood in front of the women's hostel and serenaded the girls with obscenities.'

He waited for a reaction but did not get any. God, that must have stung, he realized with satisfaction, as he listened to the background sounds. Moans interspered with giggles, and then a dog barking with excitement. He gave a start as Kakji's voice suddenly rasped in his ear, 'What do you want, you lecherous bugger? Don't tell me you have managed to put yet another secretary in the family way?'

This time there was no question of a cutting retort. Rajguru scowled, but made appropriate sounds in response to the off-colour badinage, telling himself that a young man with arrested mental development who had come into money and power could not be expected to conform to civilized norms of behaviour. In the end it was Kakji who said impatiently, 'Okay, Okay, what do you want?'

'It is about the Dorabji case. There are complications. Some busybodies have complete knowledge of what is happening. They have been building up evidence—powerful men who are determined to make trouble.'

The revelation had a cooling effect. Kakji uttered a soft curse and said, 'I'll come and see you at the ashram. No, no; I cannot even tell you the approximate time. You wait there.'

~

Rajguru's indignation was now compounded by the cockiness with which that lout Ambika Das had spoken to him. For a long time he sat drumming his fingers hard on the table. If there was a knock he did not hear it. Then he saw that the door had opened, and Vanita Dave had come in, looking nervous and apologetic. 'It is six o'clock, Swamiji. Can I go? Or do you need me for anything?'

'Six, is it? I had not realized. Yes, I do have some business here, later, but please don't wait. Why not take the car? It is doing nothing.'

She gave him a smile. 'There's a bus from the hospital in fifteen minutes. Takes me right up to my door. Namaste, Swamiji.' She folded her hands and bent her head; the temple girl bending to receive blessings from the family priest. He found himself staring at the scarlet dot on her forehead.

'Oh, Vanita. On this trip I'm going on, next week; to Paris and then New York. I was thinking of taking you as my secretary. Would you like that?'

Suddenly her hand went to her throat, and her eyes widened with joy. 'Paris!' she gasped. 'Oh, Swamiji...please...there's nothing I should love more than...'

The rest of her sentence was stifled by the intensity of her emotion, and only a soft moan escaped her lips as the strong arms came reaching out of the folds of muslin and the musky odour of his body engulfed her. This time she did not resist.

~

The viewing session had been disappointing. The cockiness, the air of victorious generals holding a conference to impose conditions on an enemy was absent. Rajguru scowled, the two outsiders tried to affect a nonchalance they did not feel.

On Colonel Avinash Batra, there was no file at all. 'Too junior,' Kaul said with a sneer.

However, there was a small spool on Batra's father and an uncle. The father had given ten thousand rupees to the Swatantra party, and the uncle had attended a clandestine meeting called by Jayaprakash Narayan when he had visited Jullunder in 1975.

'Surely that is serious enough,' Ekanti Ma suggested.

Kaul looked uncomfortable. He manipulated a gob of paan from one cheek to another and said, 'I am afraid not. The Swatantra party no longer exists, and as to JP, the Great Leader has decreed that he is not the arch villain any more—something of a dear old uncle, if anything. The quarrel was a family quarrel.'

That left the two generals, the Director of Intelligence and the Chief of the General Staff, Ponappa and Abhay Singh. 'I have their spools here,' Pashupat said, and proceeded to screen them.

There was nothing recent on either of them. Years earlier, Ponappa had caused a scandal by placing a British General's photograph higher than Nehru's in his office, and Abhay Singh, while he was a Lieutenant Colonel had refused to permit a political meeting on his parade ground to felicitate Krishna Menon's election victory. But since then both had towed the political line and professionally, both were highly rated.

'If they don't play up, I expect we will have to get the Defence Minister to threaten to stop their promotions,' Ekanti Ma said.

Again Kaul shook his head ruefully and made a clucking sound. He squirmed in his chair and said, 'The word is that the Defence Minister is not to be trusted. In fact there is a fear that he is a dagabaz; only waiting for a chance to defect and stab the Great Leader in the back.'

'Say something constructive, you fat fool!' the Swami exploded. 'Instead of sitting there and shaking your head at everything. It is only a small thing. All I want to know is where a certain house is situated.'

Ekanti Ma gave both Kaul and Pashupat warning looks. Kaul

visibly shrank and swallowed his paan. His nephew busied himself putting away the spools of microfilm and tripped over the wires, nearly upsetting the table with the tray of drinks.

Ekanti Ma said, 'Who was the Director of Military Intelligence before Ponappa? Surely he would know, and we may have something…'

'Bose! D.C. Bose,' Pashupat answered, his diffidence suddenly gone.

Even Rajguru had heard the name. 'Not "Blankets" Bose?' he asked.

'The same. We're bound to have a full dossier on him.'

'No need,' the Swami told him. 'Just tell me what the blankets deal was.'

'American supplies, for flood victims. General Bose sold the entire consignment in the black market.'

'And the army got rid of him, fast, and he was given a job in Kalas Kak industries. Right?' Rajguru asked.

'How well Swamiji remembers,' Kaul said ingratiatingly.

'He's a crook, though. He will make us pay for the information,' Pashupat warned. 'But a cheapie. Ten thousand will take care of him. Shall I try and get hold of him, Swamiji. Can I use your telephone?'

'No!' Rajguru said very firmly. 'I think that will be all, gentlemen. Goodnight.'

Sheepishly, the Owl and the Pussycat shuffled out of the tantric shrine. They were seething with anger but they knew they were helpless against the mysterious power the Swami exercised over the Great Leader. Also, they had never been permitted a glimpse of the films of their own dossiers which were kept along with some others in a special drawer of the cabinet which was kept locked.

'Idiots!' they heard the Swami say to the woman who ran his household so efficiently. 'Both of them need a hard kick on their bottoms. I must speak to the Great Leader about how useless they have proved.'

It was after the pair had gone and Ekanti Ma was tidying up the shrine that the Swami explained why he had dismissed the two men who had always shown themselves to be so adroit in twisting people's arms.

'I have that moron coming here later this evening. He will be the right man to tackle someone like General Bose. These two clowns were actually thinking of offering him money.'

'It was only ten thousand,' Ekanti Ma pointed out.

'Money must be given as a reward, never as a bribe,' the holy man pronounced.

'I'd better put another bottle of whisky out,' Ekanti Ma said. 'I expect there'll be a couple of his usual aides, who will leave muddy footmarks all over the carpet.'

'The unwashed unintellectuals,' the Swami said with derision. 'Oh, yes, and please send up a plateful of chilli pakoras—real hot ones.'

It was a little before eight o'clock when the tiny white car drew up to the steps of the Swami's private office and gave a sharp toot. Out of it poured four men who were all dressed alike, in saffron kurtas and white pyjamas.

The finding of the address and the telephone number of the army's safehouse in Motibagh from General D.C. (Blankets) Bose, retired, did not take quite five minutes. Rajguru did not write them down but made a mental note of them. Then he waited for his young guests to depart so that he could get down to action.

'Last time you served Royal Salute, Rajguru,' Ambika Das, who was doing the pouring, pointed out cattily.

'Costs twelve hundred rupees a bottle,' Rajguru apologized.

'Leh! Who're you to talk of money, the way you're fixed,' Kakji remonstrated. 'Even if it costs twelve thousand a bottle—what is it…'

Rajguru made warning signs and said. 'Next time, Kakji. I don't keep Royal Salute at the ashram.' There was no need for the others to know about the financial manipulations.

'You better!' Kakji said and made a threatening gesture.

After that they began girl talk, and that was a sure indication that they had no intention of leaving soon. They discussed the girls they were pursuing and the girls they had discarded. They had read much pornography and fumbled with sex, and had become convinced that they were sexual athletes. Their language was crude and laced with suggestive laughter and whisperings and gestures. They reminded Rajguru of schoolboys licking their lips over a Playboy centre spread.

He sat drumming his fingers and mentally counting the

minutes. He sipped his tea while his guests gobbled the fiery pakoras and gulped whisky. Of Kakji's three companions of the evening, he knew only Ambika Das. He had never seen the other two before. One of them took out a transistor radio from his pocket and put on film music, quite loudly. Kakji moved his chair closer to the radio and sat swaying his head in appreciation. Rajguru wished that Ekanti Ma had not put out the extra bottle of whisky.

He had willed himself into a state of disinterest when a familiar name brought him up with a jerk. They were talking about Netra Agarwal.

'In a day or two,' Ambika Das was saying, and holding up two fingers. 'Not more than two. She'll come to me, begging.'

'Yaar, you should have had her taken to a police thana and there given her your terms,' the taller of the two nameless ones said.

'Hut! This is something I want those buggers at the El-Taj to see. Question of izzat. Private revenge no good, huh! She has to come on her own to the El-Taj, ask for me and sit at my table and have dinner. Tomorrow or the day after...you want to bet?'

He glowered at the other two who, even though regular members of Kakji's entourage, were of lower rank. Neither was prepared to take a bet. 'Tomorrow evening, her telephone will be cut off,' Ambika Das went on. 'The day after, it will be the electricity. Then water. Even big newspaper magnates have been brought to their knees, begging.'

'But...but what if she just moves to some hotel?' the shorter one asked.

'There are stronger measures, the taller one reminded him. 'She'll find her car smashed by hooligans, stones hurled at her... dismissed from her job, charged under MISA—Ambikaji can do anything.'

Ambika Das nodded and smirked and inserted a pakora into his mouth.

'What happens after the dinner, yaar?' the taller one asked, looking at Kakji for a response. Kakji was lost to Lata Mangeshkar and was keeping taal with his fingers beating on the table, but the other two gave a titter of laughter and made signs with their hands.

'Why not bring her to the tower?' Rajguru offered. 'Nice and quiet there.'

'Who'll take his date to your penthouse?' Ambika Das asked. 'You think I've been bitten by a mad dog?'

'I'll know how to deal with a girl who's a judo expert,' Rajguru taunted.

Ambika Das held up two fingers like a rabbit's ears and blew air through compressed lips, which caused the two other ranks to emit squeals of laughter.

That was when Kalas Kak said. 'Ambi, you bring her to the El-Taj. We'll make a foursome. I'll bring Roshanara.'

His companions gave him disbelieving stares and even Rajguru thought he must be joking.

Roshanara, popularly known as the Begam was a divorcee, a ravishingly good-looking society woman whose name was being increasingly bracketed with that of Kalas Kak. The papers carried their photographs with monotonous regularity and they had even appeared together on a television programme which had covered a visit that Kakji had made to an exhibition of handicrafts organized by the Begam.

But hitherto, the Begam had not been seen with any of Kakji's companions. Impeccably groomed and dressed in expensive saris, she was believed to have refused to hobnob with the sort of men and women among whom Kakji felt at home, or even to pretend to conform to the image of the homespun Indian woman devoted to public welfare that Kakji's other girl friends had striven to project.

As such, among members of the Dropout Brigade, to be invited to meet the Begam at a small dinner party was sufficiently unusual for Ambika Das to turn round and ask, 'You really mean it, Kakji?'

'Of course, I do. I've seen the girl. Go and ring her now. We'll take them for a drive afterwards. May be go to the factory.'

The factory, barely eighteen miles from downtown Delhi, had two elegantly furnished suites for business entertaining.

Visibly shaken, Ambika Das had hurried to the outer office to telephone, almost as though not to give Kakji a chance to change his mind. He was back after several minutes, looking displeased. 'She would not say yes, or no,' he reported. 'Said she will let me know tomorrow.'

The two other ranks were aghast. 'Don't tell me she refused, knowing…'

'I told you she hasn't refused!' Ambika Das snapped, and broke open the other bottle of whisky. 'Sure you don't have a bottle of Royal Salute tucked away in one of your drawers, Rajguru?' he asked.

Rajguru made no answer. They had been with him for exactly half an hour, he had calculated. How long were they going to go on?

The Air Force came to his rescue. The building shook as the first of half a dozen shells exploded in the range next door, and the glass in the windows rattled.

Kakji cursed and blinked behind his glasses. He turned off the radio and said, 'Didn't you tell me you'd got them to stop these rackets?'

'Only a few weeks more. They've promised to shift to the new range at the end of the monsoon. At that they're careful not to use the range during my working hours,' Rajguru said pointedly. 'I am never here as late as this.'

There was a muffled crump, followed by a resounding bang which ended in a series of shrill whistles.

'My poor eardrums!' Ambika Das moaned.

'Chalo, yaar, drink up,' Kakji ordered. He rose to his feet and strode out of the room. The others followed him and they all piled into the car and drove off. The Gurkha guards at the gate gave them smart salutes.

CHAPTER 14

THE fan rotated at only one speed: slow. It neither cooled the air nor kept the mosquitoes away. Batra's agents must be far from demanding, Visram reflected.

Outside, the noise of the traffic had been reduced to the odd car on its way to Palam airport, heard as a faint whine getting louder and louder and then receding.

Visram set up in bed, suddenly wide awake, and grabbed the Beretta which he had kept under his pillow even without knowing the reason for his alarm. He had heard the sound of an approachig car and not heard it going away.

A car door banged, followed by a ping as though the meter in a taxi had been put back to zero. Then the engine revved up and the car sped away.

He was dressed in a loongi and nothing else. He shoved his feet into chappals and sprang up. There was enough illumination in the room for him not to barge into things. His watch told him that it was ten minutes to ten.

He tiptoed up to the window facing the street and parted the curtains slightly.

A man was walking towards the house. He came unhesitatingly over the stoneflagged path that led to the front door.

Visram scrambled to the head of the staris and stood in a crouch at the top, sheltered by the bannisters. Obviously the man knew all about the piano lock. The door opened and for a second or two his outline was silhouetted in a rectangle of faint light. Then the door was shut, and he became invisible.

'Stand against the wall and put your hands up,' Visram said curtly. 'No fooling!'

Visram heard a curse as he switched on the stairwell light from the top of the landing. The man was holding his hands high. 'Now turn and face the wall. Good! If you move, I'll shoot.'

The man stood very still, as though nailed to the wall. Visram ran down the stairs and searched him for weapons. His nostrils twitched at the smell; an exhalation of garlic and mogra hair oil.

'OK, you can put your hands down and turn,' he ordered.

'Who're you?' the man said belligerently. 'I've never seen you here before?'

'Never mind who I am,' Visram told him. 'What I want to know is who you are, and what you're doing here?'

'That's a fine thing! You know I'm not allowed to tell you that. Look, I'm tired and want to get some sleep. I expect you've pinched the room with the rubber mattress, so I'll have to go into the ground floor bedroom. But before I turn in I want some food and drink. And I want to take the weight off my feet.'

Visram let the man lead him into the sitting room, which was on the ground floor. The man walked round the room familiarly, swtiching on all the lights and then went up to the refrigerator. He shook his head and mumbled something as he took out a bottle of Limca and some biscuits and cheese. He picked up the bottle opener that was kept in the egg tray. Then he went and sat down in the chair near the window and began to eat.

Visram sat in the opposite chair, the one facing the window, so that he could keep the man covered with his gun. He was already feeling a little foolish. After all the man had known how to open the door and about the refrigerator and where the can opener was kept. And yet...

'I told the Colonel to get them to keep some proper food—at least some ham and bread and butter...bloody MI's gone broke...' the man complained.

'You must identify yourself,' Visram said with affected sternness. 'What name do you use to report your arrival?'

'Kadam Bande,' the man said, as he bit off a piece of the hard cheese.

'And who do you ring?'

'You should know...oh, well,' he gave a shrug and added. 'The duty dog at MI.'

'What number?'

He gave a gentle burp and put his head back to drink from the Limca bottle. He suddenly sat up and asked, 'You mean you'll ring the number?'

'If they vet you, I need not sit all night, guarding you.'

The man grinned. 'You know, for a moment I thought you were a Pakistani commando—like the PLO send into Israel. OK. Double-three-zero, double-two-six-one. Got it? Ask for Ranga Timmappa. That's the code.' He tipped the neck of the Limca bottle into his mouth and drank.

Visram went to the telephone in the corner. Still keeping the man covered with the pistol held in his left hand, he lifted the receiver with the right and cradled it against his neck. He was beginning to dial the number when he realized that the line was dead. He put down the receiver and went and sat in his chair.

'What's the matter?' the man asked. 'Line gone kaput? So much for bloody MI efficiency.'

'Why don't you have any luggage? Not even a piece of paper to show who...'

'Ask Colonel Batra that when you see him. Whew! The heat! I'm being boiled alive. I don't know about you, but if we must sit here all night so you can guard me, I must have some air.'

Abruptly he got up and walked to the window. He pulled aside the curtains with a flourish and threw open the shutters and fixed the latches. Then he went and sat in the sofa against the side wall, eying Visram who had turned in his seat so as to keep him covered.

It was the look of expectancy in the other man's eye as much as another whiff of mogra scent that triggered a warning. He was sitting in a well-lit room and in a chair that could be overlooked from the drive. He dived and hit the floor only a fraction of a second before he heard a crack and saw that a hole had appeared in the back of the chair on which he had been sitting.

The report had been no louder than a handclap. He remembered the scope-sighted sporting rifle with the silencer that the Swami had equipped his guards with. He darted away from the open window, keeping his head down, and as he swung back to take a shot at the man who had set him up for a killing, he heard another sharp crack and ducked. The bullet chipped the plaster only inches away from his shoulder. He ran round the room, telling himself that even a skilled marksman could not shoot a running man at night if he was using a scope to aim at him. He switched off all the three lights and crouched behind a chair. He caught a glimpse of the man jumping out of the window and heard his footsteps as he went pounding over the crazy-paved pathway.

He stood up, listening, trying to control his breathing. Outside, the sound of the footsteps ceased with an abruptness that made his skin prickle. Did it mean that the man was coming back? Bringing others with him? It was safer to be out, in the open, instead of indoors offering himself as a sacrifice to Rajguru's thugs.

He scrambled over the windowsill and began to walk towards the main road, keeping himself as much as possible to the shadows. His rubber chappals made very little sound. He had progressed nearly a hundred yards when he heard the footsteps again, this time behind him. He hitched up his loongi and broke into a run.

The main road and the strong blue glareless lights were barely five hundred yards away. They would hardly dare to give chase on a public highway, he thought. His chappals now made flapping sounds over the tarmac and one of the straps came off. He discarded both chappals and ran on, conscious that the men behind were gaining on him. How many were there? Two? Three?

It was no good shouting for help. He was as much a fugitive from the law as from Rajguru's jackals. What was more, he stood a far better chance of shaking off his pursuers than he would the police, once they were on to him.

He was panting hard and about to fall down from sheer exhaustion when he reached the road. The footsteps sounded very close. He turned and saw two men, no more than fifty yards behind. Just the right distance for the man with the rifle to lie prone on the ground and take careful aim at someone running headlong in a floodlit street.

He saw a single light, coming from the opposite direction,

which turned out to be a scooter. The thought of the absurd spectacle he must be presenting, of a man without shoes and dressed in a knee-length loongi running for dear life, made him slow down while the scooter ridden by a man in a bright green crash helmet passed him. The two men behind him had come on to the main road. Now one of them must be lying down and taking aim, he thought with a feeling of certainity, while the other kept the chase up.

The sharp, unmistakable blast of a police whistle cut into the other sounds. He cursed and stopped, his chest heaving, knowing that he was lost anyhow. The scooter had turned and was racing towards him. With Rajguru's men he would have turned round and made a fight of it, but he could never bring himself to use a gun against a policeman who was doing his duty.

At least the whistle had the effect of stopping his pursuers dead in their tracks. He thought of making a dart to the side of the road in a bid to escape, but realised how futile it would be. All that the copper on the scooter had to do was to go on blowing his whistle for other policemen to come rushing to his help; in fact it was a little odd that the policeman had not gone on blowing the whistle. The scooter came and stood beside him, its engine still running. Its rider did not get off but said in an urgent voice, 'Get up on the pillion, Mr Lal, quick!'

Visram had already jumped on the pillion seat and the scooter had put on speed when he thought to ask, 'Who the hell are you?'

'My name is Sartaj, sir. I have been trying desperately to get hold of you for the last four days.'

Sartaj, who was once in the force. That explained the police whistle. Visram Lal clung hard to his seat and tucked his lungi which had been flapping wildly.

~

The supermarket building going up near Ajmere gate had been the last familiar landmark. Five minutes later, he could not have said where he was except somewhere between the Churiwala and Sitaram bazars, in the depths of a many-tiered human anthill that had been changing shape as though with a life of its own since before the Moguls ever came to India; so that what had once been fortifications were now foundations, and old mansions had sunk below ground level to become joined by a maze of alleyways snaking in and out of one another.

The scooter was driven into a small room which had an opening at the rear and then chugged on at walking speed through a winding passage which ended in a narrow archway that had been cut into a stone wall eight feet thick.

They were now in a tiny cobbled courtyard which smelled of manure. A wooden staircase confronted them, so steeply angled that a stout guiderope had been provided for people to haul themselves up.

Sartaj parked the scooter under the staircase and led the way up, into a room with a bed and a table littered with school books and lit by a naked electric bulb hanging from a wire.

'The next room is the kitchen,' Sartaj explained, 'and then another room which is our bedroom. Both the wife and the boy are in Karnal. Sir, I think you will be safer here than anywhere else. You can use this room, if you don't mind, for as long as you like.'

'What happens when your wife and son come back?'

'I can arrange for them not to come back for some time. Oh, yes, there's a lavatory and a bathing place with a tap, next to our bedroom. I'm not a cook, but I can manage. Would you like some tea, sir? Or I could go and bring whatever...?'

Visram sat down on the tidy bed covered by a many-coloured khes, and asked, 'What were you doing on the Palam road?'

Sartaj perched on the table, leaning forward and looking oddly like a bird. He wiped the sweat off his face with a balled handkerchief. 'Coming to see you, Mr Lal. Saw you this morning just by chance, getting out of a taxi! God, what luck! I said to myself, because I had been quite desperate, looking for you since Saturday. But I thought it would be safer—for you, I mean—if I waited till ten o'clock at night, because...'

'So it was you I saw chasing me on Saturday evening.'

He grinned. 'Yes, sir. You gave me the slip when you got into that bus in Daryaganj. Now what? I said. You see I'd made an ass of myself running away from the El-Taj because I was sure you were there on police business. Then I saw you and Om's sister at

Maidens...well, chummy as anything, and realized I might have made a mistake. On Sunday morning she confirmed it...'

'Who? Confirmed what?'

'Om's sister. That you were on Om's side. Now of course I know; that they've got a MISA warrant against you, because you went and talked to that man Dorabji. For the last four days I've been looking for you like mad—I and Om's sister.'

'But why were you looking for me, Sartaj?'

'To tell you what OM sent me to Kashmir for—and what I learned there. You see, I knew that Om had set great store by the information; my ace of trumps, he used to call it. Well, I and his sister feel sure that only someone like you could make use of the information, Mr Lal. Sorry, I cannot offer you a cigarette. I don't smoke. Shall I go and get some?'

Visram was dying for a cigarette, but assured Sartaj that he did not want one. 'Tell me about Kashmir, Sartaj. Why don't you sit down here, on the bed,' and he moved to make room.

'No, no; please, sir. I'm used to sitting up here, when I take my son's lessons. This is his room.' He pulled up his feet and leaned back against the whitewashed wall.

~

Twenty minutes later, he had finished whatever he had to tell. 'Don't you have any questions, Mr Lal?'

'One or two. But you'll have to tell the whole thing all over again, for ABC. I'll save them till then.'

Sartaj sat up. 'You mean the COI? Mr Chopra?'

'Yes, you'll have to get him here, then tell him...'

'You mean call him here? To this place?'

'Yes. You see, he has a clearer idea of the whole thing than any of us, and will be in a position to make use of your information. So, unless you are very tired, it would be best to get hold of him now. I want to tell him what happened at the...the place I was living, earlier. He will know what to do.'

'Well, Mr Lal. If you say so.' The monkey face broke into pleasant creases. He hopped down from the table. 'Try and get some rest, Mr Lal.'

'Oh, and please tell Mr Chopra to bring a couple of shirts and trousers, for me. And shoes…'

'I don't think his shoes will be any good, Mr Lal,' Sartaj said. 'His feet are much bigger than yours.'

'Chappals, then,' Visram said. 'Oh, yes, and do bring a couple of packets of cigarettes. Any of the standard brands.'

~

It was well past midnight. They had moved to the larger room, the one beyond the kitchen, and were squatting on a cotton rug which Sartaj had spread on the floor. While Sartaj had busied himself making coffee, Visram Lal had told Chopra the story of the evening's events. ABC had listened without comment, nodding every now and then and looking pleased.

'I just had to send for you, sir, even at the risk of your being followed,' Visram apologized.

'I don't think I was,' ABC said dryly. 'I'm sure they don't know anything about our picnic in the lakeside bungalow. In any case, we can't go on keeping in hiding much longer, not with things coming to a head. After all both you and Batra are blown now.'

Visram was both puzzled and elated. It was good to see that ABC was not distressed by whatever had happened. He might be even thinking out his next move, now that the Swami had reacted with virulence to their prodding.

Sartaj came in and took the coffee cups away. 'Sartaj has quite a story for you, Mr Chopra,' Visram said. 'You'd better come in and take over, Sartaj. Begin at the beginning.'

Sartaj who had been trying to keep out of earshot came and sat down on the carpet, looking a little daunted by the presence of his erstwhile COI in his bedroom.

'Well, sir. Rajguru Swami has referred to his earlier life in several interviews. His book on yoga also contains glimpses of his past life. He came to Delhi from Patna. Before that he was in Haridwar. Then he goes back to his fifty years in the Tashi Lunpo monastery at the foot of Nanga Parbat. He went there at the turn of the century—or so he says. Before that he speaks of Shraddhanand's ashram and of his being reconverted to Hinduism. As you know, sir, Om Prakash was an incorrigible nastik—non-believer. He was sure that the Swami was not even born at the turn of the century. He told me to go to Patna and Haridwar and check his story.'

'I too got the Patna part checked,' ABC said. 'He ran the Harmandir Yoga School there, and became famous overnight when he able to cure Jayanarayan of his crippling back pains. That was when he was called up to Delhi to…to work his magic on the great and the glamorous. Did you discover anything else in Patna?'

'No, sir. Patna was exactly as advertised,' Sartaj said, now feeling much more at ease. 'So I went on to Haridwar. He didn't get to Haridwar till the mid-fifties. As you know, Gilgit went over to Pakistan in 1947. That left a gap—seven or eight years, at least. That's what Om had told me to nail down. Trouble was, no one remembered where he had come to Haridwar from, or even the year he came. From 1956, he was running the yoga centre near Sarvanath. After that date…well, everything was just as he had said it was. But I kept pegging away, trying to find someone who had known Lama Pulakashi before he set up his yoga…'

'Lama who?' Visram asked.

'Pulakashi,' ABC explained. 'Didn't you know? Oh, there's no mystery about that. He was still Pulakashi in Patna. Began to call himself Rajguru only after he became established in Delhi as…yoga teacher and high priest to the first family.'

'I had been in Haridwar for a week and getting nowhere when I had a brainwave,' Sartaj went on. 'You know what pandyas are?'

'Priests?'

'Sort of temple agents, really,' ABC said. 'They hang around holy places and maintain lists of people who have gone there for poojas which go back for generations. If any of your ancestors has been to Haridwar during the last hundred years, you'll find his name on a pandya's register.'

'And they have amazing memories too,' Sartaj went on. 'Some of them boast that they never forget the name of any outsider who's come to Haridwar during their times… Oh, I don't mean the Kumbh Melas, when millions come there to bathe. Well, the first elderly pandya I approached gave me a hard look to see how much I could afford to pay, and said it would cost ten rupees. He placed a finger on the side of his nose as though to assist thought and said, "Lama Pulakashi. Set up the Yoga Centre. Didn't he learn his yoga with the order of the Thirteen? In the Deoban Math?" It cost me another ten rupees to find out that Deoban Math was in Kashmir, near Gulmarg. When I came and told this to Om, he sent me to Kashmir. I had just returned from there when I was told that he had died.'

'Find anything useful there?' ABC asked.

Sartaj's forehead wrinkled. 'I don't know, sir. What I know is that I found out whatever Om had sent me to find out. That much I am sure of. Weird place, the math, tucked away behind a maze of forbidding mountains. Near Gulmarg all right, but only as the crow flies. You've to walk seventeen miles to get there. Lots of tall trees all round so you don't really see it till you're at the entrance, which is a hole in the hillside. May have been a small fort in medieval times, or a cave temple. You see, the whole place is more excavated than built.'

'Did you get to see much of it?' Visram asked.

'No. Only the mandap at the top—sort of terrace, and one or two outer rooms. That's where they come up for air. Most of the time they live in the bowels of the hill.'

'How many are there?'

'Thirteen, sir; never more. That's why they're called the Order of Thirteen. In 1947, there was a Pakistani raid in which four of them were killed. One of the four vacancies went to Pula—Rajguru. I'd better stick to one name. They only fill one vacancy in a year so the other three novitiates came one by one over the next three years. Well, of the nine who were there when Rajguru joined the math, only three are still there. One is the head priest who has taken a vow of silence—it is customary for the order. Whoever becomes the head priest must observe the same discipline as the novitiates. It was from the other two that I managed to get some information.'

'What language do they speak?' Visram asked.

'Oh, Hindi, English, Sanskrit; they're quite learned, those monks. And cheerful blokes. Got the impression that they liked Rajguru a lot even if as they told me, some of the others had reservations.'

ABC was frowning with concentration and had narrowed his

eyes. He was listening very intently, as though not to miss a word. 'What sort of reservations?' he asked.

'Well, sir. They use words which seem odd to us. It seems they felt that Pulakashi was somehow an inauspicious influence... at least that's the word.'

'Was that because he was circumcised?'

'No, Mr Chopra. They were not bothered about that. They had had two cases before, of reconverted young Hindus wanting to become monks. It was well, did I tell you that the novitiates had to observe a whole year's silence? It is a part of the disciplining process. It seems that, just before Rajguru had done his year's apprenticeship, one of the senior monks, Swami Angaraka, slipped down the khud and broke his neck.'

For a few seconds, no one spoke. Then ABC asked in a voice that sounded bored, 'Was there anything special about this man who died?'

'Angaraka? Nothing special, sir; just that he had come from the same part of Kashmir as Rajguru. Gilgit.'

'Yes, of course, Gilgit,' ABC nodded. 'Tashi Lunpo monastery, where he spent fifty years.'

Sartaj shook his head. 'That's where the story differs, Mr Chopra. Both these monks were quite sure about it. I asked them separately. It seems he came from a village in Gilgit all right but that he had been a student in Srinagar. He had actually secured admission in the college there when Gilgit fell to Pakistan. That was when he applied to become a monk.'

ABC leaned forward and stretched his legs out as though to remove a cramp. 'When was this?' he asked.

'In 1948. Late April.'

'Were you able to check on the story? I mean, at the Srinagar end?'

'I tried,' Sartaj said with a shake of his head. 'But neither the school nor the college were prepared to dig into records thirty years old. I dare say they would, if there was an official approach. But I was lucky enough to get hold of a retired schoolmaster. Remembered Pulakashi quite well. "Big strapping boy but far from bright," he said. "Came from Gilgit, didn't he?"'

'You found that out in Srinagar,' ABC said. 'From where he went to Deoban and became a yoga wizard.'

'Quite the ideal monk, from all accounts. Did his full eight-year course and left with the Head Priest's blessings.'

'Hardly "Far from bright" was it?' ABC mumbled almost to himself. 'Tell me. The two monks you talked to. You say they knew nothing about his having been at the Tashi Lunpo monastery earlier.'

'Nothing, sir.'

'Oh, well,' Chopra said. 'And you have no idea what Om had in mind.'

'None at all, sir. All I know is that he was keen to establish a firm date of Rajguru making his first appearance.'

'What do you make of it, Visram? ABC asked.

'Well, isn't it odd that Rajguru should make absolutely no mention of his eight years in Deoban? I should have thought that that spell would add to anyone's prestige. In fact it almost looks as though the man is anxious to hide that part of his past.'

'Exactly. He makes something of a boast of having been at Tashi Lunpo...'

'Knowing that no one can check on that part...'

'...but says nothing about Deoban. I think Sartaj has really put us on to some vital bit of information which Om would have known what to do about. The pity is that neither of us know as much about the case as Om did. Anyhow, I can tell you, Sartaj, that I have plans in hand which...well, with a bit of luck should enable us to see this thing through—with a big bit of luck. Meanwhile it is maddening to know so much and not be able to do a bloody thing.' ABC stopped and laughed mirthlessly and fluttered his fingers. He glanced at his watch and made as if to rise. It seemed to Visram that whatever plans he had devised, he was not prepared to discuss them in Sartaj's hearing.

Sartaj said, 'I know it is very late, sir. But there's something on which I need your and Mr Lal's advice.'

'Umhum?' ABC said, looking distinctly ill at ease. He rubbed his eyes with the heel of his hand.

'It's about Om's sister. One of these young hoodlums who have shot up into prominence has been pestering...'

'Ambika Das?' Visram asked.

Sartaj nodded but did not seem surprised that Visram should have a guessed the name. Meanwhile, ABC, whose mind seemed to have wandered, was asking, 'He's the principal sidekick of the Wonderkid, isn't he? A big wheel among the riot-starters? I remember starting a file on him and destroying it, under ministerial orders.'

'What's he up to?' Visram asked. 'Obscene phone calls?'

'No, Mr Lal. It is more a systematic campaign of harassment. He had threatened to have her telephone cut off tomorrow, and after that it was to be the electricity and water... Unless she goes and meets him at the El-Taj...'

'The same treatment that some of the disobedient newspapers got,' Visram said.

'But now there's an added complication. Just this evening he rang up to say that Kalas Kak was also going to be at the El-Taj and would bring the Begum...which really makes it a command.'

Like a sleeping dog suddenly roused by some unusual scent or sound, ABC was looking at Sartaj with his head cocked. He said very softly. 'Ambika Das, the man who built the car, *the car*. And also the man who owns the car. All in one party. Oh, my god! This could be the bit of luck that I have been praying for. Tell me, Sartaj. Has Miss Agarwal refused this... this invitation to dinner already?'

'No, sir. She hasn't yet done a thing. She merely told me about it. Naturally she is frantic with worry...'

'Ah, good, good! The sooner I am able to talk to Miss Agarwal, the better. You must arrange that. First thing tomorrow—oh, this morning, really. Meanwhile she is not to do a thing. But before that, I must discuss a few things with Mr Lal. So, if you could give us, say, half an hour?'

'Certainly, Mr Chopra; of course,' Sartaj said, dutifully accepting his dismissal.

'What sort of girl is this Netra Agarwal?' ABC was asking Lal. 'Plucky, would you say? Ready to cooperate with us in dealing with the crooks who killed her brother, would you say? Willing to...to take a little risk?'

Sartaj cursed. God! I've gone and done it, he said to himself as he shut the door of his own house. The bastards were thinking of dragging that poor girl into their nefarious plot.

~

Sartaj fumed as he trudged the empty streets. What a fool he had been to have confided in his erstwhile superiors about Netra Agarwal's predicament. They had seen it only as an opportunity to be exploited. He should have known: policemen were all alike, hard-nosed professionals before they were human beings. The one exception had been his friend Om.

He found himself walking past the vast, empty square before New Delhi's main station, and happened to glance at the clock which was partly obscured by a Thirty-Point hoarding. Nearly half-past one. He had been walking for an hour. He turned about and retraced his steps.

The door opened as he began to climb the stairs, Visram Lal, now dressed in the shirt and trousers and rubber chappals that Chopra had brought, was beckoning to him to hurry. Chopra, who was stretched out on the carpet, sat up, looking displeased. 'Thought you were never coming,' he complained. 'We've absolutely no time to waste. Come and listen carefully. Today is D day.'

'I'm afraid you're not going to get much sleep tonight—what's left of it,' Visram told Sartaj.

Sartaj's irritation was fast melting. Whatever the two had decided in his absence was now being translated into orders, and that was something that he could understand. Granting that they were heartless professionals, it was also true that they were two of the best men in the force. And in any case they were the only two people who were resolved to smash the racket that Om had been investigating. Netra's personal troubles seemed unimportant by comparison; perhaps she could go to some place in the South and escape being harassed by Ambika Das and his mafia.

Then with a pang he remembered the case of the South Indian actress who had been tortured in jail because she had not cooperated with the authorities in their efforts to trace the whereabouts of her brother or husband who had offended against the laws of the emergency. She had been released in a dying condition. The South was no refuge from the terrors of the Emergency.

But he had to clear his brain for ABC's instructions which were coming in a torrent. First he was to escort Chopra to a locality that was familiar to him so that he could find a taxi on his own. After that he was to go to Netra Agarwal and tell her to go and see Chopra in his bungalow the first thing in the morning.

'Is that prudent?' Visram asked. 'I expect she's still being watched.'

'Sartaj has been to her place once or twice before. They will just think he has come to give her some advice about Ambika Das's call—remember they listen in on her telephone calls. Also, they might not think it unusual that she should seek the advice of her brother's former chief as to what to do about her problems. And in any case, Visram, the need for caution is passed...today we go into action.'

He proceeded with his instructions to Sartaj. Sartaj was to pass a verbal message to Colonel Batra. It was a long and complicated message, and Chopra made Sartaj repeat every word of it. After seeing Batra, Sartaj was to go and buy three sets of saffron coloured shirts and loose pyjamas. 'But buy them in different shops. One of your size and the two others—well two sizes bigger. OK?'

'One of my size, sir?' Sartaj asked in surprise.

'Yes, yes. You will be, well, participating in the operation. After that, leave one set of the saffron garments at Batra's house.'

Exactly at noon when the Connaught Place shops were about to shut, Sartaj was to go into Sahib Singh's shop and ask to buy eye drops. A man would meet him there and hand him an envelope. The envelope would contain a small key, which he was to pass on to Visram Lal.

'About the key, sir,' Visram said. 'I was wondering if it is really necessary. It should be quite easy to open the hood and join wires to get the engine started. No problem. Unless the car door is locked and one can't get at the hood-release catch.'

'The door doesn't have a lock,' ABC said derisively. 'It's a Kutcha job, y'know. At that I'd much rather everything was done as openly as possible.'

'So long as the key does fit...'

'Oh, absolutely. I've had the key examined in detail. Number 427, made by Nilmani Auto Parts, of Ludhiana. They make ingnition keys for all sorts of makes.'

'That should be all right, then.'

'Nothing to it. Only let's hope the thing doesn't develope some mechanical trouble. It's a sub-standard job. You'll have to baby it. Remember not to go more than forty kilometers, the engine heats at higher speeds,' Mr Chopra attempted a laugh and asked, 'Any questions?'

'Oh, just one thing, sir,' Visram asked. 'Are you sure that Batra still will have the authority to lay on what you want him to? Didn't you say he was blown? Also, will his colleagues really do what he asks them to do. The services can get awfully sticky over procedure, particularly when they think that someone is mucking them about.'

A shifty look came over Chopra's face; like a bridge player producing a winning card, Visram thought. He leaned forward and said with unnecessary emphasis, 'I can assure you on both points, Visram. Yes, Batra will still be in charge of the Commando school. What is more, his colleagues will be only too ready to do his bidding, no matter how unusual it seems to them.'

It was not till later that Visram found himself wondering how ABC could be sure that Batra's colleagues would not jib at what they were being asked to do.

CHAPTER 15

WHEN he began his day Colonel Avinash Batra had no idea how he was going to get through all that Chopra expected him to do in the course of it. At nine he was in the office of the Pakistani Military attache, Brigadier Iftakhar Khan. Iftakhar was shocked to the core at what Batra was asking him to do. 'Either you're crackers or I am,' he said.

'What's so shocking about it?' Batra asked. 'Don't you remember that at the end of the Bangladesh war there was a standing arrangement by which both sides sent back each other's deserters whenever apprehended?'

'That was only true of the Bangladesh war—Bhutto's days,' Iftakhar retorted.

'Look, don't blame us later if General Jamal Din comes down on you like a ton of bricks. I know he's…'

'General Jamal Din?' Iftakhar asked. 'The Eastern Army Commander?'

Use Jamal Din's name shamelessly, Chopra's messenger had emphasized. Ram it down their throats. 'Why don't you find out,' Batra said. 'God! I'd hate to be in your position when he discovers how you turned down…'

'Can I give you the answer by this evening?'

'By the afternoon. Evening no damn good.'

'Okay.'

'And there's something else,' Batra pressed his advantage. 'We want a list of your deserters in the valley front between 1 April and

30 April 1948.'

'Nineteen what? Oh, come now...'

'That too only if General Din personally gives you the green signal. For my part I'm convinced that General Din will stand on his head to get his hands on the man we're offering.'

'What a lot you know about what General Din wants,' Iftakhar said sarcastically. 'If he was all that anxious, surely he would have sent me instructions.'

'Oh, and please tell him we can let you have a set of fingerprints, if he wants a double check,' Batra said as he rose to go.

By four o'clock, Iftakhar Khan had rung back to say that the answer from Rawalpindi was in the affirmative, and that the list of deserters from the Kashmir valley front in April 1948 was on its way to Colonel Batra's bungalow by special messenger.

'And, oh, yes,' Iftakhar said. 'That set of fingerprints. They said they'd appreciate it. I cannot imagine why.'

Throughout the day, Batra had been too pressed for time to feel conscious of elation or even nervousness. Now, as he waited for Iftakhar's messenger, he found himself yawning and taking deep breaths. The really difficult part lay ahead. The requests that Chopra had so glibly asked him to make were so unusual as to seem outrageous. He knew that his Air Force colleague on the Commando range, Wing Commander Dasilva, was a stickler for procedure. He would be quite within his rights to insist on a clearance from his HQ before he proceeded to give effect to Batra's plans for the evening.

Batra for one could not see Air HQ giving their OK; and that would be the end of Mr Chopra's elaborately worked out scheme.

Within minutes of the messenger from the Pakistani High Commissioner's office leaving, Batra was racing his MG along the Palam road, his nervousness mounting by the minute. He barged into Dasilva's office and proceeded to explain what arrangements he wanted made for a special exercise that he was laying on for the evening. It was only after he had finished whatever he had to say that he noticed that he was keeping his fingers crossed.

Dasilva neither asked questions nor made objections, but very phlegmatically proceeded to work out the details of his part of the operation. After that they spent the next two hours together, putting the two exercises of the evening into shape.

This was something that he had never bargained for. He was so overwhelmed by a feeling of relief at Dasilva's eager compliance, that it was only later that the thought struck him: could it be that Air HQ had ordered their man to offer his fullest cooperation to his colleague from the army?

He shook hands with Dasilva, now conscious of the scent of success in the air. After that, from his special equipment store, he picked up a small satchel of steel instruments, three powerful torchlights, a half-inch crowbar twenty inches long, and three plastic cylindrical objects that looked like tins of golf balls, each about a foot long and two inches across. These he placed in the suitcase that Chopra had asked him to bring along. He had to use a lot of woodwool padding to keep the cylinders from rattling and banging into one another.

In the bungalow in which Visram had stayed for two nights, he changed into the clothes that Chopra's messenger had delivered at his place. Then he drove back towards the Air Force establishment in Palam. After parking the car in the Officers' Mess car park, he had to sprint as far as the bus-stop in front of the Military Hospital to make the deadline at the rendezvous.

It was exactly eight-thirty. Chopra's messenger, Sartaj, was waiting. He too was dressed in a saffron guru shirt and pyjamas, and carried a suitcase, and he was intently watching the lights of an approaching car.

~

Netra Agarwal's role was far from challenging. She had to be sociable and make small talk, order exotic dishes in order to spin out the meal, and give the impression that she was enjoying the evening. She had been assured by Chopra that there was no danger of her having to go with her companions for a drive, and she had not pressed him for further information. Chopra had especially entreated her that she was not to use her judo tactics on any of her evening's companions. 'Try and act as friendly as you can.'

She had taken a taxi to the El-Taj and got there just a few minutes before eight. Ambika Das, smelling of cologne and looking a little on the defensive, was waiting at the doorstep. They had just reached their corner table and he had asked her what she would like to drink, when Kalas Kak and Roshanara joined them.

The conversation was subdued and decorous. The cabaret turn was to begin at a quarter past eight; a man and woman doing a flame dance. Netra, who was studying the menu to decide which dish would take the longest to serve was relieved when Roshanara said, 'Why don't we all plump for pressed duck a la Tour d'Argent? It takes half an hour to cook, but it's really worth waiting for.'

The pressed duck was ordered. They sat munching nuts and breadsticks and sipping tomato juice and smiling for photographers who took flashlight pictures. The Begam who would have preferred a glass of champagne or even a strong whisky as an appetizer crinkled her Grecian nose in distaste and pushed aside her glass of tomato juice. But there was no question of getting over this particular prohibition that the Great Leader had decreed that the Heir Apparent must never be seen to drink even a glass of beer in public, and he and his companions had to suffer in consequence no matter how much they drank in private. But she was instantly mollified when the proprietor, a flashily dressed Sindhi wearing a digital gold watch, solid gold cufflinks, and a gold belt buckle the size of a playing card, came up to enquire if everything was as it should be, and presented roses to both ladies. Then he brought up two giggling young women and introduced them as his daughter and daughter-in-law, both of whom promptly whipped out autograph books for Kakji to sign.

There was not much scope for making conversation. Netra glanced at her wristwatch, and when she saw it was eight-fifteen, she could hardly supress a flush of excitement.

That was when the lights dimmed and a blare of trumpets announced the coming on of the cabaret turn.

~

The blare was heard outside. A man dressed in a saffron guru shirt and pyjamas emerged from the shadows and strode purposefully towards the car parked in front of the El-Taj door. He got into the car, and as he inserted the key into the lock, realized that the car had been parked on a slope. He pressed the clutch and suddenly the car began to roll forward. Obviously the handbrake was not functioning.

He was within sight of Mori Gate when he turned on the ignition. The engine caught on and began to purr. He threw in the gear and put on speed. Don't push her; forty kilometers is high speed, ABC had warned. He kept the needle steady on forty. At eight-thirty, he arrived at the bus stop near the Military hospital in Palam. Even before he had brought the car to a stop, the two men who were waiting for him piled in from both sides, each lugging a suitcase. Visram drove on.

'We still have ten minutes in hand,' Batra said. 'The range practice doesn't start till quarter to nine.'

'What news from Pindi?' Visram asked.

Batra made a thumbs up sign.

'The list?'

'Also. But not a list, really. Only one name...and are they keen to get him back!' he gave a low whistle.

'I'll go on the Najafgarh road for another four minutes and then turn, shall I?'

Now that they were within minutes of committing themselves to an irreversible course of action, there seemed to be nothing more to say. It was only after Visram had turned the car round at the end of four minutes, that Batra asked, sounding very offhand, 'You don't know how many years they give you for housebreaking, do you?'

'Life, if there is violence,' Visram answered. 'But there won't be any question of punishment once we've got the microfilms in our possession. Enough evidence to blast a dozen Rajgurus, and anyone in a position of power will be terrified of us...half the cabinet will be jumping for joy to have got the Mafia off their backs.'

'In fact we could set up a racket of our own, couldn't we? Blackmailing people to make millions?'

'We could, at that.'

'But do we really know that the films are there—or even that the films were put on microfilm?'

'ABC seems pretty sure they're stored here. And as to...'

'And you, of course, have trained yourself to take Chopra on trust.'

'The films were made, sir. That I know,' Sartaj said. 'Sondhi, who is the Department's photographer told me. He was working on them for weeks, during the time when Mr Maney was the minister.'

'That's what ABC too told me,' Visram said. 'But it was a different name—Anglo Indian, beginning with…hell, how one forgets.'

'Not Roach, Mr Lal? Albert Roach was also employed in the department as a photographer. Emigrated to Canada last year.'

'Roach, of course. He was brought into the department by ABC and was…well, his man.'

'And ABC has made up his mind that the films are stored here. Intuition, I suppose.'

'Powers of deduction, more likely. He has been on the case for a long time, remember.'

'It's too late to worry about whether they really are here… God, the bloody guards are aiming rifles.'

They were turning into the gate of the ashram. Two Gurkha guards stood in the middle of the gateway, barring their path. Then they recognized the car. One sprang to attention and saluted while the other sprinted in front of the car to open the gate in the wooden fence between the ashram area and Rajguru's office. He was standing near the gate uncertain as to whether to offer any further assistance, when Batra waved a hand for him to go away.

~

'That guard has gone back to the main gate,' Batra reported.

'Thank God for small mercies,' Visram said almost to himself, as he brought the car to a halt near the office steps and swtiched off the engine.

'Damn!' Batra cursed. 'I had not bargained for that light being on.'

The small veranda outside the office building was furnished like that of an elegant private bungalow. It had a highly polished tiled floor and there were cane chairs and potted plants. The door was right in the centre. A scalloped marble lampshade hung suspended with brass chains, concealing an electric bulb.

'Must deal with that light first. Don't want to be caught out even before we enter the house, dammit,' Batra went on. 'Can't see a switchboard, can you? Must be inside. Come on Sartaj. Hop onto my shoulders, will you?—see if you can remove the bulb. Use your handkerchief, it'll be hot.'

They both ran up the steps. Batra bent down under the light to let Sartaj jump on his back, then slowly straightened up and helped Sartaj to stand on his shoulders by supporting his legs. Sartaj reached inside the shade, wrapped his handkerchief round the bulb and extracted it. It did not take quite ten seconds.

'Put it in your pocket,' Batra told him. 'And grab a torch each, and give me a light on the keyhole just for a few seconds, will you? Steady now.'

From his little cloth satchel, he brought out a set of a dozen or so plastic blades and selected two of uneven width, and about eight inches long. He inserted both into the keyhole and with one hand turned the blades very gently, at the same time, placing one end of the crowbar under the door handle and pressing with all his might with the other. The lock broke with a sharp crack.

Batra went in first. The other two followed him with the suitcases. Batra glanced at his watch and said, 'Still four minutes. We're going like clockwork. Drag a small table out into the veranda and put that bulb back, will you, while I take a look at the inner door. We want the outside light to be on, in case the guards do any patrolling. But wait, let me put off the switch, first.'

Visram and Sartaj hauled a small side table into the veranda and Sartaj climbed on it and replaced the bulb. They then took the table inside and Batra shut the door behind them and switched on the veranda light.

They went through the outer office into the room beyond. 'Whew!' Visram gave a soft whistle.

'Really tarted up, isn't it,' Batra said. 'And complete with a scrambler telephone.' He walked round the rosewood desk and spent a precious minute examining the door to the shrine. 'Bloody door is like a bank vault's,' he pronounced. I had feared as much. Take hours busting it—create no end of a racket too. Ah, that's better. The air conditioner inlet will be just ideal for the Bangalore Torpedo...two of them, I think. They're real beauties...oh, tremendous wallop and not too much of a mess. I've put in six-second fuses. Remember to lie flat on the ground when I do, Okay? The hole should be large enough for me to crawl through; if not, we'll have to enlarge it with the crowbar. If the filing cabinets inside have locks, I'll just have to bash the locks. No time for refinements. The sound should be drowned by the racket the Air Force will be making. Oh, yes, if the lights fuse with the bang, try and see if you can fix the fuse, will you. Here's some fuse wire.' He handed a reel of metal wire to Visram and glanced at his watch again. 'Well, zero hour, let's hope the bloody IAF are punctual.'

They were. The first bang was not too loud, almost like a gunshot, but it was followed by a machine gun stutter of increasing volume. 'I'm setting the fuse now. Lie low, with your head turned away. And keep your torches in your hands.'

The building shook with the explosion and the lights went off. A shower of plaster fell and the room was filled with smoke and dust. When Visram looked up, Batra was examining the hole in the beam of a torch light. 'Just dandy,' he pronounced. 'No need for further excavations, but try and see if you can fix that bloody fuse though.'

Outside, the Air Force was making a gratifying din, a series of crashes and bangs and whining sounds. Visram was pulling out the porcelain fuse-plugs one after the other. 'I'm going in,' Batra said, sounding impatient. 'Come on, Sartaj.'

The sounds from the Air Force range suddenly stopped. Visram heard a crack next door like a rifle shot and realized that Batra had broken open the lock of a filing cabinet. How many were there? he wondered.

Panic seized him as he visualized one of the guards coming to investigate what had happened to the lights. Then he suddenly discovered the fuse. It was one of the subsidiary small plugs that had come loose. He merely had to press it into position for the lights to come on again.

He gave a quick look round and dived through the hole. Batra was already wrestling with the crowbar at the lock of the tall steel cupboard, and Sartaj was busy putting away little yellow boxes of Kodak and 3M films into one of the suitcases.

~

A.B. Chopra had dined at the club, dawdled over a second cup of coffee, and taken himself for a walk. He reckoned that nine-thirty would be a proper time to drop his little bombshell. By that time, they would be about to finish dinner, and thinking of going on to other places. He had promised Miss Agarwal that she would have an opportunity of escaping. He was now giving it to her.

He walked into a telephone booth and rang the El-Taj number. He pressed a finger against one nostril which he knew was as good a way of camouflaging one's voice as any. 'Is Mr Kalas Kak there?' he asked.

'Who is speaking?' the man at the other end asked, very guardedly.

'It is just that I saw his car abandoned on the roadside and wondered if there had been a breakdown. Wanted to check up if everything is all right. He's there? Oh, good. No, no; no message or anything. You see I just wanted to check up that he is all right because the car...what? Just this side of the airport.'

'Wait a minute!' the man at the El-Taj was saying in an urgent voice. 'Hullo. The airport road, you said...hullo, hullo...'

~

The pressed duck had been cooked just as the Begam remembered having eaten in the Hotel de Paris in Monte Carlo even if, as she described it, the sauce was...well, less inspired. But she excused the imperfection by saying, 'They don't get the same ingredients, do they?'

The waiter was just bringing round the trolley for a second helping when the Manager walked up to their table and whispered something in Kalas Kak's ear.

Kakji flung his napkin, uttered his first swearword of the evening, and dashed out, saying to Ambika Das, 'Some bhenchods have stolen the car!'

He did not return for fifteen minutes, and when he did, explained that he had had to send Ambi to make a personal complaint to the Chief of Police and after that to go and retrieve the car. No one objected when Netra rose to leave, except that she was not allowed to send for a taxi. The management gave her a car and chauffeur to get her home.

CHAPTER 16

THE helicopter hovered over the target for a few seconds and rose in the air as though pushed by a current of air. 'Perfect weather,' the pilot said into the speaking tube. 'I can land you on a dinner plate.'

The man in the passenger seat held up his thumb and nodded.

They circled over Connaught Place and the Purana Quila for four minutes and made for the target again. 'Going in now.'

The man in the passenger seat held up his thumb and carefully detached the headphones.

~

From the terrace garden of their penthouse, Rajguru and Ekanti Ma had watched without curiosity as the helicopter buzzed overhead. They had come out into the open part of the terrace where they customarily sat after their evening meal and where Rajguru smoked his opium pipe before going to bed.

Today it was like a furnace. Even the canvas chairs placed on the patch of grass felt hot to the touch. But then Rajguru was not affected either by the heat or the cold. His only concession to the weather had been that he had discarded his muslin dhoti and was dressed only in a pair of red cotton underpants.

'I can't bear this heat,' Ekanti Ma complained. 'Stifling!'

He did not answer, but sat on the edge of his chair as though ready to spring up at a signal. His mood was dark and his face wore a scowl.

'Let's go in and get cool, shall we,' Ekanti Ma said.

He suffered himself to be led into the glassed-in part of the roof-garden. He lowered himself into his favourite cane chair and put his feet up on a cushioned stool. Ekanti Ma breathed lungfuls of the cold air and said, 'Are you ready for your pipe?'

He nodded and saw her go indoors. From where he sat, he could see the lawn with the vivid patches of colour made by the canvas chairs and the flowering bushes, and the white trellised frame on which the alamanda vine had been trained.

He was gazing vacantly at the familiar scene when he thought he saw a bush move, and behind the bush he saw a pale-green nylon parachute go billowing off over the terrace wall. Even before the sudden intrusion of movement in the pattern of colour had acquired definition, the glass door opened and a man burst in, wielding a pistol. The sound that the Swami was going to make came out as a stifled cluck.

'Make a single move and you die!' the intruder hissed. Then he gave a quick allround look and came and sat in a chair, holding his pistol aimed at the Swami's chest.

Rajguru was quick to get over his initial shock. 'Ah, Mr Lal! You do specialize in dramatic appearances, don't you. Last time you were a member of Parliament. What are you now, falling from the skies. Superman!'

'This time I have come as myself,' Lal told him. 'An officer of the law on duty.'

'My information is that you're hiding from the law, Mr Lal—evading arrest by going underground.'

'No, Rajguru. Not when I have Surbinder's microfilmed dossier. I know all about his wife smuggling out the Jaipur paintings, and selling them to Rosenthal. No wonder he cringed to you.'

Rajguru sat up with a jerk. 'What did you say?'

'Take a look.' Visram tossed a yellow carton at the Swami. 'Mr Chopra's file. You had an amazing system of indexing the spools. Stop fidgeting. I might shoot you accidentally...and remember not to raise your voice.'

Rajguru was peering at the roll of film. He gulped and said, 'How did you...?'

'Broke into your vault and confiscated the entire library...oh, in the name of the law. Real windfall!'

That was when the door at the other end of the room opened. Visram found himself pointing his Beretta at a woman's ample posterior. Ekanti Ma was walking backwards because she was carrying a tray on which she had arranged the paraphernalia for preparing the Swami's opium pipe: a lighted spirit lamp, a small silver box, a steel knitting needle and three long-stemmed pipes with bowls no bigger than coffee-spoons.

She turned, shut the door by pushing it with her buttocks, and only then saw Visram. 'Oh!' she gasped. 'I...I didn't know you had a visitor, Swamiji.'

'Tell her to come here and sit down,' Visram ordered. 'On the chair next to yours.' He motioned with the barrel of his pistol. 'And tell her to keep her voice low—for her own good.'

'Come and sit down, my dear. This is not a visitor, but...an old friend...dropped from the skies, literally. Remember he's got a gun on us.'

'What...what does he want?'

'He has not condescended to tell me, yet; he has been so busy striking theatrical poses.'

Ekanti Ma placed the tray on one of the side tables and blew out the spirit lamp. She was making as though to put out a hand to grab the lamp when Visram told her, 'Careful now... I've never shot a woman before. I don't want to do it now. Come and sit down!'

She shrugged and turned and meekly came and sat in the chair next to Rajguru's. 'What do you want, Mr Lal?' she asked.

'I'm here on duty, I told him.'

'I asked because the last time you wanted a share of the profits. I thought we could discuss that. I don't see any sensible man refusing the offer of a sum that would make him rich for life—say a million rupees.'

'I wouldn't know what to do with a million rupees.'

'My dear, he has one of these warped minds. He doesn't want money, but he doesn't want others to have it either,' Rajguru said, for the first time sounding angry. He turned belligerently to Lal and said, 'All right, you're here professionally. Then tell me what crime I've committed. Has anyone made a complaint to you? What is it to you if I and a few friends have worked out a method of siphoning off some of the funds which are illegally obtained in any case? And how do you know that those who are in charge of the funds are not our accomplices? Have you ever stopped to think that something which became apparent to outsiders like you and Chopra is not known to the Great Leader? Could vast funds have been sent abroad without the Great Leader's knowledge and even connivance? Have you not heard of the chain of motels in Canada that Kakji owns, the five-star hotel on the shore of lake Garda that is coming up? The family's vast holdings in multinational companies?'

Visram shrugged. 'I'm not investigating the loss of the NDF's secret funds. But...'

'No?' Ekanti Ma asked, looking greatly surprised.

'No, darling,' Rajguru assured her. 'He represents a sick mind that has no cure—the malady of the dedicated public servant.'

'Careful, dear!'

'The time for being careful has clearly passed, Ekanti. Let me at least get my say in. Mr Lal has read Solzhenitsyn. Among his friends he will hold forth about the horrors of Gulag. But will he ever say a word against the horrors of Tihar? He will roar like a lion, denouncing the dictatorship in Burma, Pakistan, even Chile, but not so much as a squeak against the dictatorship here. He has already become resigned to the perpetuation of the dynasty, an absolute monarchy complete with an heir apparent. Above all, his official blinkers do not permit him to look upon people like ourselves as benefactors of society, as those who are doing their mite to sabotage the brazen attempt at imposing dynastic rule. Oh, no! He is horrified. To him we are criminals because we have taken money that does not belong to us. It is terrifying, this malady of the official, with its contorted conception of duty. But who can contend with it? "Against stupidity even the Gods struggle in vain".'

Rajguru's eyes flashed fire and his face had lost its serene look. He was panting hard.

'We've gone over this ground before, Rajguru,' Visram pointed out. 'And assuming that there is a lot in what you're saying, you can hardly expect a professional cop to take a broad-minded view of murder.'

'What are you talking about?' Swami Rajguru asked indignantly. 'I have not harmed a fly in my life. I'm a man of God, don't you know, a man of peace. More non-violent than Gandhi ever was.'

Visram grimmaced and shook his head.

'Perhaps you could tell me who I am supposed to have murdered.'

'Deputy Superintendent Agarwal?'

'If you're going to hold me responsible for a road accident… I hear there are ninety or so every month; in that case I must be the biggest killer since Eichmann. Why are you looking at your watch, Mr Lal?'

Visram did not answer. He said, 'What about Dorabji?'

The Swami made a helpless gesture and shook his head. 'This is priceless! Surely, it was your own people who bumped him off? Are you going to hold me responsible for police killings as well?'

'You sent a man to kill me. One of your Gurkhas, equipped with a scope-sighed sporting rifle and a silencer…'

'You must suffer from a vivid imagination, Mr Lal. You accuse me of killings or intended killings even as you threaten to kill Ekanti Ma and myself. I'm sure you would have no compunction about killing either or both of us. But your contorted mind has an answer for committing such murders—that you killed us in line of duty. What a horrible word: duty!' Rajguru made a spitting gesture with his lips.

Visram glanced at his watch again and said, 'There are two more names…people you killed. One is that of a young man called Pulakashi who was…'

'What's that?' Rajguru almost screeched. He turned on his accuser and hissed, 'You swine!'

'That's right. A young man on his way to join the monastery near Gulmarg. And then another man, a monk from the Deoban Math called Angaraka, who was also from… Stop it, or I'll plug you!' Visram threatened as he saw Rajguru rising to his feet. 'And now I'll tell you why I keep looking at my watch. It is because time is running out. We have made a rendezvous for you in the desert, two hundred miles from here. And we must be there in three hours.'

Visram had a feeling that the Swami was not there, and that he was wasting his words. For Rajguru had shut his eyes and was taking deep, noisy breaths. The exercise, which barely lasted a minute, had the effect of enabling him to snap back into form. Visram, who had had a good deal of experience of hardened criminals, could see that he was confronted by a real artist; clever, wily, and totally unrepentent. He found Rajguru looking at him with narrowed eyes and a sneer of contempt.

'You poor misguided man,' Rajguru said almost pityingly. 'Have you thought of the retribution? What the Great Leader and the two jackals will do to you and your crazy friends?'

Visram gave the Swami a pitying smile in return. 'I must disillusion you, Rajguru. You must have known how the Great Leader was constantly talking about being stabbed in the back by a close colleague. How do you know that whoever has been gunning for the seat of power is not behind us?'

'The Defence Minister?' Ekanti Ma said in an awed whisper.

'He's bluffing,' Rajguru told her.

'I don't believe he is,' she said, looking very shaken. 'All they had to do was to pass on the films to him... He must have been only waiting for some such...'

'Have you?' Rajguru asked.

'You won't get me to name names,' Visram told him. 'But I can tell you this. For better or worse, someone other than the Great Leader holds the whip hand now. You don't suppose that the arrangements we have made for your journey would have been possible without orders right from the top overriding all procedural obstacles?'

'You idiots!' the Swami hissed. 'You utter fools. Don't you realize that you are playing with fire? Handing over the country to the forces of anarchy? Surely even you realize that only chaos and ruin will be the outcome of this folly!'

Visram shrugged. 'You may be quite right,' he said equably. 'Who can foresee the results of this convulsion. But the point is that the problems of this country will not affect you where you are going—Naik Fida Ali.'

'Where I am...' Whatever else he was going to say came out as a series of clucks, and the muscles of his face suddenly went slack.

'Are you all right, darling?!' Ekanti Ma exclaimed. She made an effort to rise from her chair but sat down again when she saw the barrel of Visram's pistol shift in her direction. 'Naik Fida Ali?' she gasped.

'Yes. Born in 1928, in a village called Pandu, in Gilgit. The Pakistani High Command seem to be itching to get their hands on him.'

For a couple of seconds, Rajguru and Ekanti Ma stared at one another, aghast. Then he turned to Visram and said, dramatically. 'I would much rather you shot me dead, right now. Don't you know what barbaric punishments they dole out for the commonest offences? Like chopping off your hands and feet? Come on, you bastard! Kill me—kill me if you dare!'

'I'm not interested in killing you. We want to leave you to your fate. If they chop off your hands and feet, I shall not lose a night's sleep; if you somehow escape punishment, I shall not grieve.'

'You have not said anything about her,' Rajguru said. 'Ekanti Ma.'

'I have nothing against her.'

'You mean...you mean she can go where she likes? To a foreign country?'

'As far as I am concerned, go away or stay on here.' He glanced at his watch again and said, 'We shall have to leave in ten minutes.'

'In that case, I should like to use one of those minutes to...to think over my future plans. Concentrate all my mental faculties on the problem, as it were.'

'So long as you do it here. Careful now. No tricks.'

But Rajguru was not up to any tricks. He tumbled off the chair and stood on his head, with his legs held rigidly, straight up. After exactly sixty seconds, he cartwheeled right back into his chair, as it were. He looked relaxed and even cheerful.

'Will you answer a simple question, Mr Lal,' Rajguru asked very politely. 'How exactly are you going to take me to my own people. Supposing I don't cooperate?'

Visram found himself grinning. 'You'd better cooperate. You see it is all arranged with what they call military precision. Unless we're at a certain place which is seven miles away, in twenty-three minutes from now, two of the toughest men who are trained in unarmed combat will be dropped here by parachute. Remember we're desperate men, and have gone to a lot of trouble to get you in our hands. If necessary, we'll carry you on a stretcher...'

Rajguru gave a delicate shiver. 'You mean use violence?'

'I'm afraid so. But only if you make it necessary.'

'I told you I am a man of peace, Mr Lal. Tell me, what happens when we get to your...RV? That is how you describe it, don't you, in twenty-three minutes, did you say?'

'Twenty-one now. An aeroplane will be waiting, with its engines running. It will ferry you beyond the Chenab, near Kasur. It has been given permission to go inside the border for five miles. Jamal Din will have sent an escort to meet you.'

'You mean the plane will be allowed to land?'

'Certainly not. They'll drop you and turn back.'

'They? You will not be with us, then? I was so hoping you would be. And drop me, you said?'

'Yes, Rajguru. By parachute. As a flying man, you should not be unfamiliar with parachutes.'

'Never tried it, to tell you the truth. But then there's always a first time, isn't there?' the Swami said almost to himself. 'I suppose the thing will open?'

'They usually do.'

A faint smile appeared on the Swami's face. 'Jamal Din. General Jamal Din. You know, Mr Lal, I think I'm going to enjoy meeting the man. I do wish I was, less informally dressed. Oh, I'm quite looking forward... Mr Lal, this calls for a drink. Champagne. Surely, you have a minute or two...'

Visram laughed. 'As it happens, I do have a minute or two. But I'm sorry to say that I don't trust you, Swamiji. Now, if you and Ekanti Ma will keep close together, we'll all walk up to the lift and go. And let me remind you again that I'm just itching to bang away at you in sheer exuberance so don't try any stunts. A car is waiting for you, driven by a man you may not have met. Chopra. A tough customer, and remember he has a score to settle. I advice you to be on your best behaviour.'

'Since we're talking about best behaviour, Mr Lal. I take it that you will arrange to send back Ekanti Ma here...find a taxi for her, and also...'

'Not to worry. I'll drive her back myself.'

'That is kind of you. But I was going to ask: when will you give the two of us a few minutes together.'

'Impossible.'

'But, my dear Mr Lal! This is so uncivilized. Even a condemned man is permitted to say a few words in private to his woman! Here you are separating us for ever without so much as...'

'Why can't you say whatever you want to in my presence?'

'How like a policeman?' Rajguru said with sarcasm. 'Or a man who has not been loved by a woman. You fear that I will tell her to do something that will wreck your operation, don't you, Mr Lal. How can I convince you that I have no such designs...that in fact I am quite looking forward to whatever life has in store for me in Pakistan. I will tell you what. Surely you will have no objection to our saying goodbye on the tarmac just before I get into the plane You and your friends can keep us covered in case I try and make a dash...'

'That, certainly, Rajguru. Yes, you can say goodbye on the tarmac. There will be four of us with guns,'

'Thank you. Oh, I am most grateful.' He was smiling expansively. 'You know you should not have denied yourself that drink, Mr Lal. It would have put a punctuation mark on the occasion, as it were. A chapter closing...another opening, a chapter full of promise. I don't know if you will believe me if I tell you that I have a feeling that you have done me a good turn. There was nothing left for me here. I would have had to make new friends, adjust myself to the free-for-all of a democracy. The thought makes me shudder. People like myself thrive best in the kind of regime that the Great Leader provided. If there is always a time to make an exit, I cannot imagine a better time for me to make mine.'

Visram was listening avidly. He took a deep breath and shook his head. 'If I let you talk much more, Rajguru, I'm sure you will make me do something which I shall regret.'

Rajguru grinned in response. 'I say,' he said. 'When you drop Ekanti, do have a drink then. Toast your own success and my future. Please. Shall we go now?'